The Sam Pig Storybook

ALISON UTTLEY

THE SAM PIG
STORYBOOK

illustrated by Cecil Leslie

faber and faber

First published in 1965
Reset and published in this edition in 2000
by Faber and Faber Limited
3 Queen Square, London WC1N 3AU

Photoset by Avon DataSet Ltd, Bidford on Avon, B50 4JH
Printed in England by Mackays of Chatham plc, Chatham, Kent

A CIP record for this book
is available from the British Library

ISBN 0-571-20635-2

2 4 6 8 10 9 7 5 3 1

Contents

The Billy Goat

In a small thatched cottage by the side of a shady lane lived four young pigs, whose names were Tom, Bill, Sam, and Ann. With them was their guardian, Brock the Badger, the wise old friend who took care of them.

Tom did the cooking, and Bill looked after the garden. Ann had charge of the workbasket and sewed the buttons on as fast as they flew off. Sam got in everybody's way for he was young and simple. The Badger wound up the clock and gave advice, and did all the clever things in the house.

Tom Pig was a fat little cook for he always tasted everything he made, whether it was acorn soup, or omelette of pheasants' eggs, or mushroom pie. Sometimes he tasted so much he couldn't eat his dinner until he had burst a button or two off his clothes. Later, while Bill washed up, and Sam dried the pots, careful Ann took her needle and thread and sewed the

I

buttons on again, a little nearer the edge so that Tom could breathe easily. He was a good cook, as all tasters are, and he never under-buttered the toast, or left a caterpillar in the cabbage.

Bill the gardener was not thin, for he spent quite a lot of time resting on his spade, or leaning over the garden gate, gossiping with the hedgehogs. He slept among the cabbages on hot afternoons, with a carrot in one hand and a lettuce in the other. When he awoke he took a bite, and curled himself under the shady leaves again till tea-time. Bill was a good gardener, and flowers grew and vegetables were fine and plump because he looked after them.

Ann Pig kept the wheels of the house running smoothly by doing everything that had been forgotten by others. She ran up and down stairs, and trotted from garden to orchard, always busy, so that she had no time to get fat like her brothers.

As for Sam, the youngest, he turned cart-wheels along the garden path, or rolled in a ball down the slopes, so that his clothes were worn in holes, and Ann had to mend them every day. He was the stoutest little pig of the family.

The most important member was Brock. He belonged to an ancient family which had lived before Man came into the world. Badger still ruled the woodlands, and every creature gave way before him. He had a long head with black and white stripes down it, which helped him to remain unseen when the light flashed among the trees. His hair was dark brown and his feet black as jet. The little pigs admired him for his strength and courage, and his wisdom. He could climb high walls when they ran round squealing. He could squeeze through narrow spaces when they were too fat to get through. He had a big armchair in which no one else might sit, and a tankard from which no one else might drink.

Every morning after breakfast he went off for a walk in the forest, and he didn't return till dusk. The fringe of the wood was pleasant, for the sun shone through the leaves and dappled the ground with spots of light. Here grew tall beech trees and little hazel trees, and the pigs took their baskets in autumn and filled them with beech-mast and brown nuts. Here were oak trees, laden with acorns, crisp and green, and crab-apple trees, with red crabs full of juice, and mountain ash with scarlet berries. There was all that four little pigs could wish for on the edges of the wood, but further in the forest became dark. The trees grew close together, with heads touching as if they were whispering about all the things they saw. They locked their boughs together like children who hold hands, and the sun could not look at the ground. So the little pigs never went there, and Brock the Badger warned them to keep away.

One fine summer's day when the roses and sweet williams were all blooming in Bill Pig's garden, and the cherries hung ripe on the tree, an odd person walked up to the door and rapped loudly. Never since the trouble with the Lone Wolf had the pig family allowed a stranger to enter the cottage but this extremely thin visitor was a very distinguished stranger.

His beard hung in matted strands from his bony chin, his golden eyes stared about in a bold manner. He was haughty and proud and the little pigs stood humbly before him.

'Is this where the noble family of Pigs dwells?' he asked in a fine, polite voice, and he wagged his long beard and blinked his bright eyes. He was a Billy-goat, without home or relations, seeking protection and comforts.

'Yes,' replied Bill, flattered at this praise. 'Yes. Here we all live. Won't you come in, Sir?'

'Oh I say, Bill,' whispered little Sam. 'Oh, he can't come in you know.'

But the Billy-goat had already put his hoof in the doorway. He bowed his head to avoid the beam and entered the kitchen.

'Yes. It's a very nice house,' said he, looking round. 'It's the kind of house your distinguished ancestor, Sir Honey, might have lived in before he removed to his silver dwelling-place.'

He shook the cushions on Badger's armchair and sat down without waiting to be asked.

'Sir Honey?' whispered Bill to Sam. 'Who is he?'

'Sir Honey?' said Sam to Tom. 'Who is he?'

'Sir Honey?' murmured Tom to the kettle on

the hob. 'Have we an ancestor called Sir Honey?'

The Billy-goat overheard. 'Yes,' said he. 'Sir Honey Pig-Hog, who lived in a silver sty and was loved by a lady of high degree. Surely you remember the ballad about him?'

The pigs shook their heads. 'Never heard it,' they cried.

The Billy-goat leaned back in the chair and crossed his legs. Then he sang in a high bleating voice the song of the Lady and the Swine.

> *'There was a lady loved a Swine.*
> *"Honey," said she.*
> *"Pig-hog, wilt thou be mine?"*
> *"Hunc!" said he.*
> *"I'll build thee a silver sty,*
> *"Honey," said she.*
> *"And in it thou shalt lie."*
> *"Hunc!" said he.*
> *"Pinned with a silver pin,*
> *"Honey," said she,*
> *"That thou mayst go out or in."*
> *"Hunc!" said he.*
> *"Wilt thou have me now,*

"Honey," said she.
"Speak or my heart will break."
"Hunc!" said he.'

'The Pig-Hog was your ancestor,' said the Goat, looking at them with his crafty eyes, as they applauded his fine singing.

'I've never heard of him,' said Bill and the others agreed that they too knew nothing of their famous ancestor.

'Sir Honey Pig-Hog kept a good table,' remarked the Billy-goat. 'I haven't had any dinner today.'

He gazed at the half-open door of the larder, and the plate of cakes and the row of pies on the shelf.

'I have been looking for a house like this for some time,' he continued, as his glance fell on the barrel of herb-beer. 'I think I will honour you with my presence and stay here as your Paying Guest.'

'What's that?' asked Sam bluntly. He didn't want the Billy-goat to sit in Badger's chair as if he owned it.

'A visitor who pays,' explained the Goat stiffly. 'I shall live here, and you will feed me and mend my clothes. In return I shall honour you with my company, and pay you too.'

'What will you pay us?' asked Bill anxiously, as he noticed the Goat's torn coat and his hungry look.

'I'll give you the Seal of Solomon,' said the Billy-goat.

'What is it?' whispered Bill to Tom. 'What is the Seal of Solomon?'

'I am sure I don't know,' whispered Tom, 'but Ann will tell us when she comes home. It sounds very grand indeed.'

'You can bring me my dinner now,' continued the Goat, 'and then show me your best bedroom. I am rather weary.'

So Bill and Tom cooked a good dinner for the Goat, who ate it all up and asked for more.

When Ann came home he was still eating. The three brothers ran down the garden to meet her, and they excitedly told her about the Paying Guest.

'We don't want a Paying Guest,' she cried.

'A young cuckoo is a guest, and the hedge-sparrows have told me about his manners. We don't want a cuckoo in the house.'

'He isn't at all like a cuckoo,' explained Bill. 'He has no wings or feathers. He knew our ancestor Sir Honey Pig-Hog, and he will give us the Seal of Solomon for looking after him.'

'Solomon was a great wise king who lived long ago,' said Ann, opening wide her blue eyes. 'I should think his seal is a beautiful thing, carved in ivory and set with pearls. Yes, it must be one of the world's wonders.'

She opened the door and looked at the Billy-goat, who rose and bowed to her. She was impressed by his long beard, and his golden eyes, his shaggy hair and his neat polished hooves. She spoke quietly and bade him welcome.

After dinner the Billy-goat went upstairs and lay down on the bed in Badger's room. He couldn't sleep in the small room Ann offered him. He was used to the best, he told her. He put his hooves on the linen sheets and drew the home-spun blankets round his head. He would take a nap, for he had walked far.

'It is very nice to have such a grand visitor, with horns to protect us while Badger is away,' said the little pigs. 'We will hang the Seal of Solomon over the mantelpiece, when we get it.'

Every morning little Sam ran to the brook for a bucket of water to wash the Billy-goat's white beard. Then he combed it and brushed it and curled it till it was as wavy as his own small tail.

Every day Bill Pig worked in the garden, digging up vegetables for soup, shelling peas, gathering beans, picking herbs for the pot. He worked till he didn't know whether he was standing on his head or his heels.

Every day Tom Pig did the cooking. He made soups and stews, roasts and boils, rissoles and savouries, jellies and jams, puddings and spices. He cooked till he didn't know his right foot from his left.

Every day Ann Pig sewed and knitted and mended and darned, and made new clothes for the Billy-goat, till her fingers were pricked and her eyes were sore.

The dormice and hedgehogs and moles ran to peep in at the garden gate. They wanted to get a glimpse of the Paying Guest who was honouring the Pig family, the famous Goat who knew King Solomon and the Pig in the silver sty. The Goat never went out, and nobody saw him but the four pigs who were heartily sick of him.

Each night when the washing-up was finished, the little pigs fell over with tiredness.

The clock struck nine, but no one could go to bed, for that wicked Goat wanted just one more cup of camomile tea, just one more tansy cake.

'When shall we get the Seal of Solomon?' asked Bill. 'He's been here a month and said nothing about paying.'

'You ask him, Tom,' said Ann. 'You're the eldest.'

'No,' Tom shook his head. 'You're the land-lady.'

So Ann went up to the Billy-goat who sat snoring loudly in Badger's armchair, with Badger's handkerchief over his head. He was a stout, heavy fellow, twice the size he had been when he arrived.

'Please, Sir, will you kindly pay us and go?' asked Ann bravely, although her heart was beating very fast for she was afraid of the Billy-goat's horns.

The Billy-goat opened his golden eyes and stared angrily at her.

'Here I am and here I stay!' he shouted.

'*Will* you, *won't* you, *will* you pay?' sang little Sam in a very small voice, but the Billy-goat heard him and frowned.

'I'll stay and I'll pay,' he roared. 'The Seal of Solomon is in the wood, and you can find it for yourselves!'

He shut his eyes and pulled the handkerchief over his head and the pigs backed out of the room.

'There is no such thing as the Seal of Solomon,' sighed Ann, and her brothers agreed with her.

There was no rest for anybody after that. Never could they stroll through the fields to see the ripening corn. Never could they dance among the flowers in the meadow. They could not sup with a neighbour or take tea with a friend. It was work from dawn to eve, looking after the Paying Guest who filled the small kitchen with his vast body.

'Badger would get him out,' muttered Bill to Tom. 'If only Badger would come home! He has never been away so long in the summer.'

'But what about those horns?' asked Tom.

'The Billy-goat would stick his horns into Brock. He pricked me only this morning because I didn't run fast enough with his porridge.'

'Brock would know what to do,' said Sam confidently.

The three brothers were standing in the garden, looking at the broken ground. The vegetables had all gone and the trees were robbed of their fruit. They wondered what they would do for food if the Goat stayed much longer.

Then Ann came running from the house.

'I shall go and find Badger,' she wept. 'The Paying Guest has tossed my workbox into the frying-pan, and he threatened to toss me after it. His horns are as sharp as darning-needles.'

'You can't find Badger. You will get eaten up and then who will sew on our buttons and darn our socks?' said her brothers.

'I am too thin. Nothing will eat a bag of bones,' sobbed Ann.

'You will get lost,' cried Bill. 'The robins will bury you, like a Babe-in-the-Wood.'

'No. I'll take a bag of pebbles and drop

them. Hop-'o-my-thumb did that. Then I can find my way back if I don't get to Badger's castle.'

They all thought this was a good plan and Sam collected the white stones in a calico bag while Ann put on her cloak. Bill cut a crooked stick for her protection, and, grasping it in one hand and the bag in the other, the little pig set out on her journey. Deep into the wood she walked and every few minutes she dropped a pebble.

The brown rabbits, sitting at their doors, the squirrels in the tree tops, the deer peeping through the trees, all directed her to Badger's winter house. She went far into the bracken-filled wood, struggling through the brambles and undergrowth, wading through the streams, up to her knees in the bogs.

Evening came, and the bit-bats flickered and darted shrilly overhead. The blackbird sang its late song, and darkness came down to hide the earth. But the little glow-worms lighted her onward, and the hooting owl kept her company. Fierce eyes peered at her as she plodded on, sharp noses sniffed round her feet, but the wicked creatures muttered 'She is too thin', and they drifted away.

At day-break she came to Badger's castle, with its strong door let into the earth.

She knocked but there was no answer. Wearied out she fell asleep with her head on the heather-mat. There Brock found her when he returned from hunting.

'Why have you come here? What's the matter?' he asked, and he unlocked his door and took her in to the dark chamber, with its bracken-covered floor.

'We have a Paying Guest who won't go,' cried Ann dolefully, and she took off her cloak and ate the food the kindly Badger prepared for her. 'I've come to you, dear Brock, for help.'

'Why did you let him in?' asked the astonished Badger.

'Because he knew our ancestor Sir Honey Pig-Hog, who lived in a silver sty,' said Ann.

'Pshaw! Sir Honey Fiddlesticks! How much does he pay?'

'Nothing yet,' confessed Ann. 'He promised

the Seal of Solomon, and then he said we could get it for ourselves from the wood.'

'That's true,' said Badger slowly. 'I know the Seal of Solomon.'

'He won't go away. He sits in your chair, and sleeps in your bed, Brock,' said Ann.

'What! Sleeps in *my* bed, and sits in *my* chair!' roared Brock. 'I'll see to this Paying Guest.' He looked so fierce little Ann jumped up in a fright.

'Off we go at once, Ann,' cried the Badger and away they went without waiting for Badger to take off his hunting kit. On the way Ann described the Paying Guest, for Badger couldn't imagine who had ventured to live in the small house with the four pigs.

'He has very sharp horns,' she said.

'One or two?' asked Badger. 'He may be a Bull, or he may be a Unicorn. It all depends on the number of horns.'

'Two horns,' replied Ann. 'He has a long beard and golden eyes, and he is always very cross.'

'It's a Billy-goat! That's better! Only a

silly old Billy! I can easily settle a Billy, however sharp his horns. If it had been a Bull it would have been more difficult, and I am not sure how to deal with Unicorns, but a Billy is easy.'

He gathered a few herbs as he went along, and gave them to Ann.

'We'll make a drink of herb-tea for your friend,' said he. 'A real soothing drink for him to calm his temper.'

Badger stopped in a dell and pointed out a beautiful plant, with long drooping leaves. A row of white bells hung like a shower of pearls from each curving leaf, and the bells had strange markings upon them.

'That is Solomon's Seal,' said Badger. 'We will put it in our garden, in memory of the Goat.'

'It is very beautiful,' cried Ann, kneeling down to see the long arch of snowy flowers. 'King Solomon must have been proud to have such a lovely Seal as this.'

Badger took the plant along with him, and the two chatted happily as they went through the wood, for Badger had much knowledge of ancient plants and strange roots.

The family came running to meet them as they came down the lane.

'Oh Brock! Oh Ann! He's been worse than ever. He tossed poor Sam out of the door into the garden this morning. He keeps asking where you are. He has torn his coat and there's nobody to sew it for him.'

'Umph!' muttered Badger. 'Where is he?'

'In bed, and he won't get up. He's very cross today.'

'I'll make him a sleeping draught, and then he won't want to get up,' said Badger.

That evening the Goat drank a soothing brew of Viper's Bugloss and Goat's Beard, of Mandrake and Poppy, which Badger had prepared. Ann took it up to him on a clean white tray, and he sipped it with the best spoon.

He slept like old Solomon himself in his tomb!

Then Badger trussed him with a couple of sheets and tied him with a rope. He hauled him down the garden, and across many a field and little wood to the distant farmyard. There he left him, still sleeping, and there the farmer found him.

'Hello!' cried the farmer. 'Here's a fine fat Billy-goat, a present from some kind friend. He's just what I want. He's rather like that Billy I had some months back, but this fellow is twice the size.'

He fastened the Billy-goat by a chain to a stout stake in the pasture and the Billy-goat opened his evil eye and stared at the farmer, who suddenly recognised him.

'Hello! It's the same old Billy I used to have, that runned away! I know that wicked eye again! He shan't escape this time.'

Sometimes a little pig crept up to look at the prisoner, and then ran home as fast as he could to tell the family that the Paying Guest was still staying at the farm.

In the borders of the little thatched house two plants were growing side by side. One was the yellow flower of Goat's Beard, with its feathery seeds which Sam never had to comb. The other was Solomon's Seal, which sprayed its fountain of white bells over the path.

'Carved in ivory and set with pearls,' murmured Ann. 'I like this better than the Seal Solomon had.'

Sam Pig Seeks His Fortune

One day Sam Pig started out to seek his fortune, and this was the reason. He came down as usual for breakfast, with never a thought except that he was hungry and there was a larder full of food. It was a sunny morning and he decided he would bask in the garden, and enjoy himself, and do nothing at all.

'Go and fill the kettle at the spring,' said Ann, when he entered the room. He picked up the copper kettle and carried it down the lane to the spring of water which gushed out of the earth. Then he staggered slowly back, spilling all the way.

'That's my day's work done,' he said to himself as he lifted it to the fire.

'Go and chop some sticks, Sam,' said Bill, when he was comfortably settled at the table.

He picked up the axe from the corner and went to the woodstack. Then he chipped and he chopped till he had a fine pile of kindling. He filled the wood-box and brought it back to the house.

'That's two days' work done,' said he to himself as he put some of the wood under the kettle. He returned to his seat but Ann called him again.

'Blow up the fire, Sam,' she ordered. He reached down the blow-bellows and he puffed and he huffed and he blew out his own fat cheeks as well as the bellows. Then the fire crackled and a spurt of flame roared out and the kettle began to sing.

'That's three days' work done,' said Sam to himself and he listened to the kettle's song, and tried to find out what it said.

'Go and fetch the eggs, Sam,' said Tom, and away he went once more. He chased the hens out of the garden and hunted under the hedge-side for the eggs. He put them in a rhubarb-leaf basket and walked slowly back to the house. His legs were tired already, and he looked very cross.

'That's four days' work done,' said he to himself, and he put the basket on the table. Then he sat down and waited for breakfast, but Ann called him once more.

'Sam. Wash your face and brush your hair,' she said. 'How can you sit down like a piggy-pig?'

That settled it! To be called a piggy-pig was the last straw! All Sam's plans suddenly changed. His life was going to be different. He had had enough of family rule.

'I'm going to seek my fortune,' he announced loudly, when he had scrubbed his face and hands and brushed his bristly hair. 'I'm going off right away after breakfast to seek my fortune.'

He put a handful of sugar in his cup and blew on his tea and supped his porridge noisily, in defiant mood.

'And what may that be?' asked Bill sarcastically. 'What is your fortune, Sam?'

'His face is his fortune,' said Tom, rudely.

'You foolish young pig,' cried Ann. 'What would Badger say? You must stay at home and help us. We can't do without you.'

'I know you can't,' Sam tossed his head. 'That's why I'm going.' And he ate his breakfast greedily, for he didn't know when he would have another as good.

He took his knapsack from the wall and put in it a loaf of bread and a round cheese. He brushed his small hooves and stuck a feather in his hat. Then he cut a stick from the hazel tree and away he went.

'Goodbye,' he called, waving his hat to his astonished sister and brothers. 'Goodbye, I shall return rich and great some day.'

'Goodbye. You'll soon come running back, Brother Sam,' they laughed.

Now he hadn't gone far when he heard a mooing in some bushes.

'Moo! Moo! Moo!'

He turned aside and there was a poor lone cow caught by her horns, struggling to free herself. He unfastened the boughs and pulled the branches asunder so that the cow could get away.

'Thank you. Thank you,' said the cow.

'Where are you going so early, Sam Pig?'

'To seek my fortune,' said Sam.

'Then let me go with you,' said the cow. 'We shall be company.' So the cow and Sam went along together, the cow ambling slowly, eating as she walked, Sam Pig trying to hurry her.

'Take a lift on my back,' said the cow kindly, and Sam leapt up to her warm, comfortable back. There he perched himself with his little legs astride and his tail curled up.

They went through woods and along lanes. Sam stared about from the cow's back, seeking his fortune everywhere.

'Miaou! Miaou!' The cry came from a tree, and Sam looked up in surprise. On a high bough sat a white cat, weeping and wailing in misery.

'What is the matter?' asked Sam.

'I've got up here,' sobbed the white cat, 'and I can't get down. I've been here for two nights and a day, and nobody has helped me. There's boogles and witches about in the night, and I'm scared out of my seven wits.'

'I'll get you down,' said Sam Pig proudly,

and he stood on the cow's head and reached up with his hazel switch. The white cat slithered along it and slipped safely to the ground.

'Oh, thank you! Thank you, kind sir,' said the cat. 'I'll go with you, wherever you go,' said she.

'I'm going to seek my fortune,' said Sam.

'Then I'll go too,' said the white cat, and she walked behind the cow with her tail upright like a flag and her feet stepping delicately and finely.

Away they went to seek Sam's fortune, and they hadn't gone far when they heard a dog barking.

'Bow wow. Bow wow,' it said.

The cow turned aside and the cat followed, after a natural hesitation.

In a field they saw a poor thin dog with its foot caught in a trap. The cow forced the trap open and released the creature. Away it limped, holding up its paw, but Sam put a dock-leaf bandage upon it, and bound it with ribbons of grasses.

'I'll come with you,' said the dog gratefully. 'I'll follow you, kind sir.'

'I'm going to seek my fortune,' said Sam.

'Then I'll go too,' barked the dog, and it followed after. But the white cat changed her place and sprang between the cow's horns; and that's the way they went, the cow with Sam on her back and the cat between her horns and the lame dog trotting behind.

Now after a time they heard a squeaking and a squawking from the hedgeside. There was a little Jenny Wren, struggling for its life in a bird-net.

'What's the matter?' asked Sam.

'I'm caught in this net and if nobody rescues me, I shall die,' cried the trembling wren.

'I'll save you,' said Sam, and he tore open the meshes of the net and freed the little bird.

'Oh thank you. Thank you,' said the wren. 'I'll go with you wherever you go.'

Then it saw the green eyes of the cat watching it from the cow's horns so it flew to the other end of the cow and perched on its tail. Away they all went, the cow with the pig on her back and the cat on her horns and the bird on her tail, and behind walked the dog.

They went along the woods and meadows, always seeking Sam's fortune. After a time it began to rain and they got bedraggled and wet. Then out came the sun and they saw a great rainbow stretching across the sky and dipping down to the field where they walked. The beautiful arch touched the earth at an old twisty hawthorn tree.

'That's where my fortune is hidden,' cried Sam, pointing to the thorn bush. 'At the foot of the rainbow. Badger told me once to look there. "Seek at the foot of a rainbow and you'll find a fortune," he said to me, and there's the rainbow pointing to the ground!'

So down they scrambled: the white cat leapt from the cow's horns, Sam sidled from the cow's back and the bird flew down from the cow's tail. They all began to dig and to rootle with horns and feet and bill and claws and snout. They tossed away the black earth and dug into the crumpled roots of the tree. There lay a crock filled with pieces of gold.

'Here's my fortune,' cried Sam Pig, lifting it out.

'We can't eat it,' said the cow, snuffling at it with her wet nose. 'It's hard as stone.'

'We can't eat it,' said the white cat, putting out a delicate pink tongue. 'It's tough as wood.'

'We can't eat it,' barked the dog, biting with sharp teeth at the gold. 'It's harsh as rocks.'

'We can't eat it,' sang the bird, pecking at the pieces. 'It's cruel as a snare.'

'What use is your fortune?' they all asked Sam.

'I don't know,' Sam shook his head and scratched himself behind the ear. 'I've found it, and that is what I set out to do.'

'I'm weary,' said the cow. 'Let us stay here all night.'

The cow began to crop the grass, and the cat supped the bowl of milk which the cow gave to it. The bird found a few fat worms where the earth had been disturbed. As for Sam, he shared his bread and cheese with the dog, and all were satisfied and at peace with one another. The cow tucked her legs under her big body and bowed her head in sleep. The cat curled up in a white ball. The wren put its head under its wing. The dog rested with its chin on its paws.

Then Sam cut a stick from the hawthorn tree. It was a knobby thorn full of magic, for it had guarded the gold for a thousand years, ever since the fairies had hidden it. Of course Sam didn't know that, but Badger would have warned him if he had been there.

'Never cut a bough from a twisty ancient thorn,' he would have said. 'There's a power of magic hidden in it.'

Sam cut the thorn and trimmed it with his clasp knife, and leaned it up against the tree over the crock of gold, all ready to catch a robber if one should come in the night. Then he lay down next to the dog.

The moon came up in the sky and looked at the strange assembly under the old hawthorn tree. She blinked through the branches of the old thorn and shot her moonbeams at the cudgel, shaking it into life. Then it began to belabour every creature there except the little wren which was asleep in the tree.

When the cow felt the sharp blows across her ribs, she turned on the dog and tossed it with her sharp horns. The dog rushed at the cat and tried to worry it. The cat scrambled up the tree and tried to catch the bird. The little Jenny Wren awoke with a cry and flew away.

Sam took to his heels and ran as fast as he could along the lanes and through the woods and across the meadows till he reached home. He banged at the door and wakened them all up.

'Where's the fortune, Sam?' asked Bill and Tom and little Ann Pig. 'Did you find a crock of gold?'

'Yes. A crock of gold,' cried Sam, out of breath with running so fast. 'A crock of gold under the rainbow end.'

'Where is it?' they asked. 'Gold is useful sometimes and it would do fine to mend the hole in our roof. Where is it, Sam?'

Then Sam told how he had found the gold under the hawthorn tree, but the tree had belaboured them soundly in the night and he had run home.

'That gold is bewitched,' said Ann. 'Best leave it where you found it.'

'I would like to see the crock of gold, and touch it, and smell it,' interrupted Bill.

'So would I,' added Tom. 'I've never seen any gold.'

'Then I will take you there tomorrow after I've had a good sleep,' yawned Sam. 'That is if you don't make me work before breakfast.'

The next morning they all went across the wood and over the meadows to the old hawthorn tree where Sam had found the crock of gold.

A cow was feeding in the thick grass of the field, and a white cat was leaning with her paw outstretched over the stream fishing for minnows. A dog chased a rabbit through the hedge and a little Jenny Wren piped and sang.

There was no crock of gold anywhere to be seen, but underneath the old bent tree grew a host of king-cups, glittering like gold pence in the sunshine, fluttering their yellow petals in their dark green leaves.

'You imagined the gold,' said Bill indignantly. 'You've led us here on a wild goose chase,' and he cuffed poor Sam Pig over the head.

'I didn't!' protested Sam. 'There's the cudgel I cut from the tree.'

On the ground lay a thick stick, knotted and thorny and dark. The pigs leaned over it without touching it; then they began to gather the flowers.

'Quite true,' they nodded. 'Quite true, Sam Pig. You did find a fortune after all. There it lies, all turned into yellow flowers, much more use than metal to a family of pigs. Let the human kind take the hard metal, and we'll take the posies. King-cups are good for pains and aches; their seeds make pills and their leaves are cool poultices and their flowers are a delight to our sharp noses.'

They gathered a bunch and walked slowly home through the fresh fields wet with dew. All the way they talked to Sam kindly and treated him as if he had indeed brought a fortune to them.

'Badger will be pleased with you, little Pigwiggin,' said they and this was high praise for little Sam Pig.

Magic Water

It was raining as if it would never stop, and the drops pattered on the footpath and rolled in silver beads down the windowpane. Sam Pig sat on his three-legged stool staring out at the storm. He pressed his round nose against the glass and flicked his curly tail. He drummed his small hooves on the floor with a rat-rat-tat in time with the beat of the rain. He was the only person who really liked rain, and he listened to the singing noise as the water spurted in the rain barrel and ran down the gutters. Now high, now low it went, like a fiddle played by invisible fingers.

'Crowds of silver rain-drops dancing on their toes,
Leaping in the rain-tub, swinging on the rose,'

he warbled, and the rain hummed and murmured in the garden as the dry earth sucked it in. The drops hung like rainbow buttons from the twigs of the pear tree, and the streams of water were silver threads weaving among the cabbage roses.

'Where does it all come from, Sister Ann?' he asked, and he turned to his sister who was working close by.

Ann Pig glanced up from her complicated knitting. She was making a three-cornered cap out of sheep's wool and blackthorn flowers. Tom had found the fleecy wool clinging to the hedge where the flock of sheep had struggled through and he had collected the soft strands for Ann. Bill had washed them and dyed them green. Sam had picked the blackthorn flowers, and had made a pair of knitting-needles from sharp blackthorn twigs. Now Ann was knitting a pointed cap which could be worn on Sam's head or used as a basket for carrying mushrooms and blackberries.

'Knit one, purl one,' said Ann, frowning, and she twisted the wool over the thorns and disentangled a butterfly which settled on her work. Sam had left the white starry flowers on the knitting-needles, and although Ann thought they looked very pretty, it was difficult to knit with bees and butterflies settling on one's needles.

'Where does the rain come from, Sister Ann?' repeated Sam Pig.

Ann put down her work and considered.

'From the rain-clouds,' said she.

'And how does the rain get into the clouds?' asked Sam.

This puzzled Ann. She shook her head. 'I expect it just runs backwards,' said she, but when Sam opened his mouth to ask when, where and why it ran backwards, she stopped him.

'Be quiet, Sam. How can I make a pointed cap if you talk? Knit one, purl one, insert a blackthorn flower, and knit two together.'

There was silence except for the click of the knitting-needles and the buzz of bees which sucked the honey from the white flowers. Sam peered at the darkening sky, and the drenched earth. He could see Bill working in the garden, carrying a watering-can. Tom had gone fishing round the corner. He was lonely and Ann wouldn't talk. Only the rain murmured on, so Sam chanted to it.

> *'Rain, Rain, on my window pane,*
> *Won't you come in, O Shining Rain?'*

'We don't want the rain indoors, Silly Sam,' cried Ann.

'Will you sew some raindrops on my coat?' asked Sam, leaping off the stool and coming to her.

'No. Of course I won't.' Ann laughed good-humouredly and tweaked Sam's twitching ear. 'No one can sew raindrops.'

'You can, Sister Ann. You can do everything,' whispered Sam, and he looked at the wonderful knitting on Ann's lap.

Ann pondered his words. Was it possible? She wanted some little buttons for Sam's coat, and although her brothers had brought various kinds from the woods, nothing was right. She turned over the assortment in the workbasket. A dozen acorns, a bunch of rosy berries, a collection of pebbles, and some beans. Certainly a row of glistening raindrops would be much nicer.

'And I could drink them if I was thirsty,' added Sam hopefully.

Ann went to the door and caught the raindrops on a leaf. She threaded her needle and tried to sew them, but they ran together as quickly as she slipped her sewing-needle through, and fell in a pool on the Sunday coat.

'It can't be done,' she sighed. 'They would make pretty little buttons, Sam, but I can't sew them.'

Then Badger came in. His thick coat was dark with rain, and his feet made large prints on the floor.

'Sewing raindrops, Ann?' he said, shaking himself and sprinkling Sam in a shower-bath.

'I can't do it, Brock,' sighed Ann.

'No, I don't think it can be done,' said Badger, holding a raindrop in his paw. He looked admiringly at the silvery globules. Then he drew out a hair from his tail and threaded the raindrops on it.

'Look, Ann! Now you can sew them on the coat.'

So Ann stitched the raindrops, and gave the

coat to Sam. He danced round the room, and the buttons twinkled like diamonds, shaking and changing colour, but clinging to the threads.

'His buttons were made of raindrops, of raindrops, of raindrops. His buttons were made of raindrops, and his name was Samuel Pig,' he sang shrilly.

Bill the gardener came stumping in, with his wooden spade and his watering-can.

'Whatever are you doing with a watering-can on a wet day like this?' scoffed Badger.

'Watering the primroses and bluebells,' said Bill, and he swung the can up and down, sprinkling the leafy carpet.

'Can't you see it's raining already?' asked Badger crossly.

'Yes. I'm trying to use it up, Brock. There's such a lot of it all going to waste.'

'He's been filling the watering-can and emptying it all day,' explained Sam eagerly. 'Now he's bringing the rain indoors, where I wanted it.'

Badger grunted. 'Time he had more sense,'

and he flung the can in the garden.

Then Tom Pig came in. He carried a fishing-rod and a creel. He wore a green mackintosh and he held a rhubarb-leaf over his head for an umbrella. The rain poured off the mackintosh in a pool and Ann ran with a floorcloth to wipe it up.

'It's as wet indoors as out,' she groaned. 'You all come in with your rain and your muddy hooves.'

'Do you want us to leave our feet on the doorstep as if they were galoshes?' asked Bill sullenly. He was upset about the watering-can, for he had been working hard all day.

'Look what I've got,' cried Tom Pig, opening his creel, and the family of pigs crowded round and forgot their irritation when they saw the shoal of little fish lying in the bed of grasses. There were blue fish and red fish and purple fish, all plump and shiny, glimmering like rays of light.

'Caught 'em myself,' boasted Tom. 'Fished 'em up, and caught 'em and brought 'em home for supper.'

'Where did you get such lovely little fishes?' asked Ann astonished, and they all exclaimed with delight and held up the slippery morsels.

'You'll never guess! In the rain-barrel!' said Tom. 'I've been fishing in the rain-barrel all morning. There was nothing at first, and suddenly there was a swarm, like butterflies swimming about, and I netted them.'

'Butterflies don't swim,' grunted Brock. He padded to the door and went outside to the end of the cottage where the rain-barrel stood. He peered inside and put in a paw. He brought up half a dozen little coloured fish, green and scarlet and silver, so he dropped them wriggling and squirming back again.

'Never knew such a thing!' he exclaimed. 'Never knew such a lot of fish in our rain-barrel! Needn't go to the river now. Fish for breakfast every day.'

'And for dinner and tea and supper,' added Sam, eagerly.

'Fried in fat and stuffed with parsley,' said Bill.

'Roast and boiled and pickled,' said Ann.

Tom put the frying-pan on the fire and cooked the supper and the little fish frizzled and leapt in the pan with the hissing sound of water falling on hot coals. The four pigs and Badger had a merry meal with the piled-up platter of tasty fish.

'Get your fiddle, Sam, and play us a tune, for this rain is beating on the house with a fearful racket,' cried Brock, when he had finished. He leaned back in his armchair and stretched out his short legs. Tom and Bill washed up the supper-things, and Ann went on with her knitting. The little fleecy cap was nearly done and very nice it looked with its starry white flowers set among the sheep's wool. Yet something was missing, and she wondered what it was.

Sam reached his fiddle from the hook where it hung from the rafters. He held it under his chin and tuned it. Then he began to play the tunes the rain had taught him. As the music came twinkling and dropping out of the fiddle, Ann knew what she wanted. She went to the door into the night. A watery moon was shining and the rain had ceased. Everything was quiet, as if listening to the soft strains of Sam's fiddle. She gathered some more raindrops and then she knitted them into the cap. It was as easy as possible.

When the music stopped, she popped the cap on Sam's head.

'There you are, Brother Samuel. A new cap to wear,' said she.

'It's all sparkling like a waterfall.'

'It's a rainbow in candle-light,' said Badger admiringly.

'It's a dunce's cap,' cried Bill rudely.

'It's a rain-cap,' said Sam, and he tossed his head and played another tune.

Now whether it was the effect of the raindrops on Sam's coat and cap, or whether it was the fish from the rain-barrel he had eaten for supper, I cannot tell, but Sam played as he had never played before. His fingers danced over the strings and his little hooves tapped on the floor like a myriad raindrops falling on a wooden roof. He was singing his little song to himself.

'Rain, Rain, Shining Rain,
Come and sing to us, Summer Rain.'

In the midst of the music, as Bill and Tom flicked the drying-cloth about, and Ann beat time with her knitting-needles, and Badger waved his pipe, there came a knock at the door. It was a muffled knock but everyone heard it.

'Only the rising wind,' said little Ann, and she dropped her needles.

'Or the branch of the pear tree tapping,' said Tom, and he broke a cup.

'Or the watering-can fallen against the door,' said Bill, and he knocked over the candle.

'Or a friend come to visit us,' said Badger, frowning at the family of nervous pigs.

'Or the ra-a-a-ain,' whispered Sam, and his fiddle squeaked on the highest C.

The door was slowly pushed open and a Stranger appeared. He stood in the doorway and the rain poured from him in dancing cascades to the floor. He was dressed in black and a long cloak hung from his shoulders. His hair was shining with water; the hands which

held the great cloak around him were wet and
rain fell from the long, pointed finger-tips. His
bright eyes were like stars shining from the
darkness. He carried a sheaf of long arrows,
glittering like glass, fine as spun gold,

thousands of them packed into the silver sheaf.

'Let me take your cloak, stranger. You are very wet,' said Badger rising, and all the pigs stood waiting near. The Stranger slipped the cloak from his shoulders and held it out with never a word.

It was lined with silver and shining like a fish, wet and glistening with the water which ran down it in streams.

'It's a bad night for you to be out, sir,' continued the Badger.

The Stranger smiled and the rain beat against the door with sudden fury and the wind howled round the house in a hurricane.

He sat down in the chair that Badger offered him and he sipped a glass of wine. Then he stretched out a long arm and took the fiddle which Sam had hung up when the Stranger entered.

'I heard your call,' said he to Sam, and his voice was deep and full of echoes and tremors, so that Sam stared amazed. Across the room hung the silver cloak and underneath was a pool of water. Little streams rolled down the silken folds and fell on the floor with a patter like a thousand tiny feet. Ann got up and fetched her mop, but the water dripped and ran like a brook under the door and out to the garden. Sighing at the thoughtlessness of strangers, she returned to her seat.

The Stranger was tuning the fiddle with his long slim fingers, and they all waited breathlessly. He drew the bow across and the low wail of a coming storm filled the room. Then he changed his tune, and played airs so entrancing they brought pictures which seemed to float before their eyes, of rainbow days when light flashes after rain, or spring days when sun and rain strive for mastery. He played like the doves crooning in the woods. 'Coo-roo-roo,' their voices came from the fiddle, and the listeners could see the changing colours of the doves' breasts. He played like the cuckoo calling in the wet ash trees, and the blackbird fluting in the pear tree where it has built its nest, and the thrush singing with beak uplifted to the rainy sky on the topmost bough of the sycamore tree.

The water dripped from his black gown, and the streams ran across the floor, but the family were listening to the nightingale singing to the new moon. They were staring at the Stranger whose bright eyes glittered like the raindrops on Sam's cap, whose face was shadowed and misty as a cloud. He gave the fiddle back to Sam and sat with his legs crossed, his eyes fixed on the fire. But the fire sank low, and the room was filled with damp curling mists and the pigs shivered. They crept silently into their beds and left the Stranger on the hearth.

'Who is he?' asked Sam, but nobody knew. Even Badger shook his head.

'He's very wet, poor fellow,' sighed Ann.

'He never gets any drier,' remarked Bill. 'He will put the fire out and drown us.'

'Maybe he'll go away tomorrow,' said Tom, hopefully.

'I can't send him away,' said Brock. 'There's some magic power in him.'

They came downstairs the next morning and found the floor covered with water. There stood the Stranger, tall and slim, with the raindrops falling from his clothes. He took his cloak from the peg and swung it round his shoulders so that the silver lining flashed and a fine shower of water fell. Then he picked up the sheaf of bright arrows, fine as light-rays, and slipped them under his arm.

'Thank you for your hospitality,' said he, bowing low. 'I've not stayed under a roof for many a year, but when I heard that fiddle's music and when I saw that cap of raindrops, I knew I should be welcome.'

'Who are you, sir?' asked Brock, as the Stranger opened the door and stood for a moment on the step. The sun was shining and the world looked beautiful after the storm.

The Stranger didn't speak. Instead he threw back his cloak with a proud gesture, and lifted his long arm with the arrows in his hand, and he seemed to grow in stature to a mighty size. He flung the shining arrows over the earth, and they sped like quivering sheets of rain. He tossed his cloak in the air and it formed a black cloud-streaked with silver. He walked swiftly away, and his feet never touched the earth. Birds flew after him, fluttering their wings in the mist of raindrops which encircled him. A rainbow appeared, a great bow across the sky, and the Stranger walked into it and disappeared.

'Who was it?' they asked one another. 'Who was it?'

Brock answered them. 'It was Rain himself,' said he. 'Rain come to visit us.'

They went back to the house, but already the sun was drying the pools of water. The raindrops on Sam's coat rolled away and his cap steamed in the heat. The many-coloured fish swam out of the rain-barrel and dissolved like a mist of moonbeams. The flowers raised their heads and tossed the beads of moisture away. The storm was over.

Ann picked up her knitting-needles and the remainder of the fleecy wool. She cast on the stitches and flicked away a bumble bee from the white flowers of her needles.

'I think I will make a sun-cap this time,' said she. 'It might keep the poor Rain dry. Do you think he would find it if I hung it in the pear tree, Brock?'

Brock thought that Rain might be glad of it. So Ann knitted another pointed cap and Sam climbed the pear tree and hung it on a high bough. The sun dried it and the moon bleached it, but whether Rain ever took it away I cannot tell you. Certainly the cap disappeared one night in a storm and the next day there was sunshine. Sam thought Rain had worn the cap, and perhaps he was right.

Sam Pig's Trousers

Sam Pig was always hard on his trousers. He tore them on the brambles and hooked them in the gorse bushes. He lost little pieces of them in the hawthorns, and he left shreds among the spiky thistles. He rubbed them threadbare with sliding down the rocks of the high pastures, and he wore them into holes when he scrambled through hedges. One always knew where Sam Pig had been by the fragments of check trousers which clung to thorn and crooked twig. The birds were very glad, and they took bits to make their nests. The rooks had little snippets like gay pennons dangling from their rookery in the elms, and the chaffinches and yellow-hammers mixed the threads with sheep's wool to line their beds. It seemed as if Sam Pig would provide material for everybody's home in the trees and hedgerows, but trousers won't last for ever, and Sam's were nearly done.

Sister Ann patched the seats and put pieces into the front. She stitched panels in the two sides, and then she patched and repatched the patches until there was none of the original trousers left. They were a conglomeration of stripes and plaids and spotted scraps, all herring-boned and cross-stitched with green thread.

'Sam's trousers are like a patchwork quilt,' remarked Tom, when Ann held up the queer little garments one evening after she had mended them.

'Pied and speckled like a magpie,' said Bill.

Sam Pig leaned out of the truckle bed where he lay wrapped in a blanket, waiting for Ann to finish the mending. They were the only trousers the little pig possessed, and he had to go to bed early on mending nights.

'I like them patched,' said he indignantly. 'Don't mock at them. I love my old trousers and their nice patches. It's always a surprise when Ann finishes them. Look now! There's a green patch on top of a black patch, on top of a yellow patch, on top of a blue one. And there's lots of pockets hidden among the patches, spaces where I can keep things. When Ann's stitches burst I stuff things in between.'

'Yes,' frowned Ann. 'I've already taken out a ladybird, and a piece of honeycomb, and some bees and a frog that was leaping up and down, and a stag-beetle that was fighting, not to mention sundry pebbles and oak-apples and snail shells! No wonder you look a clumsy shape with all those things hidden in your patches, Sam! All corners and lumps, you are!'

Sam curled himself under the blanket and laughed till he made the bed shake. She hadn't found the most important thing of all, something that was hidden under the largest patch! If she did –!

Just then Ann gave a shrill cry and dropped the trousers.

'Oh! They've bitten me! Your trousers bit my finger!' she exclaimed, and she put her hand in her mouth and sucked it.

'Trousers can't bite,' said Tom, but Sam dived deeper under the blanket, and laughed all the more.

'What is it, Sam?' asked Tom sternly. 'Confess! What is hidden there in your trousers?'

There was no answer, but from the patch came a pair of ears and two bright eyes. A white mouse poked out its little head. It stared at Ann, it peeped at Sam, and then it bolted down the table leg and into a hole in the floor.

'Now you've lost her! You've lost Jemima!' said Sam crossly, coming up from the blankets. 'She was my pet mouse, and you've lost her. She was a most endearing creature. I kept her in that patch and fed her on crumbs. Is her family safe?'

'Family?' cried Ann, shrilly.

'Family?' echoed Bill and Tom.

'Yes. She has four children. They all live in

the patch. They have a nest there. I helped Jemima to make it. I'm the godfather to the children. They know me very well.'

Ann hurriedly unpicked the stitches and brought out a small round nest with four pink mice inside it.

'There they are! Aren't they charming creatures?' cried Sam.

'But they will be lonely without their mother. You must put them by the hole in the floor, Ann, and Jemima will come for them. She'll miss her warm home in my trousers, and the food I gave her.'

Ann carried the nest and placed it close to the hole. In a minute the mother appeared and enticed her brood away.

'Goodbye, Sam,' she squealed in a shrill voice, thin as a grasshopper's chirp. 'Goodbye, Sam, and thank you for your hospitality. We are going to travel. It is time my children saw something of the world.'

'Goodbye,' called Sam, leaning out of bed. 'I shall miss you terribly, but we may meet again some day. The world is small.'

'Hm!' sniffed Ann Pig. 'The world may be small, but surely there is room in it for a family of white mice without their coming to live in a patch in your trousers, Sam.'

She threaded her needle and took up a bodkin and cleared away all the odds and ends the mice had left, their pots and frying-pan and toasting fork. She tossed the bits of cheese in the fire and frowned as she brought out a bacon rind.

'Bacon in the house of the four pigs is an insult,' said she sternly.

'It came from the grocer's shop, Ann. Really it did! Jemima's husband brought it for the family,' protested Sam.

'Then it's quite time you had a new pair of trousers, Sam. Jemima's husband bringing bacon rinds! I won't have it! These mice are the last straw!' cried Ann, and she banged the trousers and shook them and threw them back to Sam.

'Yes,' agreed Bill. 'It is time you had new breeks. We can't have a menagerie in our house. You'll keep ants and antelopes hidden

57

in your patches, Sam, if you go on like this.'

'Bears and bisons,' said Tom, shaking his head at Sam.

'Crocodiles and cassowaries,' whispered Sam, quivering with laughter.

'It's no laughing matter. Trousers don't grow on gooseberry bushes.'

'I don't want a new pair,' pouted Sam. 'I know this pair, and they are very comfortable. I know every stitch and cranny, and every ridge and crease and crumple.' He pulled the trousers on and shook himself.

'These will soon be quite worn out. One more tear and they will be done,' said Ann. 'We must get another pair, and where the stuff is to come from in these hard times I don't know. You'd better go collecting, all of you.'

'Collecting what? Trousers? From the scare-crows?' asked Sam.

'No. Sheep's wool. Get it off the hedges and bushes and fences. Everywhere you go you must gather the wool left by the sheep when they scramble through gaps and rub their backs on posts. Then I'll dye the wool and spin it, and make a new pair for you.'

Each day the pigs gathered sheep's wool. They picked it off the wild rose trees, where it was twisted among the thorns. They got it from low fences under which the sheep had squeezed, and from the rough trunks of hawthorns and oaks where they had rubbed their backs. Sam found a fine bunch of fleecy wool where the flock had pushed under the crooked boughs of an ancient tree to sleep in the hollow beneath. It was surprising what a quantity of wool there was lying about in the country lanes, and each day they brought back their small sacks filled to the brim.

Ann washed the little fleeces and hung them up to dry. The wool was white as snow when she had finished dipping it in the stream. She tied it to a stout stick and swung it in the sunshine till it was dry and light as a feather.

Bill filled a bowl with lichens and mosses and pieces of bark, and Ann dyed the wool.

'What colour will it be?' asked Sam anxiously peering at it. 'I don't want brown or grey or anything dull.'

'It looks like drab,' confessed Ann.

'Oh dear! What a dingy shade!' sighed Sam. 'I don't want miserable gloomy trousers, or I shall be a gloomy little pig.'

'I'm afraid they *are* going to be sad trousers, Sam,' said Ann, stirring them with a stick. 'I'm sorry, but this is the colour, and there's one good thing, it is the colour of dirt.'

'Gloomy and black as a pitchy night in winter,' said Sam.

So off he went to the woods. He picked some crimson briony berries, and scarlet rose-hips, and bright red toadstools. He brought them back and dropped them into the dye.

'Ann! Ann! Come and look,' he called, and he held up the fleece on the end of the stirring stick.

'Oh Sam! Bright red! A glorious colour,' cried Ann.

'Like a sunset,' exclaimed Tom admiringly.

'Like a house on fire,' said Bill.

Out rushed Sam again, for blueberries and blue geranium, and borage. He dipped another wisp of sheep's wool into the juices and brought it out blue as a wood in bluebell time.

They dried the wool, and Ann fastened it to her little spinning-wheel. She spun a length of red yarn and then a length of blue. Then she knitted a new pair of trousers, in blue and red checks, bright and bold, with plenty of real pockets.

When Sam Pig walked out in his new trousers all the animals and birds came to admire him. Even the Fox stopped to stare at Sam.

'As red as my brush,' he murmured, and the Hedgehog said, 'As pretty a pair of trousers as ever I seed in all my prickly life.'

When Sam met the white mouse and her family they refused to visit his new pockets.

'We like something quieter,' whispered the mouse. 'You are too dazzling for us nowadays, Sam. Besides, we have found a lodging in an old boot. It suits us better.'

'As you will, Jemima,' shrugged Sam. He sauntered off to show himself to acquaintances in the fields, to visit his old haunts in wood and lane.

Soon his trousers lost their brightness, as they

took on the hues of the woodland. They were striped green from the beech trunks, smeared with the juices of blackberry and spindle, parched by the brown earth herself. The sun faded them, the rain shrunk them, and the colours were softened by the moist airs.

'I declare! There is no difference in Sam's trousers,' Ann remarked one day. 'These might be the old check trousers; they are marked and stained in just the same way. I haven't patched them yet, but I can see a hole.'

'Yes,' said Sam, slyly, and he brought a dormouse from his pocket. 'Here is a little friend who lives with me, and he's waiting for a patch to make his winter sleeping-quarters, Ann.'

'Get along with you,' cried Ann, and she chased him out with a besom. But her eyes were twinkling as she watched her young brother dance down the garden path with his dormouse perched on his arm.

Sam Pig and the Wind

It was washing day and Ann Pig decided that it was time Sam's trousers were put in the washtub. They were new trousers, you will remember, made of sheep's wool, dyed red and blue in large checks, but they were dirty, for Sam had fallen into a pool of mud and stuck there till he was rescued.

So Ann scrubbed and rubbed them and hung them up to dry on the clothes-line in the crab-apple orchard, where they fluttered among pyjamas and handkerchiefs and the rest of the family wash.

Sam Pig stood near watching them, for he was afraid the Fox might steal them if he got the chance. It was a warm day, and Sam enjoyed having his little legs free.

'I'll stand on guard,' said he, 'then nobody can take my trousers for their nests or anything.'

The pair of trousers bobbed and danced on

the clothes-line as if somebody were shaking them. It was the wind, which was blowing strongly. It came out of the clouds with a sudden swoop, and it puffed them and it huffed them, and it stuffed them with air. They really seemed to have a pair of invisible fat legs inside them as they swung to and fro and jigged and turned somersaults over the line.

The wind must have taken a fancy to those trousers for it gave a great tug and the wooden clothes-pegs fell to the ground. Sam Pig stooped to pick up his trousers, but they leapt away out of his grasp and across the orchard. Sam sprang after them in a hurry. They frisked over the wall, struggled among the rough stones, and disappeared. Sam was sure they would be lying on the other side, and he climbed slowly and carefully to the top. Alas! The little trousers were already running swiftly across the meadow, trundling along the ground as if a pair of stout legs were inside them. Sam jumped down and ran after them at full speed. He nearly reached them, for the wind dropped and the little trousers flapped and fell empty to the ground. Just as Sam's arm was outstretched to grab them the wind swept down with a howl and caught them up again. It whirled them higher and higher, and tossed them into a tree.

'Whoo-oo-oo,' whistled the wind, as it shook them and left them. There they dangled, caught in a branch, like a dejected ninny. Sam Pig was not daunted. He began to climb that tree. He was part way up, clasping the slippery trunk, panting as he looked for a foothold, when the trousers disentangled themselves and fell to the earth.

'Hurrah!' cried Sam, and he slithered down to safety. 'Hurrah! Now I can get them.'

No! The wind swept down upon them. They rose on their little balloon legs and danced away. The wind blew stronger, and the trousers took leaps in the air like an acrobat. They turned head over heels; they danced on one leg and then on the other, like a sailor doing the hornpipe. Never were such dancing trousers seen as those windy wind-bags!

'Give me back my trousers, O wind,' called Sam Pig, and the wind laughed 'Who-o-o-o.

Who-o-o,' and shrieked, 'Noo-oo-oo,' in such a shrill high voice that Sam shivered with the icy coldness of it.

The trousers jigged along the meadows and into the woods, with Sam running breathlessly after them. He tripped over brambles and caught his feet in rabbit holes and tumbled over tree trunks, but the trousers, wide-legged and active, leapt over the briars, and escaped the thorns as the wind tugged them away. When the wind paused a moment to take a deep breath Sam Pig got near, but he was never in time to catch the runaways. Sometimes they lay down for a rest, but as Sam crept up, stepping softly lest the wind should hear, they sprang to their invisible feet and scampered away.

'What's the matter, Sam?' asked the grey donkey when Sam ran past with his arms outstretched and his ears laid flat. 'Why are you running so fast?'

'My trousers! My trousers!' panted Sam. 'The wind's got them, and it's blowing them away.'

'My goodness! It will blow them across the world, Sam. You'll never see them again,' cried the donkey, staring after the dancing garment. He kicked up his heels and brayed loudly and then galloped after them with his teeth bared.

'Hee-haw! Hee-haw! Stop! Stop!' he blared in his trumpet voice. But he couldn't catch them either, so he returned to his thistles, hee-hawing at the plight of poor Sam Pig.

The trousers were now running across a cornfield, and as they leapt over the stubble Sam was sure there was somebody inside them.

It was an airy fellow, whose long transparent arms and seagreen fingers waved and pointed to sky and earth. A laughing mocking face with puffed-out cheeks nodded at Sam, and a pursed-up mouth whistled shrilly. Wild locks of hair streamed from the wind's head. The thin eldritch voice shrieked like pipes playing, wailing and crying, now high, now low.

'Catch me! Catch me! Get me if you can! I'm the wind, Sam Pig. The wind! I'm the wind from the World's End. From the caves by the mad ocean, from the mountains snow-topped I come. I've flown a thousand leagues to play with you, Sam Pig! Catch me!'

'Wait a minute,' said Sam, rather crossly, and he trundled along on his fat little legs.

The wind turned round and danced about Sam, pulling his tail and blowing in his face so that the little pig had to shut his eyes. Suddenly the wind blew a hurricane. It picked him up and carried him in the air. How frightened was our little Sam Pig when he felt his feet paddling on nothing! His curly tail stuck out straight, his ears were flattened, his body cold as ice. He tried to call for help but no words came. Breathlessly he flew with his legs outstretched, his little feet pad-padding on the soft cushion of air.

Then the wind took pity on him, and dropped him lightly to the ground. He gave a pitiful squeak and lay panting and puffing with fright. He opened his eyes and saw his trousers lying near. He edged towards them and put out a hand, but the trousers stood up, shook themselves full of air, and went dancing off.

Sam Pig arose and followed after. He was a strong-hearted little pig and he was determined not to lose his beloved trousers.

The wind carried them to the farmyard, and sent them fluttering their flapping sides among the hens. The cock crowed, the hens all ran helter-skelter, and the trousers trotted here and there among them, ruffling their feathers, blowing them about like leaves. Sam Pig scrambled over the gate and ran to them, trying to catch the elusive trousers, but getting the cock's tail instead.

'Stop it! Catch it! Catch the wind!' cried Sam.

'Nobody can catch the wind,' crowed the cock. 'Cockadoodle doo! Take shelter, my little red wives!' And the little hens crouched together in a bunch.

'Puff! Puff! Whoo-oo-oo!' screamed the wind, blowing out its cheeks, and prancing in the little check trousers belonging to Sam Pig.

'Quick! Catch it!' called Sam lustily, and he puffed and blew and scampered on aching little legs trying to get the wind, as it whirled round the farmyard.

The wind blew in a sudden gust and the trousers flew over the gate into the field where the cattle grazed.

'Boo-hoo-oo-oo-oo,' it howled, and it raced round the field blowing the cows so that they fled to the walls and stood within the shelter. But the pair of trousers with the wind inside leapt to the back of a young heifer and sat astride, puffing into the hairy ears, holding her horns with long thin fingers.

She leapt forward in a fright and the wind rode on her backbone, standing on one leg, like a circus rider. After her went Sam Pig calling, 'Stop! Catch the wind! Give me my trousers!'

'You can't catch the wind, Sam Pig,' mooed the cows from their shelter. 'You can hide till it's past but you can't catch it.'

Down from the cow's back leapt the trousers, and away they jigged and pranced over the grass, twirling at a great pace, with Sam Pig's little legs plodding faithfully after. He was running so fast his legs seemed to twinkle, but the wind went faster, and the trousers now rose in the air like a kite and now paddled over the ground, luring Sam on by pretending to droop and die.

In the next field was Sally the mare. With a whoop and a cry the wind seized her mane and dragged at her long tail. She turned her back and even when the little trousers leapt to her haunches, she took no notice.

'Get on! Gee-up! Whoo-oo-oo to you,' cried the wind, angrily kicking her ribs with invisible toes, and thumping her sides with the empty legs of the check trousers. The mare stood stock still, head bent, eyes closed, refusing to budge an inch. Sam Pig came hurrying up to his old friend.

'Oh Sally! Catch the wind! keep the wind from taking my trousers away. Hold it, Sally!'

'You can't catch the wind, little Sam. It's free to blow where it likes, and nobody can tame it,' muttered Sally. 'But I won't move for any wind that blows.'

So the wind leapt away and skipped across the fields. The long grasses all turned with it, and tried to follow, but the earth held them back. The trees bent their boughs and the leaves tugged and broke from the twigs and flew after the swift-moving wind.

'There goes the wind,' cried the trees, and they stretched their green fingers in the way the wind had gone.

The wind blew next along a country lane, and the little trousers scampered between the flowery banks with Sam Pig following after. They reached the high road, and Sam hesitated a moment, for he never went alone on the King's Highway. But he was determined to catch his check trousers. Clouds of white dust rose and came after them, pieces of paper were caught and whirled in the air, and a poor butterfly was torn from its flower and swept in the whirlpool of motion after the flying trousers with the wind inside them.

An old woman walked along the road. Her shawl was tightly wrapped around her shoulders, her bonnet fastened with a ribbon, and her black shoes latched on her feet. In her hand she grasped a green umbrella of prodigious size. It was the old witch woman going to the village to do her marketing.

'Drat the wind! It's raising a mighty dust! It will spoil my best bonnet,' she murmured to herself as she saw the cloud of white dust sweeping upon her. She opened the big umbrella and held it over her bonnet. But the wind shot out a long arm and grasped the green umbrella. It snatched it from her hand and bore it away inside out.

She gave a cry of dismay and bent her head to keep her bonnet from being torn from its ribbons. She clutched her shawl and shut her eyes, which watered with the dust.

'My poor old umbereller! It's gone! It's seen many a storm of wind and rain, but never a gust as sharp as this!'

The wind passed on, and she ventured to raise her eyes. In the distance she could see the green umbrella flying along, and a pair of trousers running under it, and after them a short fat pig.

'Poor crittur!' she cried. 'A little pig, and it looks like my own friend little Pigwiggin as came to see me once on a time! He's blown away by this terrible varmint of a wind!'

The wind and Sam came to a church with a weathercock on top of the tower. The iron cock looked down in alarm. It spun round on its creaking axis, and crackled its stiff feathers. Backward went the wind, and back went the weathercock, groaning with pain, and back went Sam Pig, and back went the trousers and the umbrella and all. Away they went over the fields, taking the shortest cut, over the brook and up the hill. Sam Pig saw that the wind was heading, or legging, for home. His own little legs were tired and bleeding, his feet were sore, and his eyes red with dust and wind, but he kept on.

There was the little house at the edge of the wood, and there the little stream with Ann filling the kettle, and there the drying-ground with the clothes-line, empty and forlorn between the crab-apple trees.

The wind bustled over the grass and stopped dead. The pair of trousers fell in a heap. The green umbrella lay with its ribs sticking out. Its horn handle and thick cotton cover were unharmed for it had lived a hundred years already and weathered many a gale.

'Give me back my trousers,' said Sam, in a tired little voice.

'Take thy trousers,' answered the wind, and it shook the trousers and dropped them again.

Sam Pig leapt with a last great effort upon his trousers, and held them down. They never offered to move, for the wind had died away, and the air was still.

'Where are you, wind? Where have you gone?' asked Sam when he recovered himself sufficiently to speak. There was silence except for a faint whisper near the ground. Sam put his ear to a hare-bell's lip, and from it came the clear tiny tinkle of a baby wind which was curled up inside and going to sleep.

'Goodbye, Sam Pig,' said this very small whisper of a voice. 'Goodbye. I gave you a fine run, Sam Pig, and you were a good follower.'

'Goodbye, wind,' murmured Sam, and he sighed and lay down with his head on his trousers. He fell asleep in a twinkling.

There Ann found him when she came to the orchard to collect the clothes-pegs. On the ground lay Sam, with his face coated with dust, but smiling happily. His little feet were stained and cut, his arm outstretched over his torn trousers. By him was a green umbrella, inside out, a gigantic umbrella which would shelter all the family of pigs and Badger too, if they sat under it.

Ann carefully turned it the right way. Then she stooped and gave her brother a shake.

'Sam! Sam! Wake up!' she called. 'Sam! Where have you been?'

Sam rubbed his eyes and yawned. Then he sat up.

'Oh Sam! There was such a wind as you never saw! It blew the clothes off the line and I found them lying here, all except your trousers. Oh, poor Sam! I thought it had blown them right away, but here they are, under your head.'

'Yes, Ann,' said Sam, yawning again. 'The wind carried them off. I saw it with my own eyes. It ran a long, long way, but I ran too, and I caught it and got my trousers back again.'

'You caught the wind? You got your trousers

back from the raging, roaring wind?' asked Ann in astonishment.

'Yes,' Sam nodded proudly, and he opened his mouth, and shut it again. 'I ran about a hundred miles. I raced the wind, and I wouldn't let it keep my trousers.'

'And what's this?' asked Ann, holding up the green umbrella.

'Oh, that belongs to the nice old witch woman. I passed her on the way, and the wind snatched it from her. I'll take it back some time. I'm so sleepy, Ann. Do leave me alone.'

Sam's head dropped on the trousers, and he fell fast asleep. So Badger carried him in and put him to bed. Ann mended the adventurous trousers which the wind had torn. She turned out the pockets and found a small ancient whistle, which somebody had left there.

'Don't touch it,' warned Badger. 'Don't blow it. It's the wind's own whistle. Don't you know the saying, "Whistle for the wind"? If ever Sam wants the wind to come he has only to blow the whistle. We don't want it now, but if ever we do it will come.'

He put the whistle in a safe place on a top shelf, and there it lay for many a day, forgotten by everybody.

'It's an ill wind that blows nobody good,' observed Bill wisely. 'That long run has made young Sam as slim as a sapling. It is remarkable what a difference the wind makes to a fat little pig's figure.'

'But it was a good run,' said Tom. 'To think that our little Sam caught the wind.'

'Nobody else could do that,' said Ann. They were all very proud of little Sam Pig.

Sam Pig and the Dragon

Of course Sam Pig had always believed that Dragons were extinct, like Unicorns and Ogres. Otherwise he would never have entered Dragon Wood. It was a pretty little wood, filled with primroses and bluebells in the spring, and many birds nested in the trees. Nobody knew why it was called Dragon Wood, and even old Badger laughed at the name. Butterfly Wood or

Dragonfly Wood seemed more suitable for such a charming spot, for many brilliant butterflies flitted among the open spaces, and green dragonflies hovered and darted over the little pond. Sam often went there with his net, but either the meshes were too large or the gossamer threads of the net were too fragile, the little flying creatures always broke away.

One day he went to the wood with a basket for primroses. They grew in clusters under the shade of the rocks, and he soon filled the little rush basket. Then he sat down on a convenient rock. It was rough and black, but ferns grew in the crevices, and lichens patched the surface in orange-coloured discs like coins spilled over it. The sun had warmed it, and Sam lay back staring at the blue sky, watching the clouds through the young leaves of the overhanging trees. He shut his eyes and let the sun beat down in its spring warmth upon him. He was filled with content, and he was nearly asleep when he was startled by a slight movement under his body. The rock seemed to rise and fall in slow even motion.

He sprang up alarmed, and looked round. There was nothing unusual. The rock lay there, dark and massive, the ferns glowed like transparent green water, the clouds floated in the sky above. Only one thing was different. A little disturbed earth had fallen upon the mossy ground near the rock, and the primroses had spilled from the basket.

Sam Pig rose slowly to his feet. 'I think it was an earthquake,' he said to himself.

He listened, holding his breath, and there came a deep sigh. Perhaps it was a sigh, perhaps it was the wind moaning. Then he thought he saw an eye flash at him. Perhaps it was an eye, perhaps it was the sun in the glittering rain pool. Sam didn't wait any longer. He picked up the basket, stuffed the primroses in it, and went home. He turned his head now and then, and saw nothing alarming, but he couldn't help wondering.

'I've been to Dragon Wood,' he announced when he entered the house. 'And I heard – and I felt – and I saw –'

'Well?' cried Tom impatiently. 'What did

you hear and feel and see? A dragonfly?'

'Nothing,' said Sam, hesitating. Then he added, 'But it was like something. A nothing that was like something.'

He didn't go near Dragon Wood again for months. He stayed away till the flowers had gone and the trees were beginning to change the colour of their leaves.

'I want some blackberries for jam,' said Ann one autumn day. 'Go to Dragon Wood and pick some, Sam. There's plenty on those bushes, and nobody ever goes there.'

'Dragon Wood,' said Sam slowly. 'Dragon Wood. Well –. Yes, I'll go, Ann. I'll take my fiddle for company. I feel a bit queersome in Dragon Wood when I'm all alone.'

'All right. Take your fiddle, Sam. Maybe you will wheedle the blackberries off the bushes by playing to them, and I'm sure the rabbits will enjoy your music,' laughed Ann.

So away went Sam. There were the finest blackberries on a bank where the trees were scarce, and the rocks broke through the earth. He picked the juicy fruit and filled the little basket, and ate a good few himself. Then he put the basket under a tree and wandered on with the fiddle under his chin, playing a tune as he walked. The wood seemed to listen, the birds cocked their heads and sang in reply, the trees waved their branches in slow lazy rhythm, and Sam Pig felt happy and carefree. He saw the rock which had once moved and there it was, solid as the earth, weather-worn and black with rain. Yet when he stared at it he thought it was somehow different. He could trace a kind of shape about it, a bulging forehead, heavy brows, and even eyelids, long slits cut deep in the rock, half covered with bright moss. He didn't feel inclined to sit upon it, but he went on playing, to make himself brave.

Now whether it was the sweetness of Sam's music, or the warmth of the autumn sun, I do not know, but the bracken began to wave, the earth quivered and shook, and the rock was slowly uplifted. It was a scaly dark head, very large and long, with half-shut eyes concealing a glimmer of light like stars in a cloud. Ferns and lichens rolled away, the little silver birch trees toppled over, and a large oak tree crashed to the ground as the huge beast stretched itself. Then it opened its mouth and yawned, and it was as if a pit had opened in the wood. Sam gave a shrill cry and backed away. The Dragon blinked its liquid eyes and looked at Sam. The glance was kindly, and Sam stopped.

'Hallo,' said the Dragon, in a voice which seemed to come from under the earth, so deep and rumbling it was. 'Hallo, I've been asleep I think! What time is it?'

'About twelve o'clock,' said Sam in a shaking voice, and he glanced up at the sun. 'Yes. About twelve.'

'What day?' asked the Dragon, after a long pause.

'It's Saturday,' faltered Sam.

'I mean, what year,' said the Dragon, very, very slowly. 'It's always Saturday. What year is it?'

'Oh, it's – er – er – nineteen hundred and something,' stammered Sam. 'I can't remember what.'

'Too soon,' growled the Dragon, like low

thunder. 'Too soon. I've waked too early. I had to sleep till twenty hundred.'

'When did you go to bed?' asked Sam, forgetting his fright in his curiosity.

'Oh, in the year a hundred or thereabouts. The Romans made it so uncomfortable for me, marching about with their legions and tidying everywhere, I went to sleep and covered myself up. But I've waked too soon. My sleeping time is two thousand years. Have they gone yet?'

'Who?' asked Sam.

'The Romans,' said the Dragon.

'I'm not sure,' said Sam. 'But there's only me and Badger and my brothers and sister Ann living near. Not any Romans.'

The Dragon seemed to ponder this, and there was a long silence.

'Hadn't you better go back to bed again?' asked Sam, staring uneasily at the great head. 'I'll cover you up.'

'Now I'm awake I'll just look about me,' said the Dragon. 'I like your music, young fellow. Play to me again.'

The Dragon yawned once more and showed

its long white teeth and its curving scarlet tongue. A faint blue smoke came from its nostrils, and it blinked and snorted.

'I can't breathe properly,' it grumbled. 'Play to me. My throat's sore. I must have got a chill in the damp ground. I expect it's been raining and snowing a bit while I've been sleeping there. I hope I shan't get rheumatics.'

Sam played his fiddle and the Dragon waved its head in slow awkward jerks, up and down, stretching its scaly folds, loosening the thick stony skin.

'That's better,' said the Dragon. 'You've done me good. I am not so stiff now, and my throat's more comfortable.'

Sam thought it was time he went home, but the Dragon had taken a liking to him. So when he started off, the Dragon followed after. Sam quite forgot his blackberries, and he walked quickly, not caring to run from the great beast. The Dragon scarcely seemed to move, but it arrived as soon as Sam.

'You'd best wait outside,' said Sam. 'They'll be a bit surprised when they see you. I'd better warn them. You see, you are too big to come into our house. We're not used to Dragons, but I'm sure everybody will be pleased to see you.'

The Dragon agreed, and it lay down in the field.

'I am much obliged to you,' it murmured in its deep rumble. 'I can breathe easily now. The change of position has done me good, and the ancient warmth inside me has wakened.'

Indeed it had! From its nostrils came a cloud of smoke and from its mouth spurted little flickering flames of fire.

'You're burning,' cried Sam. 'Shall I fetch some water from the spring?'

The Dragon shook its great head, knocking over the palings and the clothes-props in the crab-apple orchard. 'I never drink water. It puts me out. It's my nature to smoke. You'll get used to it.'

So Sam ran up the garden path and flung open the door. He was breathless with excitement. 'Ann! Tom! Bill!' he shouted. 'There's a Dragon outside.'

'Dragon!' scoffed Bill. 'Where are the blackberries? We've been waiting to make the jam. Why have you been so long?'

'There's a Dragon outside,' repeated Sam. 'I forgot the blackberries because I found a Dragon. I've brought it home with me. At least,' he corrected himself, not wishing to appear boastful, 'at least, it followed me. It's waiting outside.'

They stared in amazement at their young brother, and then they ran to the door. They could see the monster lying outside the garden gate, with its head in the lane and its tail in the paddock. Little spirals of smoke came from the Dragon's nostrils, and its green eyes stared unblinkingly from the rocky head.

'Now, Sam,' said Ann, crossly, 'whatever did you bring a Dragon home for? You went for blackberries, not Dragons. What shall we do with it? We haven't a stable for it, and we can't have it in the house.'

'Stable! House!' scoffed Tom. 'If it whisks its long tail our house will be knocked clean over, and if it moves its head the orchard will be destroyed. It is singeing the crab-apples already.'

'It may ripen the crabs,' said Sam eagerly. 'It's very warm.'

'If it breathes hard we shall be roasted into roast pork,' said Bill mournfully.

'But it's a nice, gentle Dragon,' interrupted Sam, 'and I found it. I think it is lonely.'

'Well, go and speak to it,' said Tom, shrugging his shoulders.

Sam went down the garden to talk to the Dragon. It lay very still, breathing quietly, staring at the blue sky.

'You had best stay outside,' said Sam, 'and please behave yourself, for Sister Ann is rather worried about you.'

The Dragon nodded so hard that Sam was blown backward by the force of the wind. It promised to behave if only Sam Pig would let it stay. It curled itself round the house and garden, and shut its eyes.

Then the rest of the Pig family went closer to look at it. Its head was near the garden gate, but not near enough to scorch it. Its tail swept under the wall, and away into the orchard. There was just room to walk past without getting harmed by the Dragon's breath. They agreed it was quite a nice beast, and very unusual.

Badger was much surprised when he came home that evening. He hummed and hawed as Sam told the exciting story. The Dragon was dozing, and Badger watched it.

'It belongs to an ancient family,' said Brock. 'It is probably the last one left in the land. It will be lonely without companions. It's a pity you waked it, Sam. It may cause us a deal

of trouble. I'm not used to Dragons.'

'I am,' said Sam. 'It likes my music, and it's quite tame. Let us keep it, Badger. I will be its companion.'

The little pig looked imploringly at Brock, and Brock hummed a little tune and gazed at the Dragon. It was rather awkward having that great hot beast so near to one's garden gate. Nobody would come to visit them, but of course it was as good as having a watchdog. In any case Brock didn't know how to get rid of the Dragon. There it was and there it would stay.

They soon got used to having a Dragon round the house. It was very tame and gentle, and no trouble at all. The little animals of the woodland played on its scaly back, rabbits leapt upon it, and robins perched on its eyelids. The Dragon lay very still, just breathing, opening an eye now and then when Sam played to it, smiling at the little pig.

Ann Pig stretched a clothes-line over its head, from the lilac tree in the garden to the wild sloe in the orchard. Then she hung out the washing to dry in the fire of the Dragon's breath. The clothes dried even in wet weather, which was a great saving of time and trouble. The crab-apples ripened, the flowers sprang up anew in the hothouse of the Dragon's presence. When the days were short and winter came, the Dragon kept the house warm as toast. The snow fell and the frosts made the earth like iron, but the Dragon lay there, a warm comforting beast. They sat on its back in the coldest weather, and picnicked on the moss-covered scaly tail. The Dragon told them stories of long ago, tales of the days when wolves and wild boars and shaggy bears lived in the country. It told them of its brother Dragons, and its ancient mother, famous throughout the world for her strength. Then a tear of loneliness would trickle down its face, a tear so hot that steam rose from it. Sam rose to fetch his fiddle to cheer the sad beast, and the Dragon sighed and winked away the tears, and forgot its ancient greatness.

Brock brought his friends to see the wonderful visitor and everyone said the pigs were honoured by this King of Reptiles who was so considerate and kind.

Spring came, and Sam sat on the garden gate with his fiddle. The cuckoo called and the nightingale sang. The Dragon moved its head in its sleepy bliss, and puffed the white flames from its mouth. It was always content, never asking for anything, neither eating nor drinking – a perfect guest.

Then one fine day a cow disappeared. Sam Pig had seen it coming up the lane, and he ran indoors to fetch his milking-pail and the three-legged stool. When he came out the cow wasn't there, so the pigs had no milk for their tea. It was very strange, and Sam hunted in the fields for the lost cow. She had completely vanished.

A few days later another cow went. She had been feeding in the meadow, near the Dragon's tail. The farmer's dog came to look for her, and he eyed the Dragon suspiciously. The Dragon's eyes were shut, and the great beast lay with a look of happiness on its stony face.

The sheep-dog spoke to the pig family. 'It's my opinion,' said he, sternly, 'it's my good opinion that that there Dragon knows something about our Nancy. Aye, and about our

Primrose too, as went the other day. She was a good milker was Nancy. Well, you can't have it both ways. You can't keep a Dragon, and have your gallon of milk regular.'

'It can't be the Dragon,' protested Sam. 'Why, there's a blackbird's nest on its back, and there's a brood of young rabbits living beneath it. Everybody knows our Dragon, and it's as gentle as a dove.'

'That's as may be,' returned the dog. 'I'm only telling you. I've my suspicions. Cows can't fade away like snow in summer.'

The pigs talked it over and Sam decided to sit on the Dragon's back and keep watch. The Dragon never noticed who was on its back, it was too thick-skinned to feel any difference. Sam had once seen the roadman empty a cart-load of stone upon it when he was mending the lane, but the Dragon never flinched. Only the carthorse shied, and was restive till he was led away.

So Sam sat light as a feather on the Dragon's back, and kept guard. He felt he was acting the traitor's part to his friend, and he carried his fiddle ready to play a tune to soothe the

Dragon's feelings if he had misjudged it.

Up the road came a cow, going to the milking. It loitered here and there, picking up a blade of grass, snuffling at the herbage. When it got to the Dragon it put out its red tongue and licked the salty scales of the beast. Sam waited breathlessly. The Dragon snapped open its mouth, and in a twinkling the cow had gone. Like a flash down the flaming red lane of the Dragon's throat.

'That settles it,' said Sam quietly, and he slid to the ground, and went round to face the Dragon.

'You'd best be going back to bed, Dragon,' said he in a determined way, but the Dragon opened its sleepy eyes and gazed lovingly at Sam.

'Not yet, Sam dear,' said the Dragon. 'Not yet. I'm so happy where I am, dear Sam Pig.'

Sam was not to be cajoled. He took his fiddle and played a marching song.

'Follow me,' he commanded the Dragon. 'Fall in and follow me. Quick march! One! Two! One! Two!'

The Dragon stirred its great length, heaved its heavy body from the orchard and meadow grass, and shuffled after Sam.

Back to Dragon Wood Sam led the Dragon. He took it right to the place where he had found it. There was the hollow, where its head had lain, and the wide ditch where its body had rested.

'Now go to sleep,' said Sam. 'I'll play a lullaby, and you must shut your eyes and go fast asleep.'

Sam played a gentle rocking tune and the

Dragon gazed at Sam. A great warm tear rolled down the Dragon's cheek, and then another tear fell with a splash on the ground. The Dragon shut its eyes obediently and settled itself in the moist earth. Soon there was no movement in the vast body. The Dragon was asleep.

Sam covered it up with leaves and grasses and planted ferns and spring flowers upon its back. Then he turned and looked at it. Only a great black rock stuck out from the earth, with little silver birch trees waving their branches near. There was no trace of a Dragon in the wood.

Sam stroked the rugged surface of the rock, and then he went sadly home. Many a time he returned to Dragon Wood, and climbed on the dark rock, to visit his ancient friend. He played and sang and talked to the Dragon, but there was never a movement. Not till the year two thousand or thereabouts would the Dragon waken again.

Sam Pig and the Cuckoo Clock

On the mantelpiece in the house of the four pigs stood a clock, with a white face covered with a glass window, a brass pendulum and a hole for winding up the works. It was Badger's duty as head of the household to wind it, and nobody else ever dared to touch it. There it stood between Badger's herb-baccy box and the moneybox with the slit for pence. Every night Badger lifted it down and opened the glass window. He took the key from its hook and then wound up the clock with a whirring clicking noise which always pleased little Sam Pig.

'Can I have a go, Brock? Can I wind up the clock? Can I look inside at the works?' he implored, but Brock shook his head.

'Nobody must wind it but me, for clocks are ticklish creatures, and they don't like clumsy paws meddling with their innards.'

The clock ticked with a cheerful sound, and the four pigs loved to listen to the familiar voice, saying 'Tick tock', night and day, and to watch the little brass pendulum which they could see through the glass window. It seemed to talk to them, to say, 'Now it's time to put the potatoes in the hot ashes to cook for dinner', or 'Now it's time to fill the kettle for tea'. They ran to obey.

When Badger went away for his winter's sleep the clock stopped, just as if it were lonely without him. The little pigs looked up at the white face, and listened for the tick, but the hands said 'A quarter to five', and they never moved day or night. Two friends were gone, Brock and the clock, and they missed them. When Badger returned, the first thing he did was to wind up the clock and start the little wagging pendulum. Then the clock called 'Here I am! Here I am!' and the four pigs rejoiced.

Of course there were plenty of ways of telling the time besides the clock, but they were quiet ways. There was the sun moving majestically across the sky from East to West, sending shadows which got shorter and shorter till midday when they were the shortest. Then they began to lengthen till the sun went down.

Badger put a stick in the garden and showed the family how to tell the time by it. He pointed to the stick's black shadow, which became only a very tiny fellow. 'The sun is the best clock of all,' said Brock. But sometimes the sun didn't shine and then there were no shadows.

Ann Pig said a good way to know the time was to pick a dandelion clock and blow the little white seedlings. 'One, two, three, four,' she puffed, and away flew the parasols to make new dandelions in the garden ready for salad.

Sam Pig liked a ticking clock, one that struck the hours and told everybody the time. He liked the brassy voice, and the loud call. So when the clock stopped and nobody was allowed to wind it up, Sam was very sad.

One day he climbed on a chair and reached for the clock. He fitted the key in the hole and turned it with a grinding noise. Clicketty Click went the clock, and Sam pressed it to his chest and dragged the key round and round with all his strength. He went on turning for a long time, and the clock didn't like the pain in its stomach. When Sam put the clock down there was a whirring buzz, and it began to strike. One, two, three, four, five, it went on striking all the hours and many more. It went into tomorrow and the next day. The hands whirled round and the clock ticked so madly that nobody knew what it said.

Ann was in a terrible fright when she heard it chattering like a cageful of magpies. Bill said the clock was saying, 'You shouldn't have done it. You shouldn't have done it. You shouldn't have done it.' Tom said that Badger would rage when he came home.

All the pigs ran about very fast, trying to go to bed, to get up, to eat and cook and do the work, but they couldn't keep up with the hastening clock. Ann was breathless, and Sam didn't know where he was. Tom burnt the dinner and let the kettle boil dry. The fire flared up in a fury, and the sticks crackled and spat. Everyone was in such a hurry and such a confusion that they fell on top of each other.

Only Bill sat in a corner watching the whirling fingers of the clock.

'It can't go on for ever like this,' he told them

calmly, when Ann cried to him to hurry for it was tomorrow fortnight. 'It will be the end of the world soon, so we may as well take it easy while we can.'

'The end of the world?' Ann burst into tears. 'I won't have my end of the world without Brock,' she sobbed.

Then Sam went into the garden, scampering out and scampering in at double speed.

'The shadow-stick is moving quite slowly,' said he. 'The sun isn't running across the sky. It's the same as usual. It's only today. I think something's going to happen to this clock.'

Sure enough the clock struck one thousand, one hundred and one. It whirred and buzzed and chuffed. Then it was silent. Never was there such a silence. The four pigs stood staring, motionless. The birds in the garden stopped singing, and even the wind was quiet as if it couldn't understand what had happened in the house of the four pigs.

Then everyone began to talk. The birds sang, the wind whistled and all the pigs shouted, 'It's broken. Time has stopped.' They asked each other what Badger would say! They were very much upset! They looked inside the clock and touched its snapped springs, and its toothed wheels and its slim fingers.

'We had best get another clock before Brock comes home,' said Bill.

'But where shall we find one?' asked Tom.

'We are the only family that has a clock,' said Ann.

'And there may not be another in all the world,' said Bill.

'Oh, yes! I've seen clocks on church towers,' interrupted Sam eagerly.

'All right, Sam. You'd best get a clock from a church tower,' said Tom coldly. 'You broke our clock, and you seem to know all about them. You go and get one.'

Sam's face fell. 'I can't climb a church tower,' he explained. 'It's miles and miles high, and when you get to the top the church clock is as big as a house. We could all live inside a clock like that, we should be deafened by the striking.'

'That's your affair,' said Bill crossly. 'You

broke the clock and you must get another from somewhere.'

'Yes. That's fair enough,' said Tom. Only Ann was sorry for the little pig who stood looking so disconsolate.

'Never mind, Sam,' she whispered. 'I'll say a word to Brock and he will forgive you.'

'Forgiving won't give us back our clock,' said Bill, who overheard. 'Now, Ann, leave him alone. He must go off and find a clock.'

'And he mustn't come back with a dandelion clock either,' added Tom sternly.

So Sam packed his pyjamas in his knapsack, and a piece of soap and a toothbrush with them. Ann gave him a rock bun and a clean handkerchief, and away he went clock-hunting.

But clocks don't grow on oak trees, and although Sam searched high and low in the woods he couldn't find anything like a clock. The Jay watched him and hopped from bough to bough of the trees to try to find what Sam Pig was looking for. The wood pigeons called 'Tak two coos, Sam. Tak two coos,' but that didn't help. The cuckoo called 'Cuckoo. Cuckoo,' and flew over Sam's head.

'Has anybody seen a clock?' called Sam Pig, but the birds only whistled and sang with joy because Spring had come with the cuckoo.

So Sam Pig sat down and ate his cake and thought it over. He couldn't go back without a clock, so he decided to go to an old friend for advice. He decided to visit the old witch, who wasn't a witch at all, but an old woman who lived alone in the wood.

That was a good plan, he was sure, and he sprang to his feet and started off through the long deep woods towards the little cottage. It was late at night when he arrived, but the old woman had a candle burning in her window and a bright fire blazing on her hearth. The light of it flickered down the wood among the trees, and Sam hastened to the garden and up to the door. He tapped and waited.

'Come in. Come in, whoever you may be,' said the witch.

'Why, it's my little Pigwiggin come to see me again,' she cried when Sam pushed open the door and stepped into the room, blinking at the light.

She threw her arms round Sam Pig and kissed him on the nose.

'How are you, little Pigwiggin?' she cried.

Sam said he was very well, only tired and hungry. So she gave him supper and aired his pyjamas, and all the time she talked to him about her Owlet and her cat. The Owlet was now full grown, she told Sam, and he no longer rode on her shoulder, he was too heavy. He sat on a chair and stared with round eyes at Sam Pig. As for the cat, she turned her back and took no notice whatever.

'And what brings you here?' asked the old woman at last when Sam had said nothing. 'I hope you haven't run away from home.'

'No, although I sometimes want to when Bill and Tom are angry with me,' said Sam fiercely. 'No. They turned me out.'

'What? Packed you off into the wide world?'

'Yes. They sent me away,' said Sam.

'But why? What have you done?' asked the witch sorrowfully.

'I broke our clock,' said Sam, 'and they sent me out to find another.'

Then he told how he had wound up Badger's clock, which went buzzing along till it broke.

'Do you know where I can find a clock?' asked Sam. 'I came to ask you, because you are the wisest person I know, except Brock.'

He looked anxiously at the witch over the edge of his bowl of milk. There was a comforting ticking sound in the room, and he knew the witch had a clock for he had seen it on his first visit.

'You've come to the right place, Pigwiggin,' said the witch. 'I've got a clock I never use, for it makes such a to-do, such a chatter, I get weary of it. I want to be quiet in my old age. You shall have it with pleasure, for there is the old grandfather clock in the corner, and he keeps me company. I don't want my little noisy clock.'

Sam thanked her over and over again, but she stopped him.

'That's enough, Sam. You've said "Thank you" as often as a striking clock. Say no more but go off to sleep. Tomorrow I will get the clock down from the attic. It's a queer one but it keeps good time, and you can wind it yourself.'

So she made up the bed on the hearth-rug, and Sam lay down in his warm pyjamas. Just before he fell asleep he heard the old woman call 'Tirra-lirra', and a mouse ran out of a hole to be fed. Sam smiled sleepily at the Owl and nodded at the sulky cat. Then he shut his eyes and knew no more till morning.

The next day they all had breakfast together of porridge and cream. The porridge had curls of treacle on the top.

'What's this?' asked Sam. 'What is this sweet- ness that isn't honey?' He had never seen treacle before of course, for it comes from the sugar- cane, and not from the honeycomb.

'It's treacle, my Pigwiggin,' said the old woman. 'Have you never tasted it before? You shall have a tin to take home with you.'

'It's delicious,' said Sam. 'Even the bees would desert their honey-tree for this tin, I think, and the Fox would run a mile for a taste.'

The old woman nodded and smiled and gave

him more till his buttons were nearly bursting off. Then she took him to the garden to see her daffodils and pinks. It was such a warm sunny corner of the forest the flowers all bloomed at once and they kept in blossom till the snows came.

Overhead flew the Jay. 'Witch! Witch!' he shrieked and he swooped down to snatch a crust from the bird-table which the old woman had set for him and his friends.

'Pretty Jay,' she said. 'He comes here every day to see me, and he always speaks so kindly to me.'

Sam Pig frowned at the Jay, and the Jay mocked and jeered at Sam Pig.

But the old woman went back to the house and brought out the clock. It was a most beautiful clock in the shape of a little house, with a window just under the thatched roof, and the clock face over the front door. Two fir cones dangled from beneath it and the old woman showed Sam how to wind it up. She pulled down one fir cone, and the other moved into the house. It was quite easy, and the clock at once began to tick in a loud and cheerful manner.

'Put it under your arm,' said the witch. 'Don't jerk it, but carry it carefully, and when you get home ask your brother to hang it on the wall. It is going now and will tell you the time all the way home.'

Sam thanked her again and away he went, with the clock under one arm and the tin of treacle under the other.

The old woman stood at her gate waving to him till he got out of sight.

'The good little Pigwiggin,' said she to herself.

Sam trotted along towards home, and he hummed a song of happiness because he was carrying a clock for Brock the Badger. The clock ticked loudly against his heart, and the treacle tin sent out a good sweet smell.

'It's a very pretty clock,' said Sam, taking a peep at it. 'They will be surprised when they see it. A house with two fir cones!'

There was a sudden whir and the little window flew open. Out flew a tiny cuckoo and shouted 'Cuckoo. Cuckoo. Cuckoo,' nine times. Then back it flew and the window shut and the clock went on ticking as if nothing had happened.

'Goodness me!' cried Sam, holding the clock at arm's length. 'There's a cuckoo inside it! And it knows the time, for it *is* nine o'clock!'

He hurried along the woods, but every hour the cuckoo came out and sang its merry song and fluttered its little feathers. Sam tried to catch it, to make it speak of other things, but the cuckoo flew back to the dark interior of the clock and shut the window fast.

'Ho, cuckoo! Stop a minute!' called Sam. 'Let me in! Open your window! I want to look inside your house.' He rapped at the door and tapped at the window, and peered down the chimney, but he could see nothing.

'Tick tock! Tick tock!' went the clock, and the house door remained firmly closed.

'Why are you hurrying so fast, Sam Pig?' asked the Fox, stepping out of the bushes. 'What have you got there?'

'Nothing for you,' said Sam quickly, and he tried to push past, but the Fox snatched the clock from him.

'A house,' said the Fox. 'And who lives in it, Sam? Some honey-bees perhaps. There is a sweet smell about you, Sam Pig.' Sam Pig had pushed the tin of treacle in his pocket, and now he stood waiting.

'Tick tock!' went the clock, very loudly, and then it made a little buzzing noise.

'I think it is going to explode,' said the Fox, holding it at arm's length. 'I think this house is a queer one.'

Out flew the cuckoo, and shouted 'Cuckoo. Cuckoo,' in the Fox's face, and flapped its little wings against his nose.

'The bold bird! Take it back! I don't want such a magical thing. It's a trap or something. You take care, Sam Pig, or that bird will peck your eyes out. It nearly got mine.'

So Sam Pig went home with the cuckoo clock safe and sound, and the Fox ran through the woods to tell his family that Sam Pig had a magical bird in a little magical house, and it would peck your eyes out as soon as winking.

The pigs were delighted when Sam showed them the new clock, and they hung it up on a nail in the kitchen. They all stood listening to the noisy tick tock, and gazing at the little house. The roof was thatched with green reeds, and the little door had a brass knocker. Sam explained that he had knocked and banged at the door and tapped on the window but nobody came out till it was the hour for striking.

'It's four o'clock,' said he. 'Now you shall see for yourselves.'

The window sprang open and out flew the little cuckoo, and called the hour.

It flew round the room, calling 'Cuckoo. Cuckoo!' It blinked its eyes and shook its feathers, and tossed its head and then it returned to the little house.

The pigs could talk of nothing else all even-ing, and as each hour approached they waited for the bird to come out and sing to them. It was striking eight when Badger entered the room.

'Hallo,' he cried. 'What's this? A little cuckoo flying round? Where has it come from? It's the smallest bird I ever saw in all my life.'

But the bird flicked its tail, called eight

times and flew back through its window.

'It's a clock,' said Sam. 'I broke your clock, Brock. This is a new one, from the witch's house. It's a cuckoo clock.'

Brock stood looking at the little house, admiring the neat thatching of the roof, and the overlapping wooden shingles, and the sweet-scented fir cones which hung from their chains. Then he lifted the brass knocker and tapped at the tiny door.

'It's no good knocking there,' said Sam. 'It's not a real door. Nothing happens.'

But even as he spoke the door swung slowly open and they could see inside the little house. There was the cuckoo, sitting in a bare little room, with its feathers drooping and its shoulders hunched. It glanced at them, and then turned its head away.

'Hush,' said Sam Pig. 'It's going to sleep,' and they closed the door.

But early the next morning Sam Pig slipped down to the kitchen, and waited to see the cuckoo come out. It darted from its window and flew cuckooing out of the door, and into the woods. Away it flew, and it didn't come back for an hour. With it came another cuckoo, small and stiff like itself, with quick bright eyes and grey-barred breast. They both flew in at the little window of the cuckoo clock, and the shutter closed after them.

'There's another cuckoo come to the clock,' said Sam, when Brock came down to breakfast. 'I expect our cuckoo was lonely.'

Brock tapped at the door and pushed it open a crack. There were primroses on the table, and on the hearth a little fire gleamed. Two cuckoos sat talking by the fireside, speaking in low whispering voices.

Brock closed the door silently and nodded to Sam.

'Did you see the little fire burning and the candlestick on the mantelpiece and the prim-roses?' asked Sam.

'Yes. Look at the smoke coming out of the chimney. The cuckoo is making himself at home.'

Indeed it was so, for a tiny column of blue smoke came curling from the chimney of the wooden house. Every hour the cuckoo came out to call the time, and with him came his wife, two birds which flew round the room and then disappeared into their own little dwelling.

The Theatre

'Have you ever been to a theatre, Badger?' asked Sam Pig one day when the little family sat at dinner.

What a strange question to ask! Bill Pig stopped with a roast potato half-way to his mouth, and Tom Pig dropped his bread on the floor. Ann opened wide her small blue eyes and gasped with astonishment. What was brother Sam talking about now! Only Brock the Badger took it calmly. Not one of his black-and-silver hairs quivered, not a muscle moved. He took up a piece of toast and dripping and had a bite before he answered the young pig.

'No,' he drawled. 'I can't say as I've ever been to a theatre, Sam.'

'But what is it? What is a theatre?' they all asked quickly.

'It's a play-acting house, where anyone pretends to be somebody else,' explained Sam, proud of his knowledge.

'Like the Wolf pretending to be a poor lone sheep?' asked Ann. 'I shouldn't like that at all.'

'Like the Fox pretending to be dead?' asked Bill.

'Like a falling leaf pretending to be a butterfly?' asked Tom.

'Well, something like those things,' said Sam. 'I've never actually been to a theatre, but I've been talking to Sally the mare, and she says there's a theatre on Midsummer Eve.'

'Where? Oh where?' they asked in a gabble of suprise.

'At the farm, in the stable or barn, I don't know exactly. We are all invited, and they asked me to take my fiddle,' said Sam.

'It's Midsummer Eve tomorrow,' said Badger. 'Well, I've never seen a theatre, so we will all go together, and see the fun, whatever it is.'

There were great preparations. Sam Pig had a bath in the washtub the night before, and on the morning of Midsummer Eve he scrubbed his face so that it shone like a lamp.

'If there wasn't a moon we could see by the light of your face,' said Bill.

Then Sam threw a clod of soil at Bill, and Bill tossed it back again, and Sam had to wash once more.

Tom got out his blacking-pot and the brushes and he polished everybody's hooves. Ann gave a twist and curl to all the little tails and she swept a little furze brush over the creamy hairs on her brothers' heads. Badger was very busy in his bedroom, making himself into a fine country gentleman. Bill brought button-holes of moss roses and parsley for each of the pigs to wear. Tom gave out sticks of barley honey for each of them to suck. Barley honey is made out of honeycomb and ground barley, and very delicious it is.

Badger cut stout staffs to help them on the journey, and Sam as usual got in everybody's way as he ran here and there trying to help.

At last it was time to depart. The moon had risen and the stars were peeping through the soft clouds. A little breeze ruffled the leaves and the woods sang their evening hymn to the coming of night. The fields were silvery with dew, and a nightingale sang in the oak tree.

'Jug. Jug. Jug. Tirra la-a-a. How happy I am! Sweet. Sweet,' it sang and they all stood listening to its exquisite voice.

'We're going to a theatre. Tirra la-a-a,' piped Sam in his thinnest wee voice, as he tried to rival the bird.

'How happy I am! I have a mate and a nest with a brood of young ones,' sang the bird in rapture.

'Be quiet, Sam,' chided Brock. 'Animals are silent when they walk the woods by night. Only the nightingale and the owl may raise their voices. Come along softly and don't walk in the moon shadows, or the goblins will get you. They'll pull your tail and swing you on their backs and carry you off.'

Sam looked quickly behind him at the blue shadows. Then he saw that Badger was laughing at him, so he pressed close to his friend and trotted quietly along.

When they arrived at the farm they tiptoed very gently over the lawn and round the flower-beds, for it would never do to leave a trail on the soil. The watch-dog lay in his kennel with one eye watching them. He gave no alarm, for of course he knew about the festivities. The farmhouse was in darkness with the shutters closed and never a glimmer of light showing. On Midsummer Eve it was considered danger-ous to be abroad, for strange things happened.

The animals padded across the yard to the stable from which came a faint glow. They pushed their way through the little crowd in the doorway and gazed around in admiration.

The horses' stalls were festooned with green leaves, and from the roof hung a horn lantern with a light like a pale moon. The mangers were filled with forget-me-nots and the walls were decked with streamers of ivy. In the wallholes where usually the horse-brushes and currycombs were kept, there stood hollowed turnips with candles burning within. A multitude of glow-worms lay among the flowers and leaves on the walls, and gave out their clear green light, tiny and fairy.

One part of the stable was screened off with a leafy curtain and from behind it came muffled laughter, high squeals, and subdued whispers. The curtain scarcely reached the ground and Sam Pig could see little black feet jumping up and down behind it.

The horses were in the stalls, and these were the best seats of all, for of course it was their theatre. Although their backs were to the stage their long heads were turned and their brown eyes gazed in mild surprise. On the partitions of the stalls, perched on the curving oak ledges, were red and white hens, and a couple of cocks splendid in burnished feathers and glittering spurs. They were in the gallery. They were noisy creatures and never ceased pushing and chattering, crowing and cackling even in the most pathetic moment when the heroine lost her slipper.

The body of the stable was occupied by Sally the mare, by the farm pigs, the young calves, and a dozen or more sheep and lambs. The sheep were huddled together looking rather frightened, but the sheep-dog reassured them.

'It's only pretence,' said he, and everybody told everyone else. 'It's only pretence.'

Badger modestly led the way to the back of the stable but the farmyard animals gave up their seats at the front. The door was closed, so that even the moon could not look at the curious scene. Somebody blew out the lamp in the roof, and then the stable was lighted only by the turnip candles and the glow-worms, but a faint gleam came from behind that magical curtain of leaves upon which all eyes were fixed.

The Alderney cow shook her head so that her bell tinkled. Sally the mare twitched the curtain aside, and nibbled a few leaves in her excitement. Everybody cried 'Oh-o-o-o-o-o-o!'

There were the seven little pigs from the pig-cote, dressed as fairies, in pink skirts with wreaths of rosebuds round their pink ears. They danced on their nimble black toes, and swung their ballet skirts. They pirouetted until the hens cried out to them.

'Stop a minute! It makes us giddy to watch you!'

'Hush,' said Badger indignantly. 'Hush! No talking!' and the hens stopped clucking for a whole minute and stared down at Badger's black-and-white head.

A band of music-makers played in a corner. There was a lamb with a shepherd's pipe, and a Scottish terrier with bagpipes and a kitten with a drum.

'Come along, Sam, and join us,' they beckoned, and Sam stepped shyly through the little dancing pigs who never stopped whirling.

He tuned his fiddle and sat down in the corner. Soon he was sawing with might and main, trying to keep time with the squealing of the Scottie's bagpipes, the fluting of the lamb's pipe and the drumming of the little cat.

The farmyard pigs sang their own shrill songs, and the audience joined in the choruses of 'John Barleycorn' and 'A Frog He Would a-Wooing Go'.

They gave an acrobatic display and leaped through hoops of leafy willow on to Sally's broad back. They bowed and bowed again and then the curtain was drawn. It was the interval.

The mother of the dancing pigs handed round refreshments, elderberry wine and cowslip ale, and cakes of herbs and bunches of hay.

They were all eating and drinking when the Alderney rang her bell. The mare twitched the curtain back, and the lantern went out. Quickly they stuffed their cakes in their mouths and hid their drinking-mugs in the ivy. There was now to be acted the famous play of Cinderella and her straw slipper.

The smallest pig sat in rags by the empty

fireplace, and the fine sisters went off to the ball, flaunting their long skirts and their pheasant feathers.

In came a pair of rats drawing a pumpkin across the stable floor. There was such a rustle and flutter among the cocks who wanted to fly down and attack them, such a hiss from the cat, and such a growl from the Scottie, Badger had to stand up and quieten them.

'It's all pretence,' said he, and they echoed 'Pretence', and were quiet.

The Fairy Godmother waved her wand, and Cinderella's rags fell off. Behold! She was a pink-skirted pigling! Away she went to the ball, riding on the pumpkin, trundling herself along the floor with her little hooves which were covered with shoes of yellow straw.

The next scene was the ballroom, where everyone in the stable danced. Badger danced the polka with the Scottie, and Ann Pig turned with a lamb. Little Sam Pig was chosen by Cinderella herself and he was in great confusion as he tripped and skipped and stumbled over her straw slippers. But the stable clock struck twelve, and Cinderella ran away. Sam tried to hold her but she escaped and hid in a corner out of sight. One of the slippers lay on the floor. Sam Pig picked it up and put it in his pocket.

'Sam Pig! Sam Pig!' called the sow. 'You must go round the theatre and see whose foot is small enough to fit into the little straw slipper.'

'But I know!' answered Sam quickly. 'It belongs to the little Cinderella pig.'

'Hist! Do what I tell you! This is a theatre and it's all pretence,' said the sow sternly. So Sam walked round with the little straw slipper, and everybody tried it on. The mare held out her great hoof, the Alderney held up her delicate foot. The sheep held up their little hooves, and the hens clucked and fussed and stretched out their long thin toes. Little Ann Pig got the slipper on and tried to keep it, but Sam refused to give it up.

'It's not yours, Ann,' he whispered crossly.

Even Badger held out his hairy pad, but Sam pushed it aside.

'I told you so! I told you so! It isn't yours and you can't have it. It belongs to that nice little

Cinderella pig, and I don't know where she is.'

He pushed the ugly sisters aside, and there, hiding among the besoms and harness and horse-rugs, was little Cinderella. She held out a neat little hoof and Sam Pig dragged the straw slipper upon it. It fitted like a glove!

'Hurrah!' they all cried. 'The Princess is found.' As for Sam he was so excited he leaned towards her and gave her a kiss. You remember the old woman in the wood who kissed him? Sam never forgot that nice feeling. Now he kissed Cinderella.

'Hurrah!' cried everybody. 'Hurrah! The Prince has kissed Cinderella.'

'But it's all pretence,' they told one another.

The stable door flew open, and they all flocked out into the cool night air. The sheep scampered away to the pasture, the Alderney walked sedately to the field. The pigs hastened to the pig-cote and nestled together in the shelter of their little home. The cocks and hens scurried back to the hen-place, escorted by the Scottie. The Fox was staring over the wall, wondering what was happening that midsummer night, but he turned aside when he saw Hamish the Scottie. The cat came out last, and she climbed up on the stable roof.

Brock and the four pigs trundled over the fields to their little home, chattering softly of all they had seen.

'So that's a theatre!' said Brock. 'It was grand! And you, Sam Pig, were the Prince!'

Sam said nothing. All his thoughts were on the little pigling called Cinderella whom he had kissed by the light of the turnip lanterns.

'But it's all pretence,' murmured Ann, and the others echoed, 'Yes. All pretence.'

The Boat

One day Badger called to Sam Pig. 'Get your axe, Sam, and come with me. I want you to cut some saplings for me later on.'

Sam hastened to the woodshed where his axe lay, and then he ran after Badger who was already walking at his steady even pace to the woods.

'Wait a minute, Brock,' he called, and the Badger stopped.

'You'll make the birds jealous, Sam,' said the Badger, for Sam was whistling with all his might. The little pig was so happy that Brock had honoured him by asking for his company that he warbled like a blackbird.

'Shouldn't have thought it possible for a piglet to make such a noise,' said Brock. 'Like a wood at sunrise you are, Sam.'

'And what's the difference between now and sunrise?' asked Sam, and he took another little run and skip.

'At sunrise the birds all wake from their night sleep and they are so glad to see their friend the great sun steal up silently from under the earth that they all shout together in a chorus. "Welcome, O sun," they sing, and the sun is glad to hear them.'

'I should think so!' said Sam. 'He must be glad to get a welcome after his journey. I never call out to him, Brock.'

'No, because you are fast asleep. Nobody takes much notice except the birds. Even Man doesn't care, but sometimes a farm boy going to fetch the cows at dawn whistles to the sun.'

'I will, too,' said Sam. 'I will join the chorus, and welcome him.'

They were marching deeper in the woods as they talked, and Brock told Sam many things about birds and their migrations, about fish and animals and plants. They came to a clearing where some trees had been felled by the wood-cutters. Badger went from one to another, touching them, smelling them, considering their merits, and Sam also looked at them. Oak and ash and holly he recognized by the shapes of the branches and the roughness of the bark.

'Too strong and too big for my purpose,' said Brock. 'I must find a willow.'

Near the river they found willow saplings which were of even thickness and Sam cut them with his axe. Badger trimmed off the leaves and twisted several saplings together in a fan shape. Then he wove other saplings in and out so that a framework was made.

'Cut me some reeds, the broadest leaves you can find,' said Brock, and Sam went to the water's edge and hacked off the thick reeds. He thought he knew what Brock was making, for it began to take the shape of a large basket, or a cradle perhaps.

Brock covered the framework with the leaves, threading them till there was never a chink uncovered. Then he stood upright and grunted. 'There. What do you think of that? How do you like it?' he asked.

'Is it a bread basket?' asked Sam. 'Or a basket for all the eggs the birds lay in a year? Or to hold all the apples in the orchard?'

'It's a boat,' said Badger shortly. 'I thought

you would have sense enough to see.'

'A boat?' echoed Sam, opening his eyes. 'To go on the river, like my raft?'

Badger nodded and stooped down to tuck in a rough end.

'Yes. It will hold two piglings, not more. I can take you out in it. Now I must caulk it.'

'What's that?'

'Make it watertight. I use the resin from the fir-trees for that,' said Brock, and he went to the firs and got the brown gum from the bark. He rolled it between his paws and munched it between his teeth till it was soft. Then he pasted it over the bottom of the little oval craft.

'Now we'll try it,' said he, and he carried it, light as a feather, to the river. The little boat floated like a cockle-shell. It bobbed on the water like a dancing water-beetle.

Badger drew it back by its rope and climbed in. The little boat's edge was near the water with his weight, and when Sam touched it, it overturned.

Badger shook the water from his coat and climbed to the bank.

'I must alter the shape. It's too flat and shallow,' said he. He twisted the willow frame and then he got in once more. This time the boat swung into the stream in safety when Sam joined Brock.

They hid the boat in the reeds and went home, talking quietly of all the things they could do on the river.

The next day Badger took Sam Pig fishing. They had a rod and bait and a pail to carry the fish. They took sandwiches, too, and a bottle of herb beer. Badger had made a pair of oars from a leafy bough to paddle them along. When they came to a quiet shady spot Badger began to fish. Soon he had caught a dozen trout. They took them home and Tom fried them in the pan for supper.

The next day they went off again to fish, and there was a little crowd on the bank waiting for them. Everybody was talking of Sam Pig's basket-boat, which was so much safer than a raft, and easier to manage than a log of wood.

'Oh, Badger. Make us a boat,' they implored, and the good-natured Badger promised he would. Many an animal brought a pile of willow boughs, long and short, to the house of the four pigs, and Badger sat in the garden weaving little baskets.

'A regular workshop this is,' grumbled Bill, as he swept up the litter. 'A boat-shop. Boats of all sizes. I shall put a notice up: "Boats made to order or not to order, to fit every size of animal." '

Badger wove baskets for water-rats – who really didn't want them for they could swim – for hedgehogs and rabbits and fallow deer. He even made little boats for the black cock and his wife, who came over from the farm at the risk of their lives to see the fun. The water-way instead of being a quiet river became a highway of little creatures each paddling himself along. Sometimes the boats were overturned and then there was a scramble and a shout and a throwing of lifebelts, which were made of bark from the silver-birch trees. The wet animals got ashore and rubbed themselves dry in the grasses, and then returned to their drifting boats, none the worse.

Now the only animal who hadn't a boat was the Fox, and Badger refused to make one for him. The Fox was much annoyed about this, for although he could swim he did not care to wet his thick fur. When he saw all the little boats sail off, with their small owners swishing the water with little boughs, he gnashed his teeth with rage.

'There they go, rabbits and delicious morsels, and that Sam Pig, all rowing and laughing, and I have to run on the bank,' he grumbled. 'Even the cock and hen venture there out of my reach. If I had a boat I could join the happy company. I could talk with the ducks and race the rabbits.'

But Brock took no notice of the Fox's rages. There was no boat for the Fox.

One day when Sam Pig went down to the river his boat had gone. He borrowed another from a large hare, but it wasn't big enough for him. His fat little body filled it to overflowing, and he had to move very slowly lest the boat should topple over with him.

He drifted down the stream, not daring to

paddle, looking to right and left for his own boat which he thought must have broken from its moorings in the reeds. He wasn't very good at tying knots and perhaps the rope had come unfastened. Then he spied the boat under the branches of an overhanging tree. Lying in it with his legs crossed and his head on the leafy cushion Ann had made for Badger, was the Fox. Sam thought he was fast asleep, and very carefully he wafted the little boat alongside. But the Fox was wide awake. He was watching Sam out of the corner of his eye, waiting to know what Sam would do!

Sam leaned over and shook the basket-work side.

'Wake up, Fox,' he shouted. 'Wake up. That's my boat you've got.'

The Fox gave a loud snore, and Sam rocked the boat violently. He forgot all about his own frail craft, which was too small to allow any sudden movement. In a moment it turned over and he was thrown in the river.

'Help! Help!' he called, but the Fox only snored the harder and watched through half-shut eyes. Sam waded indignantly ashore and walked home wet and angry.

The Fox lay shaking with laughter. Then he saw a couple of boats coming down the river with rabbits inside. The little animals rowed near, calling 'Sam Pig! Sam Pig! We know you are there, hiding in your boat.' They came close and the Fox shot out a hairy arm and seized them. Then he rowed home and had rabbit pie for supper. Yes, it was a clever plan to use Sam Pig's boat for poaching.

The next day he drifted into a company of ducks, and before they were aware of him he snapped up a couple. He also caught the adventurous black cock and his wife, who had gone for a sail. Nothing was safe from the Fox, neither the water-hens who ran scurrying to the bank, not the furry water-voles in their homes on the island. The Fox could go anywhere with ease, and the innocent creatures were at his mercy.

Sam Pig told his brothers and sister Ann about the wicked beast. Badger was away in the forest and they couldn't get his help or advice.

'The Fox has stolen my boat, and he sleeps on your cushion, Ann,' said he. 'He rows up to the poor ducks and grabs them. He can go anywhere, for it is such a beautiful boat. It's the only one big enough to hold him. What shall I do? I can't get it back, because I can't swim and I can't push him out because I'm not strong enough.'

'Nobody ventures on the river now,' said Bill. 'They are afraid to use their wicker boats. As soon as anyone sails away, your boat comes from the reeds and the Fox chases them. There is no escape, so all the little boats are in the harbour under the alder trees and there they will stay.'

'It's a pity Badger ever made a boat,' said Tom. 'It all comes of our pride. Pigs are not sailors.'

'I wish Badger would come home,' groaned Sam.

'The Fox can't eat *us*, but we are losing so many of our friends,' said Ann mournfully.

They talked all evening, making plans and rejecting them. Bill suggested they should wait till the Fox went home with his prize, his rabbits or ducks, and then steal out and recapture the boat. But the Fox was too cunning for that. Nobody ever saw him go home with the fat ducks on his back or the rabbits slung on his arm. He rowed far away up the river and eluded his watchers.

Tom suggested they should put a poisonous herb pie in the boat, a pie made of Viper's Bugloss and Deadly Nightshade. They made the pie, but they couldn't get near the boat with it.

Ann said she had heard that cats sometimes wore bells round their necks, and if the Fox wore a bell everybody would be warned. They thought this was a splendid plan. Sam took the little brass dinner bell to hang round the Fox's neck.

'Here's a present for you, Mister Fox,' he called over the river to the Fox who was idly sculling.

'Thank you. Thank you, Sam Pig,' said the Fox. 'What is it?'

'A bell, Mister Fox. A dinner bell. It's for you

to ring when you want your dinner. You hang it round your neck,' explained Sam hopefully.

'I get my dinner without ringing a bell, thank you,' returned the Fox very politely, and he rowed softly down the stream towards the smooth pool, where the ducks played.

'Well,' said Sam to himself. 'I shall have to lose my nice boat. There's only one thing to be done. Somebody must sink the boat with the Fox in it. Who can do it?'

Sam Pig went through all his acquaintances, and nobody was a really good swimmer. Even Badger couldn't face the river's deeps and stay down long enough to scuttle the boat. The only person was Jack Otter, Badger's friend, who lived some way up the river in the rocky wild parts. Sam decided to visit Jack Otter, whom he had never seen.

Ann packed a basket of sandwiches for him, and he took his fiddle for he had heard that otters were fond of music. The tunes might lure them to the bank.

He walked along the river-side towards the hills. He passed the Fox, comfortably lolling in the wicker boat, eating rabbit and water-hen.

'Hallo, Sam Pig. Where are you off to with your fiddle? Going to play to the fishes?' he jeered.

'Give me back my boat,' said Sam.

The Fox smiled wickedly. 'Come and fetch it, Sam. It's yours if you can get it.'

He flicked an oar in the water and the little boat spun round. Sam caught his breath as he looked at his beloved boat, which once had been so spick and span, with leafy oars and cushions and trim little seat. The Fox had lined it with feathers from the ducks he had eaten, and there was a pile of gnawed bones at the bottom. Sam shivered in disgust. If his plan succeeded the boat would be lost for ever. That would not matter; it was no longer his boat, it was the Fox's.

After some time Sam came to a place where the river narrowed and the nature of the ground changed. It became wilder and rocks sprang from the river's bed. The water churned over them in white foam. Sam's boat would have been wrecked in such rough water. He stepped over the tuffets of heather on the hillside and sprang over little wild streams which ran to join the river. He followed one of these up in the high hills, and had to retrace his steps, for there was no sign of the otters. He sat down at the riverside and ate his sandwiches. Then he tuned his fiddle and played a merry dance.

A smooth round head appeared, and he was aware of a pair of bright eyes watching him from the shadow of a rock.

'Otter! Jack Otter!' he called very softly, but the shy beast slipped away.

'Bother,' cried Sam. 'He thinks I am an enemy. I wish Badger were here with me.'

He took up his fiddle and played again, waiting for the otter to reappear. Sure enough the sleek head came out of the water, and the otter looked at him from the safety of the river.

'I'm Sam Pig, and Badger is my friend,' said Sam hurriedly, trying not to alarm the timid animal.

Silently Jack Otter climbed out of the river and trotted over to Sam.

'Badger's friend,' he said in a husky voice.

'Badger.' Then he gave a shrill whistle and a family of little otters appeared, all eager to meet Sam Pig, who was Badger's friend. They chattered with soft voices and Sam answered their questions. Yes, Badger was well. He was out hunting, and Sam hadn't seen him for a moon's time.

'He will be back with the full moon,' said Jack Otter, confidentially. 'He promised to come and see us, for my two children adore old Badger.'

'Did you make that music?' asked one of the little otters shyly.

'Will you make it again?' asked the little girl otter.

So Sam tuned his fiddle and dried it, for it was wet with river spray. Then he played to them, and the otters sat with dark eyes fixed upon Sam's fingers, their heads raised, and their keen ears alert.

'Stay all night, Sam Pig,' they begged. 'It is such fun in these hills in the moonlight, and you can play to us. You can sleep in the hollow by the hawthorn tree, nobody will find you, and one of us will keep guard. We've never met a young pig before.'

'And we will catch a fine salmon for your supper, and you shall have the choicest portion,' said Jack Otter.

So Sam agreed to stay the night with the otters on their cold hillside. He stood on the river bank and watched them dive noiselessly and leap high in the water with curving, shining bodies. They climbed the rocks and fell with never a splash. They stood on their heads and threw themselves backwards, and the water seemed to open and cover them with scarcely a ripple. It was a miracle of movement and Sam never wearied of watching their lithe antics. Then he took up his fiddle and played again, and they danced in the shining water swift as light itself. From the sky over the moorland looked down the white-faced moon, and the stars came out like gold fireflies in the blue night. Like gold sparks the water flashed, and the little otters leapt and curvetted, prancing horses in the sparkling stream, all among the reflected stars and the broken moonrays.

They brought up fish in their paws, fish all glittering with silvery scales and startled round eyes, and they held them out to Sam Pig.

'Will this suit you? Or this? This is a delicious supper,' they cried, tossing the fish high and catching it.

Sam shook his head. He preferred his fish fried in a pan, not eaten raw. He was a civilized little animal, but he looked with envy at the wild otters who bit off the heads from the salmon and ate the choicest bits and threw the rest of the fish away. No washing up, no cooking, no house.

Then he remembered the object of his journey. The Fox was a wild creature, too, and he was up to mischief in Sam's wicker boat. He called to the otters and they came out of the water, whistling and panting as they flung themselves down by his side. They stroked his trousers, and pulled his ears, and tickled his ribs, and they twanged the fiddle-strings.

'Tell us a story, Sam,' they begged. 'A tale of your part of the world, where your family lives with Badger.'

'Well,' said Sam, drawing a deep breath and looking down at the wet company. 'Well, Badger made me a basket-boat, of willow, so that I can sail on the river.'

'Can't you swim?' cried the otters, opening wide their eyes.

Sam shook his head. 'No, I can't swim, and I can't sink, I just float along like a balloon.'

'Poor Sam! Poor Sam Pig! What a calamity! He can't swim,' said the otters, mournfully, and the little girl otter actually dropped a tear.

'So Badger made me a boat,' continued Sam. 'But the Fox stole my little boat.'

'Ah!' cried the otters fiercely. They knew the Fox, an enemy, a hated sly creature, who would catch them if he were not afraid of their teeth.

'I want to sink the boat,' said Sam. 'I want to sink her with the Fox inside.'

'But the Fox will swim ashore,' said the otters at once.

'Yes he will, the clever fellow, but he won't be able to use my boat any more.'

The otters agreed.

'So I want you to sink her for me,' said Sam.

The otters talked together in quick whispers. Yes, they could swim under the boat without the Fox knowing, and bore little holes. That would do the trick. The Fox would have to swim for his life, and the boat would go down to the bottom of the river.

They showed Sam the hollow hawthorn tree, for he was yawning sleepily, and they made a bed for him. He slept till dawn, but the otters were up all night, strumming on Sam's fiddle, leaping over the moonrays, gliding into the silvery water after the fish.

The next day Sam said goodbye to his new friends, and started for home. The otters told him they would swim down the river at twilight. Then if Sam waited among the reeds near the boat he would see the water flood her and sink her.

'Give our love to Badger,' they called after him in their husky, dusky voices. 'Tell him we shall be pleased when he comes here. There is good hunting for wild creatures in these moorlands.'

Sam trotted home, but it was so far he did not arrive till dark was settling over the land and the river mists were rising. It was already time to watch for the otters. He stood among the reeds, waiting, and he saw the little boat coming along. The Fox had a couple of ducks which he was taking alive to his family. They were quacking miserably in the bottom of the boat. The Fox rowed slowly, singing out of tune, pleased with himself and the easy way he had got his dinner. Life was pleasant with a boat and dinners were plentiful. Then he saw Sam Pig hiding in the reeds, and he stopped rowing to mock at the little pig.

'Ho, Sam Pig! Did you lure any fish out of the water? Wouldn't you like your boat? Your fishing rod is here, but I don't trouble to use it. Plenty of other things.'

There was a ripple round the boat, but it was caused by the oars' movements. Neither Sam nor the Fox knew that at that moment the otters were swimming below, waiting to attack. They pushed their sharp augurs, which they had made from fish bones, through the thick reedy covering into the willow shell. One after another they pierced the boat, and the water slowly entered in fine trickles. The Fox was watching Sam Pig, teasing him, taunting him, and Sam Pig was uneasily wondering whether the otters would miss the boat after all.

'Goodness me! There seems to be a leak,'

muttered the Fox, as he looked down at his damp feet. He tried to stop the water from entering by pushing the feathers down, but more and more water rushed in as the holes widened. The Fox leaped about, stuffing here and there with the cushion.

'What's the matter?' asked Sam excitedly, as he saw the Fox's panic.

'Your precious boat has sprung a leak! A rotten boat! There's holes in her. I must get away before she sinks,' cried the Fox angrily, and he sprang into the water. He forgot the two ducks in his hurry and quickly they swam away. The boat filled with water and dropped from sight to the river bottom. For a moment the otters rose up and looked at Sam. They nodded their round heads and then they dived. The Fox paddled angrily to the bank, shouting with rage.

'Sam Pig! Your boat's gone. It's sprung a leak!' he called, but Sam Pig was already galloping home with the news.

Badger was there when Sam arrived and he listened to the little pig's story.

'And my boat has gone for ever,' said Sam, mournfully. 'But I am glad, for I hated Mister Fox to have it.'

'It was my fault,' said Badger, slowly. He reached for his pipe and lighted it with a glowing coal. Then he pulled on his carpet slippers. 'It was my fault. I never ought to have made a boat large enough for the Fox. I will make another some day, Sam, a little one, just your size, and if the Fox steals it, he can't use it. Now come along, Sam. Tell me about your visit to the otters. Did you see them swim? Tell me about them.'

'They are expecting you soon,' said Sam, when he had told his tale.

'Ah, yes,' said Badger. 'When the moon is full I shall go up the river and stay with them. I shall tell them stories and hear their own wild tales. Yes, I shall visit the otters soon, and thank them, Sam.'

Badger puffed slowly at his pipe and was silent, thinking of those slim strong creatures of the river and hills, and Sam too sat very quiet, dreaming of the beautiful wild otters.

The Christmas Box

It was December, and every morning when Sam Pig awoke he thought about Christmas Day. He looked at the snow, and he shivered a little as he pulled on his little trousers and ran downstairs. But the kitchen was warm and bright and a big fire burned in the hearth. Tom cooked the porridge and Ann set the table with spoons and plates, and Sam ran out to sweep the path or to find a log for the fire.

After breakfast Sam fed the birds. They came flying down from the woods, hundreds of them, fluttering and crying and stamping their tiny feet, and flapping their slender wings. The big birds – the green woodpeckers, the blue spangled jays, the dusky rooks and the speckled thrushes – ate from large earthen dishes and stone troughs which Sam filled with scraps. They were always so hungry that the little birds got no chance, so Sam had a special breakfast table for robins and tom tits, for wrens and chaffinches. On a long flat stone were ranged rows of little polished bowls filled with crumbs and savouries. The bowls were walnut-shells, and every bird had its own tiny brown nutshell. Sam got the shells from the big walnut tree in the corner of the farmer's croft. When autumn came the nuts fell to the ground, and Sam carried them home in a sack. The walnuts were made into nut-meal, but the shells were kept for the smallest birds.

After the bird-feeding Sam went out on his sledge. Sometimes Bill and Tom and Ann rode with him. Badger had made the sledge, but he never rode on it himself. He was too old and dignified, but he enjoyed watching the four pigs career down the field and roll in a heap at the bottom.

'Good old Badger,' thought Sam. 'I will give him a nice Christmas present this year. I'll make him something to take back to his house in the woods when he goes for his winter sleep.'

Badger of course never retired before Christmas, but when the festival was over he disappeared for three months and left the little family alone.

That was as far as Sam got. Ann was busy knitting a muffler for Badger. It was made of black and white sheep's wool, striped to match Badger's striped head. Bill the gardener was tending a blue hyacinth which he kept hidden in the woodshed. Tom the cook had made a cake for Brock. It was stuffed with currants and cherries and almonds as well as many other things like honeycomb and ants' eggs. Only young Sam had nothing at all.

There was plenty of time to make a present, he told himself carelessly, and he swept up the snow from the path and collected the small birds' walnut-shells.

'Christmas is coming,' said a robin brightly. 'Have you got your Christmas cards ready, Sam?'

'Christmas cards?' said Sam. 'What's that?'

'You don't know what a Christmas card is? Why, I'm part of a Christmas card! You won't have a good Christmas without a few cards, Sam.'

Sam went back to the house where Ann sat by the fire knitting Badger's muffler. She used a pair of holly-wood knitting-needles which Sam had made. A pile of scarlet holly-berries lay in a bowl by her side and she knitted a berry into the wool for ornament here and there. The black-thorn knitting needles with their little white flowers were, of course, put away for the winter. She only used those to knit spring garments.

Sam sat down by her side and took up the ball of wool. He rubbed it on his cheek and hesitated, but Ann went on knitting. She wondered what he was going to say.

'Ann. Can I make a Christmas card for Badger?' he asked.

Ann pondered this for a time, and her little needles clicked in tune with her thoughts.

'Yes, I think you can,' said she at last. 'I had forgotten what a Christmas card was like. Now I remember. There is a paintbox in the kitchen drawer, very very old. It belonged to our grand-mother. She used to collect colours from the flowers and she kept them in a box. Go and look for it, Sam.'

Sam went to the drawer and turned over the odd collection of things. There were cough-lozenges and candle-ends, and bits of string, and a bunch of rusty keys, a piece of soap and a pencil, all stuck together with gum from the larch trees. Then, at the back of the drawer, buried under dead leaves and dried moss he found the little paintbox.

'Here it is! Oh Ann! How exciting,' cried Sam, and he carried it to the table.

'It's very dry and the paints all look the same colour,' said Ann, 'but with a good wash they'll be all right.'

'It's a very nice box of paints,' said Sam, and he licked each paint carefully with his pointed tongue.

'They taste delicious,' said he, smacking his lips. 'The colours are all different underneath, and the tastes are like the colours. Look, Ann! Here's red, and here's green and here's blue, all underneath this browny colour.'

He held out the box of licked paints which were now gaily coloured.

'The red tastes of tomatoes and the green of

158

wood-sorrel and the blue of forget-me-nots,' said Sam.

Badger was much interested in the paintbox when he came in.

'You will want a paint-brush,' said he. 'You can't use the besom-brush, or the scrubbing-brush, or even your tooth-brush to paint a Christmas card, Sam.'

'Nor can he use the Fox's brush,' teased Bill.

Badger plucked a few hairs from his tail and bound them together.

'Here! A badger-brush will be excellent, Sam.'

'What shall I have to paint on?' asked Sam, as he sucked the little brush to a point and rubbed it on one of the paints.

That puzzled everybody. There was no paper at all. They looked high and low, but it wasn't till Tom was cooking the supper that they found the right thing. Tom cracked some eggs and threw the shells in the corner. Sam took one up and used the badger-brush upon it.

'This is what I will have,' he cried, and indeed it was perfect, so smooth and delicate. Bill cut the edges neatly and Sam practised his painting upon it, making curves and flourishes.

'That isn't like a Christmas card,' said Ann, leaning over his shoulder. 'A Christmas card must have a robin on it.'

'You must ask the robin to come and be painted tomorrow,' said Brock. 'He will know all about it. Robins have been painted on Christmas cards for many years.'

After the birds' breakfast the next day Sam asked the robin to come and have a picture made.

'I will sit here on this holly branch,' said the robin. 'Here is the snow, and here's the holly. I can hold a sprig of mistletoe in my beak if you like.'

So Sam fetched his little stool and sat in the snow with his paintbox and the badger-brush, and the robin perched on the holly branch, with a mistletoe sprig in its beak. It puffed out its scarlet breast and stared with unwinking brown eyes at Sam, and he licked his brush and dipped it in the red and blue and green, giving the robin a blue feather and a green wing.

'More eggshells,' called Sam, and he painted so fast and so brightly that the robin took one look and flew away in disgust.

'That's a bird of Paradise,' said he crossly.

Sam took his eggshells indoors and hid them in a hole in the wall, ready for Christmas Day.

'Have you a Christmas present for Badger?' asked Ann. 'I have nearly finished my scarf, and Tom's cake is made, and Bill's hyacinth is in bud. What have you made, Sam?'

'Nothing except the Christmas card,' confessed Sam. 'I've been thinking and thinking, but I can't find anything. If I could knit a pair of stockings, or grow a cabbage, or make a pasty I should know what to give him, but I can't do nothing.'

'Anything,' corrected Ann.

'Nothing,' said Sam. 'I can play my fiddle –'

'And fall in the river and steal a few apples, and get lost and catch the wind –' laughed Ann. 'Never mind. You shall share my scarf if you like, Sam, for you helped to find the sheep's wool and you got the holly berries for me.'

Sam shook his head. 'No. I won't share. I'll do something myself.'

He went out to the woods, trudging through the snow, looking for Christmas presents. In the holly trees were scarlet clusters of berries, and the glossy ivy was adorned with black beads. The rest of the trees, except the yews and fir trees, were bare, and they stood with boughs uplifted, and their trunks faintly smudged with snow. There wasn't a Christmas present any-where among them. The willows, from which Badger had made the boat, were smooth and ruddy, with never a parcel or packet or treasure among them. Then something waved in a thorn bush, something fluttered like a white flag, and Sam ran forward. The wind was rising and it made a curious moan and a whistle as it ruffled Sam's ears and made them ache. He stretched up to the little flag and found it was a feather. A feather! Sam had a thought! Perhaps the wind blew it to him, but there it was, a feather!

'I'll make him a feather bed, and when he goes to his castle deep in the woods he will take it with him to lie on. Poor old Badger, sleeping alone on the hard ground. Yes, I'll make him a feather bed.'

When the birds came for their breakfast the next morning Sam spoke to them about it.

'Can you spare a feather or two? I want to make a feather bed for old Badger's Christmas present,' he told them.

The birds shook their wings and dropped each a loose feather; they brushed and combed themselves and tossed little feathers to the ground. They passed the word round among the tree families, and other birds came flying with little feathers in their beaks for Sam Pig. A

flock of starlings left a heap of glistening shot-
silk, and the rooks came cawing from the bare
elms with sleek black quills. The chattering
magpies brought their black and white feathers,
which Sam thought were like Badger's head.
The jays came with their bright blue jewels,
and the robins with scarlet wisps from their
breasts. A crowd of tits gave him their own soft
little many-coloured feathers, and even the
wood pigeons left grey feathers for Sam. He
had so many the air was clouded with feathers
so that it seemed to be snowing again.

He gathered them up and filled his sack,
and even then he had some over. He put the
beautiful tiny feathers in his pocket, the red
scraps from the robins, the blue petals of
feathers from the tits, the yellow atoms from
the goldfinches and the emerald-blue gems from
the kingfisher. These he wove into a basket as
small as a nutshell, for Sister Ann, and inside
he put some mistletoe pearls. Ann would like
this, he knew.

On Christmas Day Sam came downstairs to
the kitchen, calling 'A merry Christmas' to

everybody. He didn't hang up his stocking of course because he had no stockings, and he didn't expect any presents either. Badger was the one who got the presents, old Badger who was the friend and guardian of the four pigs. It was at Christmas time they made their gifts to thank him for his care. So all the little pigs came hurrying downstairs with their presents for him.

There stood Badger, waiting for them, with a twinkle in his eye. Ann gave him the black and white muffler with its little scarlet berries inter-woven.

'Here's a muffler for cold days in the forest, Brock,' said she.

'Just the thing for nights when I go hunting,' said Brock, nodding his head and wrapping the muffler round his neck.

Then Bill gave him the little blue hyacinth growing in a pot.

'Here's a flower for you, Brock, which I've reared myself.'

'Thank you, Bill. It's the flower I love,' said Brock and he sniffed the sweet scent.

Then Tom came forward with the cake, which was prickly with almonds and seeds from many a plant.

'Here's a cake, Brock, and it's got so many things inside it, I've lost count of them, but there's honey-comb and eggs.'

'Ah! You know how I like a slice of cake,' cried Brock, taking the great round cake which was heavy as lead.

Then little Sam came, with the feather bed on his back. He had embroidered it with the letter B made of the black and white magpie feathers.

'For you to sleep on in your castle,' said he.

'Sam! Sam!' everybody cried. 'And you kept it secret! That's what you were doing every morning when the birds came for their break-fast! We thought there seemed to be a lot of feathers on the ground!'

Badger lay down on the little bed and pre-tended to snore. He was delighted with the warm comfortable present from little Sam Pig.

'Never mind the weather but sleep upon a feather,' said he. 'I shall sleep like a top through the fiercest gale when I lie on this little bed.'

They had breakfast, with a lashing of treacle on their porridge from the tin which Ann had kept for festivals. Then Sam hurried out to feed the birds and to thank them again for their share in Badger's Christmas. He carried a basket full of walnut-shells stuffed with scraps, and he found hosts of birds hopping about waiting for him.

But when he stepped into the garden he gave a cry of surprise, for in the flower bed grew a strange little tree.

'Look! Look!' he called. 'Ann! Bill! Tom! Badger! Come and look! It wasn't growing there last night. Where has it come from? And look at the funny fruit hanging on it! What is it?'

They followed him out and stared in astonishment at the small fir tree, all hung with pretty things. There were sugar pigs with pink noses and curly tails of string; and sugar watches with linked chains of white sugar, and chocolate mice. There were rosy apples and golden oranges, and among the sweet dainties were glittering icicles and hoar-frost crystals.

'Where has it come from? How did it grow here?' they asked, and they turned to Badger. 'Is it a magic?' they asked. 'Will it disappear? Is it really real?'

'It's solid enough, for the tree has come from the woods, but the other things will disappear fast enough I warrant when you four get near them.'

'But where did you find such strange and lovely things?' persisted Ann, staring up with her little blue eyes. 'Where? Where? From Fairyland, Badger?'

'I went to the Christmas fair in the town. I walked up to a market stall and bought them with a silver penny I had by me,' said Brock.

'But did nobody say anything to you?' asked Sam. 'How did you escape?'

'They were all so busy they didn't notice a little brown man who walked among them. They didn't bother about me on Christmas Eve. Miracles happen on Christmas Eve, and perhaps I was one of them. Also I carried the Leprechaun's shoe in my hand and maybe that helped me.'

Then Sam Pig brought the little feather basket and hung it among the icicles for his sister Ann. She was enchanted by it, and strung the mistletoe pearls round her neck.

'But where are your Christmas cards, Sam?' she asked suddenly. 'This is the time to give them.'

'I sat on them, Ann,' confessed Sam. 'I put them on a chair and sat down on them.'

'Crushed Christmas cards,' murmured Tom the cook. 'They will do very well to give an extra flavour to the soup. Those reds and blues and greens will make the soup taste extra good I'm sure.'

It was true. The Christmas soup with the Christmas card flavour was the nicest anyone had ever tasted, and not a drop was left.

As for the Christmas tree, everybody shared it, for the birds flew down to its branches and sang a Christmas carol in thanks for their breakfasts, and Sam sat underneath and sang another carol in thanks for their feathers.

So it was a very happy Christmas all round.

Sam Pig Goes to Market

One day Sam Pig found a penny. It had been lost by little Bill Wigg on his way to school. It slipped through a hole in Bill's pocket and dropped in the grass. There it lay for many a week, until Sam Pig came along with his nose close to the ground, peering and peeping at ants and beetles and snails. Sam Pig gave a shout of joy. He picked it out of the leaves, brushed away the net of webbing the creatures had spun over it, and he rubbed it on his trousers. It was surely a lucky penny to lie in the flowers, with daisies and forget-me-nots covering it with their petals and wood animals dancing over it.

'I will go to market,' thought Sam. 'Yes, I'll go all the way to market and do my shopping. Perhaps I could get a bicycle or a musical box for my penny.'

The market was miles and miles away, but Sam Pig started off early in the morning when the dew was on the grass and the birds were singing their merriest songs. Sam stuck a feather in his hat, cut a stick from the hedge, and put a pebble in his pocket to rattle against the penny. He whistled a tune as gay as the yellow-hammer's song about a bit of bread and no cheese, he called to the cuckoo, and he danced a few steps and then marched a few steps – left, right, left, right – with his stick held like a gun. His knapsack hung on his back ready for all the things he was going to buy with his lucky penny. Badger would be surprised when he saw all Sam's fairings!

After a time there was a cloppety clop of hooves behind him, but Sam Pig marched on. There was a rattle of wheels on the stones of the highway and a farm cart came bumping alongside. The farmer leaned over and looked at the little figure walking so bravely on the road.

'Whoa, mare!' he cried. 'Whoa, Sally! There's little Sam Pig as came to help our Irishmen at hay harvest. Would you like a lift, Sam?'

'Oh, thank you, Master,' cried Sam, and he

171

climbed up the wheel and sat as pleased and proud as Punch at the farmer's side. Never in all his life had he been so honoured! A ride in a cart!

'How's the grass, Master?' asked Sam affably, as he settled himself comfortably on the high seat and drew the old rug round his knees.

'Tollerble! Needs a drop of rain,' said the farmer, and he touched Sally with his whip, for she was trying to look round at Sam.

'And how are you keeping, Master?' asked Sam, shouting to make himself heard over the rattle of the cart wheels.

'Pretty middlin', except for a touch of rheumatics,' said the farmer. 'How's yourself, Sam?'

'Nicely, thank you,' said Sam. 'Will you want help this year at hay harvest, Master?'

'Well, I could do with a little 'un like yourself if you like to come and bring your fiddle, Sam. The Irish spoke well of you last year. Yes, I'll take you on again, Sam.'

'Thank you, Master.'

'Where are you going, Sam, all by your lonesome, trotting along the road?' asked the farmer after a pause.

'To market, Master. I've got a penny to spend.'

'You don't say so! A whole penny!' The farmer laughed, and the mare pricked up her ears when she heard.

'Well, you can buy a fine lot of things for a penny. Mousetraps, boot-laces, curranty buns, twenty marbles, all cost a penny, Sam. If you stand by the mare while I have my shave at the barber's shop I'll give you another penny to add to it.'

'Oh, thank you, Master. Oh! Oh!' Sam's eyes sparkled, and the mare kicked her heels for she dearly loved a talk with Sam Pig, and while the Master was being shaved there would be time for a gossip.

So they drove along the lanes and the farmer pointed out the fields of mowing grass, and the pastures, the cornland, and the crops, the cattle and sheep, the ploughs and the harrows. Sam Pig nodded his head and answered so wisely the farmer was much impressed. The mare trotted slowly along the road, enjoying the talk, glad to be out with her friends.

When they reached the barber's shop Sam stayed in the cart and held the reins, and the mare turned her head and had a good talk about Bill and Tom, about Ann and Brock, about the cows at the farm, and the new calves, and the little pigs in the sty and the turkey who strutted in the farmyard.

Sam Pig could see the farmer through the little window. He was wrapped in a white cloth, and lathered and shaved. It was indeed a wondrous sight, something to tell Brock the Badger about when he got home. Then the farmer came out and gave Sam a penny for minding the mare.

'I'll look out for you when I go back and give you a lift again, if you feel like it, Sam. You'll be so tired of spending your riches, that you'll be glad to get a ride.'

'Thank you, Master,' said Sam.

The cart drove away and Sam passed up the crowded street where the cabbages and eggs

and baskets of gooseberries were displayed on
the pavement edge. In the centre of the market-
place were the stalls, heaped with carraway
cakes, and brandy snaps, and peppermint rock
and aniseed balls. Sam walked up and down
and round about, staring and sniffing, and
keeping himself to himself. It was difficult to
decide what to buy among so many rich and
splendid things.

He saw boot-laces, but of course he had no
boots. He saw marbles of many colours hanging in little bags, but Brock could make marbles
of clay from the stream. There was a box of
them on the shelf at home. Then he saw a nice
neat-looking mousetrap with a door and door-
knocker, and walls of bright wire. It was a little
wooden house, just the right size for a mouse to
live in. Sam paid his penny and bought the
mousetrap.

'Just bait it with a morsel of cheese, and the
mouse will go in, and bang! the door will shut,'
said the man who sold it to Sam. Sam thanked
him and went on his way delighted with it.

As he walked through the village he passed a

poor cottage, and he heard a woman bewailing.

'Oh dear! Oh dear! What shall I do? Whatever shall I do?'

Sam Pig, who was a kind-hearted little fellow,
stopped and looked through the open door.

'Can I help you, ma'am?' he asked politely.

'My little cat is dead, and there's a mouse in
my larder. It has eaten all my cheese! Oh dear!'

'Would you like the loan of my mousetrap?'
asked Sam.

The poor old woman came to the door and
looked at Sam.

'Oh thank you. I've been fair bothered by
this mouse. It's eating me out of house and
home. Just you wait while I sets the trap. I
haven't got any bait, but never mind. Just you
wait and see what happens.'

She ran to the larder and set the mousetrap,
and then came to Sam Pig, who stood by the
dresser, looking at the mugs and jugs.

'That's all I've got left in the world now. I've
got to go to the workhouse next week, and I
don't want to leave my little home,' she said
softly, rubbing the edge of the dresser with her

finger and dusting the mugs with her apron.

'It's very hard,' she continued.

'It is,' agreed Sam. He was wondering whether to give her the penny which lay in his pocket, when there was a crack! The little mouse was caught.

'We've got it! We've got the varmint!' cried the old woman, and she ran to the larder and brought back the mousetrap.

Inside the trap sat the little mouse. It was weeping bitterly, but of course the old woman didn't know that.

'Oh, why did I go into that little house?' it wailed.

Then it ran up and down trying to get out, pushing at the door, dragging at the steel bars.

'Oh, set me free! Oh, set me free! If you set me free I'll tell you a secret. I have a secret. Oh, set me free! I'll never do it again. I won't eat your cheese. I'll go home to my mother Jemima, who lives in an old boot down the lane. Oh, set me free!'

'She's squeaking,' said the old woman. 'I'll take and drown her right away.'

'No,' said Sam quickly. 'Wait a minute.'

'I know your mother, little mouse,' said he softly to the mouse. 'I know Jemima: she is an old friend of mine.'

'Oh, Sam Pig! I didn't know you in that hat,' said the mouse. 'Oh, set me free, Sam Pig.'

The mouse and Sam were talking in the mouse's own little language, and the old woman heard none of this. She poked the fire and put the kettle on ready for a cup of tea while Sam stood by the dresser holding the mousetrap, and speaking to the tiny prisoner.

'What is your secret, little mouse?' asked Sam.

'There's a heap of gold money under the floor of the old woman's house. There is! I was making my nest in it, but the coins were too hard and cold. I always eat my dinner on them, for they are round as plates, and quite unbreakable.'

'That will be good news for the poor old woman,' said Sam softly. 'Shall I take you home in my pocket, little mouse? I know where your mother lives, and I'll put you down in the lane. You are far away, you must have wandered.'

'Yes, Sam Pig,' sobbed the small creature. 'I want to go back to my mother and sisters and brothers. I won't eat cheese any more. I shall live on earth nuts and haws and all the nice things in the hedgerows after this. Never again will I roam.'

So Sam Pig opened the trap and put the mouse in his pocket.

The old woman made the tea and poured out a cup for Sam.

'I've only got dry bread, but you are welcome to it,' said she.

Sam shared the old woman's meal and talked to her about mice and mousetraps and the market outside, and all the time he was wondering how to look for the gold.

'Maybe there's a mouse's nest under your floor,' said he. 'Shall I look and see?'

'If it won't be too much trouble,' said the old woman. 'I'm nervous of mice, and I don't want any more bothering me.'

Sam found the mouse's hole and lifted a

stone flag near it. There were bits of cheese, and pieces of cloth and crumbs of bread, as well as shreds of wool lying there. Underneath was something that glittered. Sam stood aside and the old woman turned over the scraps and swept them up in her dustpan.

'What a mercy you caught that mouse! See what it has done! My wool and my slippers nibbled!'

Then she caught sight of the gold.

'Mercy on us! What's this?' she cried. 'It's a gold mine! Look ye here! Gold sovereigns. Many a lot of 'em. I shan't have to go to the workhouse after all! I can stay here! Oh, young sir, how can I thank you?'

She scooped up the gold with trembling fingers and poured it on the table. There was quite a good sum of money, and Sam Pig smiled up at the old woman's happy face.

'It was the mouse, not me,' said he. 'If it hadn't been for the mouse, we shouldn't have found it.'

'True,' said she. 'That mouse has been a blessing. I'm sorry I called it names.'

'It's in my pocket,' said Sam. 'I'm going to set it free in the lane. It's a field mouse, you know, not an ordinary mouse at all.'

'Well, I'm proper grateful to you and the mouse, and if you'll accept one of the gold sovereigns, I shall be glad.'

So Sam took the sovereign, and said goodbye to the old woman. She followed him to the door and smiled and nodded to him as he went away.

'I shan't be turned out of my little house now,' she said again, and she sat down in her rocking-chair and burst into tears of happiness.

Sam Pig went back to the market, and looked at the stalls. He could buy nearly everything with a gold sovereign. He walked about, and stared at the piles of sweetmeats, but he couldn't make up his mind what to have. At last he spent the odd penny on pink-and-white comfits. They had writing on them, and he could just manage to spell out the mottoes.

'I love you.' 'Good night.' 'You are a dear,' was printed on the flat round sweets.

Sam put them in his pocket, away from the mouse. She couldn't be trusted to leave them alone.

He heard a sound of music, loud and gay and noisy, not at all like the music of Sam's fiddle, or the music of the wind in the trees, or the song of birds. It came from a distant part of the market and Sam trotted across the square to find it.

A dark-skinned Italian turned the handle of a barrel-organ, and the merry tunes came dancing out. The village children crowded round, for seldom there came a barrel-organ to their street. Everybody seemed to listen to it, and Sam saw the farmer with his hands in his pockets watching the foreigner, and enjoying the tunes.

There were peals of laughter, and Sam went nearer. He crept between the children to see what was the matter. They were all looking at a little red-coated stranger, who sat in the man's arms. Such a sad little face he had! His wrinkled cheeks and puckered forehead and dark miserable eyes were unlike any Sam had seen before. He wore a red cap on his head and a little red jacket trimmed with gold. In his tiny hand he held a mug, and the children threw pennies into it.

Sam listened to the jabbering talk but he could not understand a word. The Italian's tunes came tinkling through the air, and the little children danced to them. Sam too joined in the dance, and skipped and hopped with the others. At last the music stopped and the monkey came walking over the ground with outstretched hand for money. It looked at Sam, and Sam put his hand in his pocket. He brought out the gold piece and dropped it into the tin mug.

'Oh, thank you! Thank you!' whispered the Italian, in quick, breathless haste. 'Oh, how can I thank you? We shall get a good meal, my little Biano and I, and we shall sleep in comfort for many a night with this. Thank you! A blessing on you.'

The little monkey came forward and put its tiny brown hand in Sam's. As the two hands touched, the little creature gave a sudden look of recognition.

'I'm Sam Pig,' murmured Sam, hoping it would understand. It shook its head, and looked at Sam, as if to tell him all its troubles. Then it crept into its master's coat, and clung to him.

Sam turned away, and as he walked across the market-place towards the blacksmith's forge, he could hear the tunes of the barrel-organ swinging triumphantly through the elm trees. The Italian was rejoicing that he had got a gold piece.

At the blacksmith's door were three horses waiting, but inside the forge, with one foot held in the blacksmith's great hand, was Sally the mare.

'Tink! tink! tink!' went the hammer, and the boy blew up the fire and sparks came through the hole in the roof, to fly upward to the stars. Sam stood outside, watching the smith and waiting for Sally. The mare seemed to know he was there, for she looked round and spoke in her silent way.

'He won't be long. He's done three hooves. Only one to do! How have you enjoyed yourself, Sam?'

'Oh, I've found a gold mine, and helped a monkey,' said Sam, casually. 'And I bought some comfits, and I've got Jemima's daughter in my pocket.'

'Who is Jemima?' asked the mare, and she moved suddenly so that the smith cried out: 'Whoa, there! Steady, there!'

'Jemima's the mouse I once looked after. Now I've found her daughter, and I'm going to take her home to the old boot.'

'Oh!' said the mare. 'I thought Jemima was a lady.'

Sam laughed and sang a little song:

> *'Jemima's not a lady,*
> *She's just a little mouse,*
> *Her daughter walked into a trap,*
> *And thought it was a house.'*

The smith looked up from the shoe he was making.

'What's that noise?' he asked. 'There's a pig somewhere about, Dick. Just go and see.'

So Sam walked away, and waited at a respectable distance from the forge, where Dick couldn't find him. At last the farmer came to fetch the mare, and Sam climbed into the cart beside him. They drove away, bumping along the roads, with the great brown market-basket packed with eatables under the seat, and a bag of meal and a sack of flour at the back against the cart-end.

'Well, Sam,' said the farmer. 'I've sold the eggs and the butter at a better price than usual, and I've done the marketing, and made a good bargain too. What have you been doing with yourself all day? Have you spent your twopence?'

'Yes, Master,' said Sam shuffling on the seat as the little mouse started to climb out of his pocket.

'Yes. I've got some sugar comfits with mottoes on them.' He took out the bag of sweets and offered them to the farmer. Farmer Green-sleeves dipped a large finger and thumb inside and brought out a pink comfit.

'What does it say, Master?' asked Sam.

'It says, "May fortune attend you",' read the farmer, and he popped the comfit in his mouth.

'They are all talking about a strange thing in the village,' continued the farmer as he contentedly sucked his sweet. 'There's a poor old woman, who was going to the workhouse next week, and what do you think happened?'

'She found some gold,' said Sam.

'Quite true! So you heard about it, too! Yes, she found a heap of gold under her floor. She said a little fellow came to her house with a mousetrap, and he lifted a flagstone and found the money. A queer tale. I'm very glad, for I was sorry for her. Now she's got enough to live on for years.'

Sam felt in his knapsack, and brought out the mousetrap.

'I bought a mousetrap with my penny,' said he, 'but I shan't use it. I don't believe in catching mice. I shall line it with red flannel and use it for somebody's bedroom.'

The farmer looked at the trap, and then at Sam. He said nothing, and Sam talked of this and that, of all he had seen at the market, of the monkey and the organ-grinder and the blacksmith's forge, but he didn't mention the old woman and the gold.

When they came to the little green lane Sam got out. He thanked the farmer and patted the mare, and stood by the roadside till Sally had trotted round the corner. Then he tiptoed through the grass to the old boot which lay among the garlic and red campion and Jack-by-the-hedge, lost in the thick flowers.

'Here's your daughter come home, Jemima,' said he, tapping at the side of the boot.

Out came Jemima, and there was such a welcome to the little mouse it did Sam's heart good.

He slipped away while they were all talking and trotted back to the road, and onward to his own home.

'I've been to market, riding in the cart with the farmer,' he announced.

'Get along with you,' exclaimed Bill and Tom disbelievingly.

'I did, so there! And I spent twopence, so there!' said Sam.

'How did you get twopence?' they asked.

'I found a penny of it, and I earned a penny of it, and I love twopence better than my life,' sang Sam, and he danced round the table.

'What did you buy?' they asked.

'A mousetrap and a bag of comfits,' said Sam, and he emptied his pockets to show them.

'The comfits are for all of you, but the mouse-trap is my own. I shall take away the door, and line the house with red flannel, and make it into a hospital for sick butterflies.'

'Sick butterflies!' muttered Bill, scornfully.

'Sick guinea-pigs,' said Tom.

They helped themselves to the comfits, and Sam told them the whole story of his adventures.

'And you gave the gold to a sick monkey?' asked Tom. 'You might have bought a bicycle with it.'

'Yes, I might,' said Sam, 'but I didn't.'

All the way home the farmer was thinking hard. Yes, he was quite certain it was little Sam Pig who found that gold under the old woman's floor. He wouldn't say anything about it, not even to his wife. If Sam wanted to keep the secret, he would keep it too. Nobody would ever know who was the little person who helped the old woman to keep out of the workhouse, for who would believe him if he said it was a small pig?

Sam Pig and the Water-Baby

Sam Pig was down by the river one day fishing with the rod Badger had made for him. It was a fine willow rod, slender and supple, with a string fastened to it and the bait on the end. The bait was a berry, a bright red berry. Sam often caught fish and he took them home in his creel for Ann to fry for supper. A creel, you must know, is a basket, and Sam's creel was woven from rushes and lined with fresh wet grass to make a bed for the fish.

It was a dull day with rain in the sky, just the sort of day for catching fish. Sam Pig wore a mackintosh and he had twisted a cabbage leaf into a fishing-cap, so that the fish wouldn't recognize him.

'Who's up there, trying to catch us?' asked one fish in a reedy voice.

'Is it a real fisherman, or is it only Sam Pig pretending to be one?' asked another fish.

There was a peal of fishy laughter, like a fountain of bells, and a trout leaped out of the water and took a squint at Sam.

'It looks like Sam Pig and it doesn't look like Sam. He's got a green cap on his head, whoever he is,' said the trout.

'I'll go up and peep at him,' said an old fish.

'I can tell in a minute, for he has often tried to catch me.'

Sam Pig got much annoyed by the behaviour of the fish, leaping out of the water, squinting at him, staring with flat round eyes, opening their mouths and shutting them tight.

'You keep still and eat my berry,' he shouted at last. 'How can I catch you if you leap about like this?'

'Yes, it's Sam Pig right enough,' whispered the little fish to one another, and they laughed behind their fins and shook their silvery tails and darted in and out of the water reeds.

Sam Pig threw down his fishing-rod in disgust and took up his net. He dipped it in the water and drew it along the waves. Then he brought it out and from every thin mesh dripped the river.

'That's something new,' said the fish. 'It's more exciting than the rod. It's a pretty thing, all made of holes. Why, it holds nothing!'

'A nothing, a nothing, it dances and skips.
It picks up the water, and away it all drips,'

sang the little fish, jeering and dancing on their tails.

'You daren't jump inside,' said Sam crossly, and he leaned over the water. The rain was falling fast and he was chilled with sitting on the wet bank.

'Yes I dare,' shrilled the speckled trout, who had first discovered Sam. 'Look at me.'

It darted into the silvery net as it lay in the water, and then it turned to swim out again. Too late! Like a flash Sam Pig caught up the net, and there was the fish, waving over Sam's head.

'Oh-oh-oh,' sighed all the fish in the river with round mouths muttering and eyes a-goggle.

'He's caught. Our brother is captured by little Sam Pig!'

Sam lifted the fish from the meshes of the net and knelt to put it in the creel. He opened the lid and placed the struggling trout on the green bed.

'Lemme go!' panted the trout. 'Oh, lemme go!'

'Never! Lie there till Ann puts you in our frying-pan,' said Sam triumphantly.

'Not I!' The fish gave a sudden jerk, and it was out of the creel, flip-flapping over the bank to the river in a jiffy.

Sam Pig rushed after it, but he was too late. The trout took a leap and turned a backward somersault into the water.

'By the skin of his teeth,' muttered Sam, leaning over to watch his lost prize.

'By the tip of his tail,' cried a frog, who had been excitedly hopping up and down the bank.

'By the spots of his back,' cried the fish, swimming round their brother and congratulating him upon his clever escape.

'I meant to do it,' boasted the fish. 'I've always wanted to trick Sam Pig.'

'Let's play another trick on him,' whispered a little fish. They all disappeared under the stones and talked together. The water reeds were waving over their heads, and Sam's net was moving about, seeking another foolish trout.

The fish came out again, towing a green

bundle. They pushed it into the net and watched it lying there.

Sam felt the weight and lifted the net quickly before the fish could escape. When he took the bundle out, it wasn't a fish at all. It was a baby, a water-baby, from the silver-green nursery among the river rocks. The fish had stolen it from its cradle and carried it away from its home.

'That will teach Sam Pig not to come netting in our water,' said they, and they swam to the surface to watch Sam. The little pig was much surprised when he saw the child wrapped in its cloak of water-weeds.

The water-baby opened its green eyes and stared at Sam. Then it puckered up its little face and began to weep. It stuck its fists in its eyes and bent its head and sobbed bitterly.

'Here! Stop that!' exclaimed Sam crossly as he shook it, and the baby cried all the more, a queer little wail like the rustle of grasses.

So Sam shut it in the creel and carried it home. All the way soft little sobs came from the basket.

'What have you got there, Sam?' asked the
Fox, as Sam went past with his burden slung
on his back. 'What are you stealing? Ducks or
apples?'

'It's a water-baby. I didn't steal it. I caught
it in my fishing-net,' said Sam gruffly.

'A water-baby? Don't have nuffin' to do with
water-babies,' warned the Fox. 'They're queer
fish.'

Sam ran on with the dripping net and his wet
mackintosh trailing behind him.

'See what I've caught,' he cried, throwing open
the door and thumping the creel on the table.

The water-baby gave a thin wail of misery
and the pigs crowded round to see what Sam
had brought.

'A water-baby,' said Sam in disgust. 'And I
wanted a fish.'

'It's the loveliest little creature,' cried Ann,
taking it up in her arms and nursing it. 'Look
at its green eyes, and its golden curls, like sun
in water. Look at its silver-green tail and the
little fins on its back and its delicate hands and
arms!'

'It's smiling at you!' said Sam, astonished. 'It only cried at me. I didn't know it could smile.'

'You didn't treat it properly, Sam.' Ann looked severely at her young brother. 'You dumped it in the creel and tossed it about, and it didn't like that.'

Then Brock the Badger came in and Ann Pig held out the water-baby for him to see. It laughed at old Badger and pulled his hairy face.

'It's a beauty,' cried Brock. 'I've seen these little ones swimming about in the moonlight, on quiet nights when nobody was abroad, but I've never seen one as young as this. It must have been taken from its cradle. It can't talk yet.'

'What shall we do with it?' asked Tom. 'Shall we keep it?'

'Oh do let me keep it for a while,' begged Ann. 'I've never had a water-baby in my arms.'

'But it can't walk,' objected Bill. 'We can't nurse it all the time. I'm not going to be a water-baby's nurse, thank you.'

'I'll nurse it, and look after it,' said Ann quickly.

'And what will it eat?' asked Sam.

'We'll try it on bread and milk,' said Brock. 'Yes, I think we might keep it for a time unless it's unhappy. Then we'll take it back to the river.'

Ann put the baby down on the softest blanket in the house, and the little creature lay there, contentedly looking round at the strange place where it found itself. The four pigs fed it with milk and bread, and gave it sips of water. Sam fetched his bath from the shed and filled it with water for the water-baby. It swam round and round, splashing with its green tail, tossing the water over its glistening scales.

'It swims better than you, Sam,' teased Bill, knowing Sam couldn't swim.

'Better than a fish,' agreed Sam. 'It couldn't ever drown.'

That night there was a terrible storm. The wind roared down the chimney, the rain poured in torrents along the lanes, and there was such a gurgling of water the four pigs thought the clouds had burst.

'It was a wild night,' remarked Tom Pig as he cooked the breakfast and beat up an egg in milk for the water-baby. 'I never remember such weather since that rain-fellow stayed with us long ago. Do you think he was somewhere about?'

'No,' said Ann. 'It wasn't the rain only. There was something else last night, a strange dull, roaring sound.'

'It can't be anything to do with the water-baby, can it?' asked Sam Pig anxiously.

'What do you mean? How could it be the innocent baby, lying here as good as gold in its cradle?' cried Ann indignantly. She picked up the water-baby and nursed it, and sang 'Rock-a-bye baby in the tree top' to it.

'Rock-a-bye baby in the river bottom,' corrected Sam.

Then he gave a start and sprang to the door. There was a mighty roar, a thunderous clamour in the air. He looked out and there was the river, rushing along the lane, with all the little fishes peeping out of the water, and a boat bobbing about on the surface.

'Quick! Quick! We shall all be drowned. The river's burst its banks,' he shouted. 'It's coming!'

It was true. The river came roaring across the orchard, and under the garden gate. It lifted the gate from its hinges and carried it along. The four pigs ran as fast as they could out of the back door. Ann carried the water-baby in her arms, Sam grabbed his fiddle from the hook, Bill snatched up a loaf of bread, and Tom the cook seized the frying-pan. Only old Brock the Badger stayed downstairs to meet the raging angry waters and to talk to them.

'What is the matter, Old Mister River?' he asked in his calm deep voice. 'What's wrong that you leave the bed where you've lived for a thousand years, and why have you come to disturb an innocent family of pigs?'

'Gr-gr-gr-gr –' went the water, muttering and grumbling as it curled round the house. 'Give me back my baby.'

'It's just like the Dragon, only worse,' said

Sam, clinging to a bough of an apple tree. 'I might try to tame it, only I'm scared of it.'

He played a little tune, but it was quavering and melancholy because the fiddle was wet. It made the river angrier than ever, and it dashed against Sam's tree and shook it until Sam nearly fell into the torrent.

'Oh goodness! Take care, River. You'll drown me. You mustn't do that. I'm a friend of yours.'

The water was making a dull moaning noise, and the four pigs were getting alarmed. The river was climbing higher, and the apple trees where they clung were half-hidden in water. The pigs climbed to the topmost branches and clung for safety. Old Brock was swimming to save himself.

'Old Mister River! What do you want?' he called.

'Give me back my baby,' muttered the river.

Then Brock saw a friend swimming towards him. It was Jack Otter, diving and playing in the river among the apple trees.

'What does the river want?' asked Brock. 'I can't understand its voice. Why has it come here? Why are you here, Jack Otter?'

'Oh Brock! We've lost our water-baby. She was the river's favourite child. The loveliest creature that ever breathed in the water. We are all looking for her – the otters, and the fishes and the little water-voles. We've been seeking all night. She was stolen by somebody when she was fast asleep. The river is going to find her if it flows all over England, into every lane and field and wood.'

'Gr-gr-gr-gr,' moaned the river again, and it lapped the tree where Ann sat with the water-baby in her arms.

Even as the otter spoke, the water-baby opened its green eyes and gave a little wriggle when it saw the river below. It leapt like a fish out of Ann's arms and dived into the shining river. Down it went, and the river held it tightly and began to sing to it. The roaring ceased and a lovely melody filled the air, as the water began to flow gently down the lane. Away it went, over the fields and woods, towards the ancient river-bed, and with it went all the fishes and otters and river animals.

Down into its bed sank the river, with the water-baby clasped in its arms, and all the time it sang the smooth sweet lullaby of rivers. It dropped the child into its green wicker cradle, and rocked it with gentle motion. It gave the water-baby a shell to play with, and it put a guard of an ancient pike to keep off all strangers. The little fish who had stolen it were sent away to swim a whole long day down the stream where there were no cool depths and great stones to hide among when the sun was hot. Then they came back forgiven.

The four pigs climbed from their perches in the apple trees, and surveyed the mud the river had left behind it.

'All this mess! It comes of harbouring water-babies,' said Bill grumpily. 'Look at the garden! Look at my cabbages and lettuces.'

'And my rose-bushes,' sighed Ann. 'But it was a nice baby, and it isn't everybody who has had a water-baby in the house.'

'Come along with your besoms and tidy the garden,' said Brock. 'River mud is good for the soil, I've heard, and perhaps your cabbages will grow even larger, Tom, for the river's visit.'

They fetched their little birch-besoms and swept and tidied the garden paths and carried away the stones the river had brought, and the dark rich mud soaked into the ground. That summer the vegetables were enormous, and the marrows were as large as those the little pigs once saw at a Flower Show. Even the roses were redder, and the lilies sweeter. Everything grew as it had never grown before.

'Thank you for coming to see us, Old Mister River,' shouted Sam Pig, as he sat by the water's edge with his fishing-rod and his net.

'Gr-gr-gr –' murmured the river, tossing its waters in contempt for little Sam Pig, and the silver fish flicked their tails and laughed at him.

Then a wave lifted and out of the depths appeared a little water-maiden. She climbed on a mossy rock and began to comb her long golden hair. She waved a small white hand to Sam, and then she dived back under the water.

'Well I never! She's grown up already,' exclaimed Sam. 'Water-babies don't take long to grow. I do wish she would come out and talk to me.'

He whistled and called, and he even dived after her, but he only got very wet and bedraggled, as he struggled up the bank.

'Sam Pig! Sam Pig! You can't catch any of us, fish or water-maidens,' sang a shrill, reedy voice, and the speckled trout laughed and leapt in the air.

Sam Pig and the Scarecrow

One day when Sam Pig went for his usual walk up Windy Whistle hill to the look-out tree on the top he saw something different. The fields were there, green and brown, with ploughed land and wheat and barley; the pastures lay in misty loveliness as the long rays of the sun shone through the hedges; the farmhouse was there in the hollow, with the walnut-tree and the orchard, but there was somebody present who seemed part of the landscape. A strange figure stood in the middle of the cornfield, and the odd thing about him was his quietness. He never took a step here or there. He stayed always in the same place. It is true he waved his lanky arms and his coat flapped in the wind. His ragged hat shook and his round face seemed to be staring up at the sky, at birds and clouds and sunlight. Sam looked hard at him, and frowned and took a step forward. Then he frowned again and took a step backward. It wasn't fair that a man should stay right in the middle of Sam's particular field, and never go away. Perhaps he was a shooter, on the lookout for rabbits and pheasants. But his arms were stretched out in a warning way, as if he wished to be alone.

Sam retreated behind the oak tree and watched the intruder. He stayed a long time, waiting for some movement, but the man never took a step. Then Sam went home and told Brock the Badger about him.

'There's a one-legged man in the wheat field. He hasn't moved for hours. He's all alone in the middle of the field, Brock. What do you think he is doing?'

'What is he like, Sam?' asked Brock, looking down at the excited little pig.

'He's like all men, stiff and stupid-looking, but he has only one leg, Brock, and he's a bit untidier and a bit more ragged than a tramp.'

'I expect it's Joe Scarecrow,' said Badger. 'He's all right. He comes out every spring and guards the seed for the farmer. Then back he goes to the barn, when the harvest is over. He's a friendly person, Joe Scarecrow.'

So the next day Sam Pig went to visit the scarecrow. There the odd-looking fellow stood waving his arms at the rooks, his coat-tails fluttering, his trousers flapping, one leg empty and the other filled with a wooden post. Round his neck was a scarf of bright cotton, with tapes and scraps of scarlet and blue ribbons dangling, and each end flew out like a streamer in the wind.

Sam Pig trotted across the field and went up to the scarecrow. He carried a bunch of flowers for the poor lonely fellow.

'Hallo, Mr Scarecrow,' said Sam, 'I've brought you these.'

'Thank ye kindly, and pray call me Joe,' said the scarecrow. 'Aye, if it isn't Sam Pig! I thought I 'membered you. Didn't I see you in the hayfield with the Irishmen at harvest time last year? Didn't I look out of the barn where I lay in a corner, and didn't I spy you with those fine Irishmen?'

'Of course,' cried Sam. 'I remember getting a peep at a man of straw, but I wasn't quite sure what it was.'

'I was half asleep, Sam. Now I'm awake and working for my living. It's a grand thing, work.'

Sam smiled dubiously, but the scarecrow flapped his arms and scared a pair of crows so that they flew away with noisy caws. He waved to a cuckoo, and shook his fist at a bold company of starlings, and fluttered his scarf fringes at a bevy of little linnets.

> *'Oh keep away, little birds,*
> *Keep away do,*
> *Or Joe the Scarecrow*
> *Will moggrify you.'*

He sang in a shrill voice, and the row of bells

stitched to his sleeves rang like music.

'Look here, Sam Pig. I'm sick and tired of standing here and I want to change, yet I don't want to let the farmer down. He's been a good friend to me, and he gives me a decent suit each year. He sadly needs me to scare the crows and to keep his corn free from those hungry thieves.'

'Yes,' agreed Sam. 'You are doing a piece of good work.'

'What I was thinking was this. If some kind body would take my place and scare the crows and rooks for me, it would give me a welcome holiday, and I'd be main glad.'

'Yes,' agreed Sam. 'But who would stay here in your place, Joe?'

'That is what I was coming to, Sam Pig. Suppose you comed here? It's just the kind of job for a young healthy pig – scaring birds, viewing the country, and nothing to do. Just the life – nothing whatever to do.'

'Well, I like doing nothing,' said Sam, and he yawned and stretched himself. 'I have to work very hard at home. You've no idea how

Brother Bill and Brother Tom keep me at it, forking up the 'taters, picking up sticks, getting the eggs, filling the kettle, scaring the Fox, gathering honey. I shouldn't mind a rest, but I'd rather stay in bed. I don't know whether I want to be a scarecrow.'

'It's a grand life, Sam,' said the scarecrow earnestly. 'You will be a farmer without a farmer's cares, a traveller without having to walk, a watcher on a ship without being tossed by waves, a benefactor to man without having to meet any of those humans.'

'Ah,' grunted Sam.

'You smell the wind on the hills, and the grass at your feet and you can see the corn grow. That's a sight few people see. You can watch it sprout and grow.'

Sam was much impressed. He went close to Joe Scarecrow and surveyed the great field. It certainly was a lovely prospect, with rolling hills, and high hedges, tall old trees and the woods far away.

'I think I'll do it,' said he.

'Ah. Thank you, Sam. But you're rather too

well dressed for a scarecrow, Sam. Suppose you change clothes with me?'

Sam didn't like this. He agreed to part with his coat and hat, and to wear the ragged jacket and broken felt hat which the scarecrow wore, but he resolutely refused to part with his plaid trousers. They had been made by Sister Ann, from sheep's wool gathered in the hedgerows, dyed with berries, red, white and blue, and they were Sam's dearest possession. No, he couldn't part with his trousers and wear the ragged breeks with holes in the knees that the straw man had. So he doffed his coat and hat and dressed himself in the scarecrow's garb. Then he stood in the middle of the cornfield, a stick in his hand, a straw in his mouth, waiting for the birds.

'Goodbye,' said the scarecrow. 'I'm off to Blackpool. I'll bring you a piece of Blackpool rock. Goodbye. I'm going to see the briny ocean. Goodbye, Sam Pig.'

'When are you coming back?' called Sam hastily. 'How long will you be away, Joe?'

But Joe Scarecrow didn't seem to hear. He

waved his stiff wooden arms as if he were
scaring the birds. He called 'Goodbye! So long,
little Sam Pig. Blackpool beach for me!' and
the last Sam saw of him was a tattered trouser
leg hopping over the stile, and a face of straw
and turnip grinning as the scarecrow disappeared in the distance.

'Well, here I am, monarch of all I survey, as
the saying is,' murmured Sam cheerfully, and
he sang a little song which made the crows
open their black eyes even wider and fly cawing
in alarm to the woods.

> *'O little birds, now will you*
> *Keep off this cornfield, or I'll kill you.'*

'That scarecrow is more alive than usual,'
said the crows. 'He's squeaking and squawking
terrible, and he's grown so fat and his eyes are
looking about him. We can't settle for a minute
without he waves that stick and shouts at us.'

Sam stood first on one leg then on another.
Then he sat down, but he sprang to his feet
when he saw a farm labourer enter the field.
The man took no notice of Sam, and Sam stood

very still just like Joe Scarecrow himself. When the labourer had gone, Sam put his hand in his pocket and brought out a mouth-organ. How thankful he was that he hadn't changed trousers with the scarecrow. He fumbled in all the pockets of the ragged coat. There was an old clay pipe, a bunch of string, a few nails and that was all. Sam played a tune on the mouth-organ, sucked the empty pipe, and made a cat's cradle with the string. Then he sighed. He was hungry and he remembered he had made no arrangements for food. Scarecrows don't eat anything, but pigs eat a lot. There was a piece of bread and honeycomb in the jacket the scarecrow had taken to Blackpool, and Sam thought longingly of it.

'When it gets dark I'll go off and find something,' he comforted himself. 'When the crows go to their nests and the men are in the farmhouse, then I'll go off.'

He waited impatiently till dark came and then he padded over the fields to the farmhouse. He went to the back door, near the dairy. The door was open a crack and he pushed it wider.

Then he crept along the passage. He drank deep from the yellow bowls set for cream, he cut a large slice of cheese and seized a hunk of bread from the new crusty loaves in the bread-mug. He pocketed a few eggs and a half-pound of butter. Then he heard footsteps coming from the kitchen. Sam Pig crouched low on his four little trotters, as a dairymaid came in with a candle.

'Who's this? Oh! Oh!' she cried, dropping the candle in a fright.

Sam scuttled through the door, brushing close to her skirts.

'Oh, Missis! Oh! A somebody, all ragged and round!' she screamed running back to the kitchen.

Sam Pig raced to the back door and was out in a flash. The dog barked, and then wagged his tail when he saw it was only Sam Pig, his old friend. The horse neighed and then nodded its head at Sam. The cows mooed and then shook their horns joyfully. The farm hands came tumbling out to see who it was. Sam ran along the lane, with the men after him. He

scrambled through a gap in the hedge and scuttled back to the middle of the field. There he stood in the moonlight, a pale scarecrow, and when the farm men got to the gate they looked up and they looked down but never a man could they see except the ragged scarecrow flapping its arms and shaking its straws and ribbons in a doleful manner in the corn.

'There's nobbut the scarecrow,' they said when they got back to the farm. 'Nobody could have runned away and not got the dog after him. Nobody could have runned across that girt field of ours.'

'It looked like a scarecrow,' sobbed the dairy-maid.

'Well, scarecrows don't eat bread and cheese and drink the milk,' said the farmer's wife. 'We must keep the door locked. There must be a bad character about.'

Yes, a bad character was about, and it was Sam Pig!

Every day Sam did his duty. He stood in the field and scared the crows so well that not one dared to put even a long pointed claw in the young corn. All day he stood, dreaming strange dreams, half asleep, singing little songs, talking to the small animals that came to visit him, the harvest-mice, the hedgehog, the moles and the weasels. At night he sallied forth and raided the hen roost for eggs, the garden for fruit, the cowshed for milk. He couldn't get into the house for they kept a watch for him, but he dodged about and climbed trees and scampered on tiptoes with his ragged sleeves flapping and his little pockets bulging with food. Even then he couldn't get enough to eat, and little Sam Pig was decidedly thinner. The rain beat down, the winds blew, and his tattered rags scarcely covered him. And the green corn grew, and never a blade was eaten by the marauding birds.

'Will Joe Scarecrow never come back?' he asked the wind and the rain, the sun and the moon. 'Has he gone for ever?'

'For ever,' replied the Echo, and Sam was very sad.

One evening at dusk Brock the Badger came trotting over the field.

'Sam Pig! We've been hunting everywhere for you! Gone from us with never a word, and we missing you something terrible! Ann cries, and Bill and Tom are in the dumps without their merry brother. We've nobody to tease, nobody to scold, nobody to play with. Why are you standing here, pretending to be a scarecrow?'

'Because I wanted to watch the corn growing,' said Sam. 'I've seen it move, Brock. It pushes up, Brock, blade by blade. It grows more quickly by night than by day, Brock.'

'Well, that's something to find out, Sam,' said Brock.

'Oh Brock, I am glad you've come. It has been lonely here, with only the moon and stars to keep me company at night, and the rabbits and screech owls.'

'Where is Joe Scarecrow?' asked Brock.

'He's gone to Blackpool beach to look at the briny ocean,' said Sam, 'and I can't go home till he comes back. I promised.'

'You must keep your promise, Sam, but I'm sorry to think that you are going to be a scarecrow all your life.'

Sam was sorry too. He was heartily sick of minding the corn, and he might have been there for ever, if little Billy Wigg hadn't stumbled across the furrows, walking where he ought not to walk. He had never been close to a scare-crow, and he wanted to see the man of straw and wood at close quarters. Sam stood as still as a post, not twitching an ear, as Billy Wigg came up.

'Hallo,' said Billy, staring open-mouthed at Sam. 'I didn't know scarecrows were real – real – real pigs!'

'Well, you know now,' muttered Sam, 'and the sooner you go home the better, trampling the corn with your heavy boots and walking where you didn't ought. Be off with you!'

So Billy Wigg went back at double speed, and he went straight to the farmer and told him about his scarecrow. Then out came Farmer Greensleeves, but he trod carefully between the furrows, so that never a blade of corn was harmed.

Sam Pig stood like a figure of wood, but he couldn't deceive the farmer any longer.

'What's this?' asked Farmer Greensleeves. 'What are you doing here dressed up as a scarecrow, Sam Pig?'

'I've taken the place of the real one, Master. He's gone to Blackpool beach, to see the briny ocean, and I've been scaring crows instead of him,' faltered Sam.

The farmer threw back his head and laughed till the hills echoed and Sam Pig laughed too, thankful the farmer wasn't cross.

'This beats the band!' roared the farmer, slapping his sides. 'Little Sam Pig from yonder wood scaring my crows, and doing it well, too. I've never seen the crop so heavy. Not a blade missing. Sam Pig with straw in his hat and the scarecrow's ragged coat on his back.'

Sam felt very proud and happy.

'What wages shall I give you, Sam?' asked the farmer. 'What do I owe you?'

'Just a drop of buttermilk, Master,' said Sam. 'I get thirsty and there's nothing to drink.'

'Be you the ragged fellow as come into our dairy one night and scared the dairymaid?' asked the farmer.

Sam nodded shyly, and the farmer clapped his hands and laughed again.

'Buttermilk! Yes, you shall have a gallon and some barleycorn too,' said he. 'And you needn't stay here any longer, Sam.'

While they talked there was a shout from across the field and a policeman came through the gate. He was arm in arm with a queer person who hopped unsteadily, and as they came nearer the farmer and Sam Pig recognized Joe Scarecrow.

'Had to arrest him. Name of Joe Scarecrow,' panted the policeman. 'He was scaring the sea-gulls on Blackpool beach. He told us he belonged to this field, so I've brought him home. He's been a deal of trouble, hopping along, waving his arms and stopping the traffic. I've never had a scarecrow to deal with before, and I hopes this is the last.'

He planted the scarecrow firmly in the ground, and marched off, flattening the corn with his great boots. Joe looked reproachfully after him and sighed.

'Well, I'm glad to get back,' said he.

'Did you enjoy yourself, Joe?' asked Sam, capering round the thin fellow, and whipping off his ragged clothes ready for the exchange.

'I did, Sam. I did fine. Ah, it was gradely to see the briny ocean and the throng of folk so thick you could walk on their heads. It was gradely to taste a winkle and to make sand pies. Ah, it was indeed a treat. But, my word, I'm glad to get me home again.'

'Change hats and coats, Joe,' said Sam. 'I'm going home now.'

'Thou art shaping first-rate as a scarecrow, Sam. It suits thee. I dunnot know whether I shall change back.'

'Change at once!' cried Sam, stamping his foot. 'If you don't I shall call that policeman back again.'

So the scarecrow and Sam changed their clothes, and Sam put his little round hat with a feather in it on his head. Then the farmer and Sam started off across the field.

'Sam! Sam!' called Joe Scarecrow. 'I've got a present for you. You'll find it in your coat pocket. It's a stick of Blackpool rock.'

Sam took the long pink bar from his coat and licked it with a happy grimace.

'Are all the rocks as sweet as this, Scarecrow? No wonder you didn't want to come away.'

'Maybe they are, Sam. I didn't have time to taste them all,' called the Scarecrow, and he grinned with his turnip face and began to sing his old cracked song.

> *'Oh keep away little birds,*
> *Keep away do,*
> *Or Joe the Scarecrow*
> *Will moggrify you.'*

The Chimney-Sweep

There was a mighty to-do in the house of the four pigs. The chimney was stopped up. Thick black smoke came puffing down the chimney into the kitchen, smothering everything in soot. There had been no fire during the summer, and now, just when everything was going so well, the chimney wouldn't draw.

Ann's white apron was blackened and Tom's face was smudged with dark smears. They ran to the door to call the others to help.

'Bill! Sam! Bill!' cried Ann, waving her apron to shake off some of the soot-flakes. 'Come here, quickly.'

'Is dinner ready?' asked Bill, and little Sam came running into the house. He soon retreated with a black face, and a cloud of darkness followed him.

'It's the chimney,' said Sam. 'It's stopped up.'

'Yes. I know that,' said Tom impatiently.

'What was there for dinner, Ann?' asked Sam.

'Apple dumplings and savoury onions,' sighed Ann, 'and now they'll be spoiled.'

Sam went into the house again, to rescue a dumpling or two. When he didn't come out the others were anxious.

'Sam! Sam!' they called. 'Where are you? We can't see you in the cloud. Do you want us to rescue you?'

There was a muffled noise, choking and

spluttering and a small black pig came out. It was Sam, who had been trying to climb the chimney.

'It's no good. I got part way up but the soot blowed me back.'

'You do look a black little pig,' laughed Tom. 'There's one at the farm, you know. He might be your twin.'

They all stood in the garden, looking up at the chimney. Not a curl of smoke came out, but through the doorway and keyhole came a dark fog which spread across the path.

'What shall we do?' asked Ann. 'Brock is away, and we can't even go indoors.'

'We'll live in the garden of course,' said Tom. 'We can eat vegetables and sleep in the cabbage patch.'

'I don't want to live in the garden, and sleep in the cabbage patch,' grumbled Sam.

'Sweep-O. Sweep-O. Any chimneys swept? Any chimneys swept?' chanted a voice over the hedge, and the little pigs started with surprise.

'Just when we wanted a sweep!' they said. 'Who is it?'

From out of the trees appeared the Fox. He was smiling and walking with a dancing step, singing his song:

'Sweep-O. Sweep-O. Any chimneys? Any chimneys?'

'Oh, Mister Fox,' called Ann quickly. 'Will you come here? Our chimney's stopped up, and we were just wondering what to do when we heard you.'

'How strange!' said the Fox. 'How remarkable! I've just been sweeping a few chimneys in

the wood. With my thick red brush I am in great demand. There is no other animal with a brush like mine. I am a champion chimney-sweep.'

He opened the garden gate and came dancing through, with that queer sidelong look on his face, and that lilting step which Sam didn't like. It was the first time the Fox had been invited into the garden of the little pigs, but of course when the chimney was stopped up and the Fox was a champion sweep, it must be all right.

'Yes, it's smoking very badly. Chimney completely stopped. Must be something stopping it. My brush is used to obstacles. There is no chimney I can't conquer,' said the Fox, smirking at the four pigs.

Sam frowned and turned away, but the Fox noticed him.

'Ha! My young friend there has already been sweeping the chimney! Your tail, Sam Pig, is not adapted to sweeping. A curly little tail like yours is neither use nor ornament. Now my tail is both! It is beautiful and it is a fine brush.'

Sam scowled at the Fox.

'Well, do it. Sweep the chimney,' said he crossly.

'And my payment, Sam Pig? Do you think I will cover myself with soot for nothing? I want payment.'

'What will you charge, sir?' asked Tom timidly, as Sam didn't answer.

'Anything you like if we can get into our little house again,' said Ann.

'I only want the key of the hen-place, over at the farm,' said the Fox. 'Sam could get that for me quite easily.'

'And what do you want with it?' asked Sam suspiciously.

'I'm going to sweep their chimney too. All the chimneys round about ought to be cleaned. Stable chimneys, cow-place chimney, and hen-house chimney. And I'm going to do it for nothing. No charge!'

'I'll go,' said Sam quickly. 'I'll run there and ask.'

'Then I'll be sweeping your chimney while you go, to save time. All I have to do is to stick my brush up, and whisk it round, and flurry the soot away.'

They nodded and admired the fine red tail and the strong hairs of it. It was a powerful brush. It would flurry the soot right away.

'You of course have no tails to speak of. Nothing except curly tips. You could never sweep a chimney with them. There is no animal with a natural brush like mine.'

He pranced about proudly and swung his long red tail to the admiration of the little pigs.

'You wait here,' he commanded Bill and Tom and Ann. 'You stay in the garden and look up at the roof till you see my tail come out of the chimney.'

So the Fox stepped softly into the house, and disappeared in the thick black smoke. Sam ran off to the farm to get the key of the hen-house.

'Sam Pig! What are you doing here?' asked the little farm pigs when Sam rapped at the pig-cote door.

'Sh-sh-sh. I want the key of the hen-house,' said Sam in a whisper.

'What for, Sam Pig?'

'The Fox is going to sweep the chimney. He's going to sweep all the chimneys here. Where is the key?'

'Oi! Oi! Oi! Ask somebody else, Sam Pig,' they grunted.

Sam climbed down from the pig-cote door and rapped on the stable.

'Sally, old mare. Sally!' he called. 'Give me the key of the hen-house.'

Sally turned her head from her manger and lumbered slowly across to the stable door.

'Sam Pig! I haven't seen you for a long time. What are you doing here?'

'Give me the key of the hen-house, Sally. Our house is full of soot and the chimney blocked, and the sweep is there.'

'Who is the sweep, Sam?'

'The Fox,' said Sam. 'He wants the key of the hen-house, and he is going to sweep that chimney too.'

'Ha! Ha!' whinnied Sally. 'You'd better ask someone else for the key. I don't hold with this talk of sweeping.'

So Sam Pig went across the yard, and called to the cow.

'Daisy, the cow. Daisy!' he called. 'Give me the key of the hen-house.'

Daisy came running up in a hurry to speak to Sam.

'Moo! Sam Pig! I'm that glad to see you I can't tell you!' said she. 'Come along and have a chat with me.'

'There's no time,' said Sam. 'Our chimney's stopped up and the house full of smoke. Nobody can have any dinner till the chimney's swept.'

'And who's going to sweep it, Sam?'

'The Fox. He wants the key of the hen-house to sweep that chimney too,' said Sam.

'Moo-moo-moo!' cried the cow. 'You'd better ask the dog.'

So Sam ran to the kennel, where lay the house-dog Rover.

'Bow-wow. Hallo! Sam Pig,' barked the dog. 'I haven't seen you since the Midsummer party. What are you doing here, Sam?'

'Give me the key of the hen-house,' said Sam.

'Our chimney's stopped up and the house full of soot. Nobody can have any dinner till it's swept.'

'Who's going to be the sweep, Sam?' asked the dog.

'The Fox,' said Sam. 'He's going to sweep it with his red brush, and I am taking him the key of the hen-house so that he can sweep their chimney too.'

'Indeed!' said the dog with a low growl. He fetched a key from the barn wall and gave it to Sam, but it was an old rusty key that had hung there for fifty years.

Then Sam ran back to the little house on the edge of the wood.

The Fox had been inside all this time, but he hadn't touched the chimney with his beautiful brush. Oh no! He had gone boldly into the larder and finished off all the pies and pasties Tom the cook had made. He emptied every cupboard, and ate every crumb. There was nothing left when Sam Pig returned with the rusty key.

The pigs stood in the garden staring at the

chimney, but they never saw the tip of the Fox's tail appear. It wasn't till Sam brought the key that the Fox came out, licking his lips, looking very pleased.

'Thank you, Sam. I've finished now. You will find it swept and empty,' said the Fox, and he took the key and galloped away.

'Has he really finished?' asked Sam.

'He has been there all this time, so it must be done,' said Tom, 'but we never saw his tail come out.' When they went to the house door they were met by thick smoke again.

Then Badger came home.

'What's all this? The chimney smoking? You

got the Fox to clean it? O foolish young pigs! Get me a bough of furze, and I'll do it for you.'

He thrust the furze up the chimney and away flew the smoke. The flames of the fire burned brightly once again. They washed the floor, and tidied the house. There was nothing to eat, of course, but luckily Brock had brought some provisions in his sack.

'Did the Fox sweep the hen-house chimney?' asked Sam, when next he met the yard-dog.

'Oh, Sam Pig! The hen-house has no chimney! You gave the Fox an ancient key, and when Reynard put it in the lock it groaned and squealed, and creaked. The farmer came out with his gun, and I rushed after the Fox. He got a few shotcorns in his leg, so he won't come after the hen-house key again in a hurry.'

'He ate us out of house and home,' said Sam dolefully. 'He robbed us instead of the hen-house, I think.'

'Never mind,' said the dog. 'You know how to sweep a chimney without a chimney-sweep now, and that's a useful piece of knowledge.'

The Cheshire Cheese

One day Sam Pig walked in the wood with his axe on his shoulder and a bag on his back. He was not gathering firewood, for the woodshed was full, nor was he going to chop down a tree. No, he was exploring, as every little pig goes a-roaming for adventure when the fancy takes him. He was looking for anything he could find. Now and then he stopped and picked up a small treasure, a curved piece of wood like a sickle, a pronged stick like a toasting fork, a smooth pebble like an egg, a scarlet bunch of berries, or a few purple toadstools. There is no end to the exciting things to be found in a wood by those who have eyes for them, and soon Sam Pig had a fine assortment of toys, of kitchen utensils, of farm implements, all made of wood and stone.

He went far into the wood and after a time he sat down on a tree stump just as an explorer would do in a forest, and he opened his bag.

Ann had packed a round green cheese and a hunk of bread for his lunch. There was a stream close by, and Sam had taken the pith from a slip of elder-wood to make a drinking-tube. As he ate and drank he talked to the small wood folk who came round begging for crumbs.

'Spare us a crumb, Sam. Spare us a bit of cheese. Spare us a bit more, Sam,' they urged in their sweet shrill voices, and Sam sprinkled his crumbs and talked and then played a tune on the elder pipe which he had made. Drinking-cups, flutes and whistles all can be made out of the stems of the elder.

Then a proud cock pheasant came up, and Sam offered him some cheese.

'My gamekeepers would never allow me to touch such a thing,' said the pheasant loftily. 'I only eat Cheshire cheese. This is very inferior stuff, Sam Pig.'

'Sister Ann made it,' said Sam, indignantly defending the cheese. 'It's got hawthorn leaves and sage and dandelions in it.'

'Cheshire cheese is made of cream,' said the

pheasant, and he spurned the cheese with his long foot.

Sam picked it up and wiped it, and scolded the bird, who took no notice whatever. His golden eye never blinked, as he stared in disdain at the little pig flustering round. Suddenly he turned his head, and gave a screech of fear. He rose in the air with a noisy flapping of wings and soared away among the trees.

Sam Pig looked round too, and he saw the sharp nose of the Fox.

'Hallo, Sam Pig. I haven't seen you for quite a long time. How are you these days? I hope I see you well and hearty.'

'Yes, thank you, Mister Fox,' said Sam, uneasily stuffing the remainder of the cheese in his pocket, and standing up before the superior being.

'What's that you've got?' asked the Fox. He sidled forward and slipped a paw in Sam's pocket. He drew out the cheese, tasted a piece with a grimace of disgust, and tossed it away.

'Like the pheasant, I only eat Cheshire cheese,' said he scornfully. 'I am sorry the cock wouldn't wait to talk about it with me. It is an interesting subject, the making of cheese, especially Cheshire cheese. Ah, Sam, those great farms, and the milky cows and the bowls of cream from which the farmer makes the monstrous yellow cheeses! You don't know what a good cheese is, Sam. You've never eaten real cheese. Why, I've tasted toasted cheese that would fetch a rat out of his hole and a lion out of his den.'

'Would it lure an apple off a tree or a pudding out of a pot?' asked Sam Pig, his eyes wide with wonder.

'Yes. My Cheshire cheese will 'tice a bird from her nest, and a rabbit from its warren,' said the Fox, with a leer.

'And how do you get a cheese like that?' asked Sam.

The Fox gazed at the upturned innocent face. His crafty eyes met Sam's blue eyes, and he turned away and laughed.

'Ha! Ha! Sam Pig. No need to travel to Cheshire. I could give you a dozen Cheshire cheeses if you pay for them.'

'How much will they be?' asked Sam.

'Just a dozen pounds of butter and a basket of eggs,' said the Fox carelessly. 'Nothing more. You can easily get that, Sam. I know your larder is full.'

'Ann wouldn't like me to take them,' said Sam. 'It's our weekly food.'

'She won't mind when she sees a dozen great yellow cheeses, Sam, each one as big as a little cart-wheel,' wheedled the Fox. 'Think of it. A dozen. Perhaps more. You go home and talk it over. There's nothing underhand or secret about it. Talk it over. If you agree, then meet me a week tonight. I will look out for you.'

'A week tonight,' said Sam.

'Yes, when the moon is up and you can see your way. I wouldn't ask you to come through the woods with only the thin slip of the moon to guide you. Come when the moon is shining, Sam.'

Sam Pig ran home from his exploring trip and told his sister Ann and his brothers about it.

'I met the Fox today,' said Sam, cutting a wedge of bread and buttering it.

'That's nothing,' remarked Bill. 'He's always somewhere in the woods, nosing about into other people's business.'

'He came up and talked to me. He didn't like our green herb cheese. He tasted a bit. He didn't like our cheese at all.'

'And why not, pray?' asked Bill hotly. 'What's wrong with it? What call has the Fox to mock at our cheese?'

'He says it's too mild and green. The pheasant didn't like it either, but although the Fox wanted to talk to him about it, he flew away.'

'When the Fox and the pheasant talk about cheese, then the world will come to an end,' said Tom coldly.

'The Fox is quite a clever animal,' said little Ann Pig amiably. 'What did he say about cheeses, Sam?'

'He said he knows a better one, a fine one, the best in the country. It is called Cheshire cheese, and those who haven't tasted it know nothing of cheeses.'

The pigs said nothing, but they pondered these words of wisdom. If there was a better cheese than theirs they would like to meet it. When Badger came home they asked him about it.

'Cheshire cheese? He's right. The Fox is right for once. Cheshire cheese is the best of all. It's yellow as a marigold, or cream-coloured like meadow-sweet. It crumbles even when you look at it,' said Brock slowly. 'I remember tasting a delicious piece of Cheshire that was red as a rose. A traveller had left it on a fallen tree, where he had been lunching. I've never forgotten the taste of that cheese.'

'The Fox says we can have a dozen Cheshire cheeses, if I take in exchange a dozen pounds of butter and a basket of new-laid eggs,' said Sam.

'I don't like to have dealings with the Fox. He is too sly for our simple ways, but it sounds all right, Sam.'

'A week tonight he will have them ready if I go,' added Sam.

'We shall see,' said Brock softly. 'Yes, we shall see.'

A week later Sam went off by moonlight with a dozen pounds of butter and a basket of eggs. It had been raining ever since Sam met the Fox, and the wood was laced with pools, so that Sam took a long time to get round them with his heavy burden. He was very glad when he saw the Fox waiting in the grove of oak trees.

'There you are, Sam. Come along!' called the Fox.

He had a fishing-net in his paws and he beckoned to Sam.

'You've brought the butter and eggs, and now I'll give you the cheese, many a cheese, fine round yellow Cheshire cheeses.'

Sam looked about him for a store of cheeses and there were none in sight.

'Look in this pond, Sam. What do you see?' The Fox put his paw on Sam's arm and drew him close to a pool of rain-water.

'The moon,' said Sam.

'The moon?' The Fox sounded surprised and pained at Sam's answer.

'How can it be the moon? The moon is up there in the sky, isn't it?'

Sam nodded. There was the full moon riding high, a great yellow moon shining down through the trees.

'The moon is in the sky, but here in the pond is a Cheshire cheese,' said the Fox slowly.

'There's a lot round about here. The farmer makes them and puts them in the water to ripen. Here they lie, and here they stay to get crumbly and sweet. Come along and see for yourself.'

He led Sam over the rough broken path and they stooped to a dozen little pools. In every one was a great round yellow cheese.

'There you are, Sam. The farmer's hiding-place. I've got a fishing-net for you. All you have to do is to fish them up and put them in your basket. You won't be able to carry them all, but they'll keep. They'll keep a month or a year or for ever.'

'Truly?' asked Sam, puzzled.

'Yes. Then take them home and mind nobody sees you. The farmer will be mad if he finds out. He likes his cheeses ripe and he'll be mad as a hatter if they've gone.'

'I won't take them all,' said Sam earnestly.

'Good little Sam,' leered the Fox and away he went. So Sam was left with the fishing-net to catch the yellow cheeses in the pools. He fished and fished, but there was nothing except broken

reflections. He scooped with his little hands, and he even tried to drink up one of the pools, but there wasn't a taste of cheese. And all the time the bright yellow moon winked and blinked in the high sky.

Sadly he went home and told the family.

'I saw the cheeses in the pools, ripening, but I couldn't catch them. They seemed to slip out of the net,' he said.

'Cheeses in the pools? Great yellow cheeses in the rain pools?' cried Brock. 'That was the moon, Sam, the full moon.'

'There's only one moon in the sky, and I saw a score of cheeses in the pools,' objected Sam.

'One moon will give a thousand reflections if there are a thousand pools,' said Brock. 'The pools are looking-glasses for the great moon on high. Never mind, Sam. I guessed the Fox was going to play a trick on you, and I think he won't be pleased when he eats the butter and eggs I gave you.'

'What did you do to them?'

'The butter was made from buttercups, so although it is yellow it is harsh and rank. The eggs were addled. I changed them, for I was sure the Fox was going to catch you with his tale of cheeses.'

Sam Pig and the Honey-Bees

Sam Pig sat in the clover patch in the meadow one spring day. It was a favourite resting-place from hard work, for there was honey to eat, sweet flowers to smell, and the busy honey-bees to watch as they came to visit the white clover.

Sam sucked the honey from the ends of the florets, where the honey-bag is kept, and he watched the bees fill their little baskets to the brim ready for storing in the hives.

'I like honey, I do,' said Sam Pig to the bees. 'I like to get it from a wild bees' nest, but your honey is nicer.'

The bees were too busy to stop their work for a small fat piglet. They loaded themselves with clover honey and pollen, and they darted back to the hives. Then they hurried to the clover patch again, never wasting a minute, or dawdling or playing.

'I should like a nice honeycomb,' said Sam Pig, lazily watching them. 'It takes a long time to get enough from sucking clover flowers. You can do it so much better.'

The bees said nothing. They had other things to think about. There was a revolution in the hive, and already the new queen was dressing for her wedding flight. They were not going with her. Their duty was to go on gathering honey for the rest of the hive, but they whispered and murmured to one another of the great doings.

Sam Pig stared lazily into the sky, where a black cloud was moving. It floated along in a curious manner, trembling and swaying, hesitating as it went over the field, then rushing forward. Sam dropped his clover flowers to watch it.

'It's going to rain,' grumbled Sam to the little bees, who still went on working with never a word to Sam. Their thoughts were on the queen and her flight that day.

'It's going to pour, for that's a very black cloud. The blacker the wetter, they say. It's closer than any cloud I've ever seen. Why, it's nearly on top of me. Why doesn't it keep up in the sky in its proper place? It's a stormy wet cloud I'm sure, and perhaps there's thunder and lightning in it. I wish I had an umbrella!'

He seized a bunch of leaves and held them above his head. The cloud passed right over and he cowered among the flowers. He heard a buzzing and humming sound like soft music, and a rustle like silk, and a roar like a tiny lion, and these strange noises came from the black cloud.

'It's a singing cloud,' he muttered. 'Now,

isn't that wonderful! I've heard a thunder cloud bellow, and a rainy cloud hiss, and now I hear a little black cloud sing and hum!'

Then he saw that it wasn't a cloud at all, but a swarm of bees, flying in a dark mass through the air. There were thousands of honey-bees, booming and humming, whirling their tiny transparent wings, shaking their small heads and circling around their queen, who flew in the midst of her subjects.

'Goodness me!' exclaimed Sam Pig. 'It's much too early for a swarm. What's the matter with the bees? It's only May!'

> *'A swarm of bees in May,*
> *Is worth a load of hay,'*

said a wise old voice, and the Mother of Toads put her head out of the ground.

'What? A load of hay, Old Mother of Toads? Worth a load of hay?' cried Sam. 'I should like a load of hay.'

'That's what it's worth, Sam Pig,' said the ancient Toad. 'And I know it. So take that swarm of bees.'

Away went Sam, and followed after the cloud which was hovering and wavering across the fields. He scampered very fast, through ditches and under hedges.

'This is what is called a bee-line, I think,' said Sam to himself. 'I'm going straight there, for I'm going to get it.'

Then he saw the swarm settle on a bough of an apple tree in Farmer Greensleeves' orchard. There it hung like a black pudding, buzzing and humming like mad.

Sam raced to the cow-house where the farmer was milking.

'Please, Master! Come quickly. Please, Master!' panted Sam Pig.

'Hallo! Who's this?' asked the surprised farmer, lifting his red face from the cow's warm side.

'Please, Master! It's Sam Pig. You know, Sam Pig as helped with the haymaking last summer. Sam Pig you took to market.'

'Ah yes,' said the farmer, slowly, and he went on with his milking. 'And what's the matter with you, Sam?'

'Would you like to have a swarm of bees, Master?'

'Indeed I should! I've got an empty skep down the garden. Where are they?' cried the farmer, and he rose to his feet and stretched himself.

'I've followed them across the fields to the orchard, Master. They are in an apple tree.'

The farmer got his skep and went with Sam to the orchard.

He shook the apple-bough gently, and Sam held the skep underneath. When the bees were safe inside he carried them to the end of the garden, to the row of straw skeps on the bench under the sunny wall.

'Thank ye kindly, Sam. I'm much obliged to ye! I'll give ye a load of hay for this swarm. It's the proper payment for a swarm in May, because that's the best time for them. When we cut the hay I'll remember and send you a load.'

So Sam Pig trotted home well content with his bargain. When he told Brock that he had mistaken the cloud of bees for a rain cloud the Badger laughed.

'There's an old saying,

"Bees will not swarm,
Before a storm."

They never go far from their hives when it is going to rain. They know a lot, do bees, and I could tell you many a tale about them.'

A month later Sam was going fishing when he saw another black cloud sailing low across the fields, rising and then dipping, as it swayed and swung in the air.

'Pouring rain, and I've forgotten my mackin-tosh,' muttered Sam, and he stood frowning at the cloud. 'It didn't ought to rain today! But it will make the fish rise.'

Then he heard the deep humming song of the thousands of tiny insects, the whir of those delicate wings, and he knew it was a swarm going off to find a new home.

'I should like to hive that swarm. It's worth two loads of hay maybe. I will go and tell the farmer,' thought Sam, and he started off.

Away he went, over the meadows and under the gates, through the hedges, following the swarm of bees till at last it settled like a black football in a mulberry tree.

Then the Old Mother of Toads popped her head out of the grass and spoke to Sam.

> *'A swarm of bees in June,*
> *Is worth a silver spoon.'*

said she.

'A silver spoon?' cried Sam. 'That will be a good thing to have. I've only got a wooden spoon at home.'

He trotted over the fields to the farmer, who was tedding the new-mown grass in Cuckoo Field.

'Master! Master!' panted Sam. 'Master, I've found something.'

'What's amiss, Sam?' asked the farmer, leaning on his fork and looking kindly at the excited little pig.

'I've found another swarm of bees,' said Sam.

So the farmer left his hay and followed Sam to the old mulberry tree. He climbed the branches and shook the swarm into the skep Sam held beneath it. He carried them carefully to the garden, and hived them.

'Now, Sam, what about payment?' said he.

' *"A swarm of bees in June,*
Is worth a silver spoon."

As it's little Sam Pig I shall give ye a little silver spoon.'

So he went to his cupboard and brought out a salt-spoon of silver. Sam was delighted with it.

'Oh, thank you, Master. I've always wanted a silver spoon for my own,' cried Sam, and he galloped away to show it to Brock and Ann and the others.

Another month passed and the haymaking was nearly done. The hay was raked into shining cocks, and loaded on the haywagons. Then it was carted to the stackyard, ready for the stacks.

Sam was waiting for the promised load of hay from the farmer. He sat on a fence thinking of all the things he would do with it when he got it. He might make a haystack for himself in the croft, or he could stuff beds with it, or sleep on it, just as it was. It would be lovely to have a load of hay to play hide-and-seek, or hunt the thimble.

A cloud rose in the west and moved swiftly across the field, hovering and wavering and then darting forward. Sam Pig stared at it in annoyance.

'Bother! Rain again, just when they are finishing the hay! Luckily they've got it nearly all in!'

Then he heard the familiar buzzing and humming of ten thousand bees, and he knew it was a late swarm going away to find a new palace for their queen.

Up sprang Sam and ran after it. He followed it till it settled on a sycamore tree in Farmer Greensleeves' spinney.

> *'A swarm of bees in July,*
> *Isn't worth a fly,'*

said the Old Mother of Toads, poking her head out of the bushes.

'Not worth a fly?' asked Sam. 'Oh, you must be wrong, Old Mother. This swarm is the best of all. I'm going to tell the farmer about it.'

Away ran Sam to the farmer, who was busy in the stackyard, unloading his last haywain on to the stack.

'Hallo, Sam Pig,' he called as little Sam came trotting through the gate, waving his hat and shouting.

'Come to ask me for that load of hay? It's coming tonight, when we've finished.'

'No, Master. I came to tell you I've got another swarm for you,' cried Sam excitedly.

'Another swarm of bees? It's too late now. Don't you know a swarm of bees in July isn't worth a fly?' laughed the farmer.

'Why not?' asked Sam. 'Why is it not worth a fly?'

'Because the honey season is over, the flow of honey has stopped,' the farmer explained.

So Sam turned away and went home with his tail uncurled.

That evening, just as the first star appeared in the sky, and the first glow-worm lighted its green lamp in the lane, there came a little procession across the fields. There was a cart made of green rushes, drawn by a nanny-goat as white as milk. The driver was little Bill Wigg, and he held a whip of plaited rushes. The cart was heaped high with a load of silvery-gold hay, made from all the choicest meadow flowers, and the scent of it was like summer itself.

'A load of hay for little Sam Pigwiggin with the farmer's compliments, and there's a pot of honey buried inside it and a honeycomb and a piece of beeswax,' said Bill Wigg, flourishing his whip.

'Whoa, mare!' he called to the nanny-goat, and the white goat stood still and waited at the gate of the pigs' house.

The cart was unloaded and Sam carried the hay to the orchard, to make a little stack. Then away trotted the nanny-goat with Bill Wigg riding and the little cart of rushes bumping and tumbling along the field paths.

'I'm going to sleep on my haystack tonight,' said Sam Pig. 'Would you like to come too?'

'Oh yes,' they shouted. 'Let's all sleep on top of a new haystack.'

'And I'm going to eat my supper with my silver spoon,' said Sam.

'You won't get much,' scoffed Bill Pig.

'But it will taste very good,' said Sam. 'My supper is honey from my bees. I invite you all to come and eat it on the haystack by the light of the glow-worms.'

So the four little pigs ate the honey on top of Sam's haystack, and each one of them had a lick of the silver spoon.

Dinner for Brock

Into the wood went a small stout figure, walking carefully, glancing down at the burden he carried. It was our little Sam Pig, taking Brock's dinner to the Badger, who was working among the trees. The dinner was in a white basin, with a saucer on the top, and it was tied up in a red handkerchief. Anyone could see it was something special by the way Sam carried it, neither swinging nor swaying it. The corners of the handkerchief were tied together to form a handle. Sam felt very important as he walked along the track. He had seen plumbers and masons and farm labourers carrying their dinners in that way.

Inside the basin was a hot-pot that Ann had made for Brock that morning. Although Tom Pig was the cook in the little household, Ann sometimes came forward to try her hand at a tasty dish for old Brock the Badger. Yes, that very same morning Ann had made it and Sam

Pig had helped her. Ann sang a little ditty as she cooked, and this is what she sang:

> '*Half a pound of twopenny rice,*
> *Half a pound of treacle,*
> *Half a pound of what-you-like,*
> *Pop goes the weasel.*'

Ann had boiled the twopenny rice, and mixed it with the treacle, and added half a pound of what-you-like to the dish. It made the delicious hot-pot that sent curls of fragrant steam through the handkerchief, flowing up among the trees like incense.

Sam sniffed and sniffed, and the rabbits came out and sniffed, and even the weasels poked their cruel, slender heads out of holes and twitched their wicked nostrils.

There was a rustle in the undergrowth, and every animal faded away into the earth, except Sam, who marched on, trying to be brave as he glanced sideways. Perhaps it was a wolf or a bear coming lolloping after Brock's hot-pot. Sam was ready to defend the pot with his life if necessary.

It was only the Fox, prowling about, attracted by the good, rich smell. The Fox looked slyly at Sam and stepped lightly up to him, tiptoeing in the bracken like a dancer, not walking in good English manner like little Sam.

'Hallo, Sam Pig. What's that you're carrying so carefully? A brace of pheasants in the pot?' he asked.

'Hot-pot for Brock the Badger,' said Sam proudly.

'Give me a taste, Sam,' wheedled the Fox. 'I've not had a square meal for a week.'

'Can't!' answered Sam. 'It's not mine to give. Brock is waiting for it.'

'Hum!' thought the Fox. 'If Brock is near I must be quiet. No chance of taking it.'

Then he said aloud, 'What's it made of? I never smelled such a grand smell as comes from that little pot you're carrying there.'

'I'll sing you the song of it,' said Sam proudly, and he put down the pot and sang:

> 'Half a pound of twopenny rice,
> Half a pound of treacle,

Half a pound of what-you-like,
Pop goes the weasel.'

'Indeed! And what kind of a thing is what-you-like?' asked the Fox.

'It's mushrooms,' answered Sam, picking up the basin. 'Brock likes mushrooms, so we put them in for him.'

'If I made it I should put half a pound of roast duck into it, Sam, or half a pound of rabbit,' said the Fox. 'You and Ann know nothing about cookery. Let me help you to make a hot-pot, a real pot, a real good one, for Brock.'

'For Brock?' asked Sam, hesitating.

'Yes, for Brock. I have a recipe which belonged to my grandmother. I should like to teach it to you.'

'Oh, thank you,' said Sam. 'Come along when we can have the kitchen to ourselves. I never get the chance to do any real cooking.'

So the Fox galloped away and Sam went on through the wood to the clearing where Brock was working. There was Brock cutting down small trees, making a rough wooden summer-house. The Badger put down his axe and welcomed Sam.

'Good lad, Sam. I was just ready for my dinner. I could smell it coming. The wind caught it and brought it to me. What is it?'

'A hot-pot, Brock. Ann made it.'

Brock untied the handkerchief and sat down on a stump with the basin between his knees. He poured out some of the stew into the saucer, and offered it to Sam.

'You have a taste, Sam. There's more than I want.'

They lapped it up and licked out the basin and saucer in the way of all well-brought-up animals. In a circle round them sat the small creatures of the woodland, watching and waiting, but there was nothing left for them.

'Very tasty, very sweet,' said Brock.

'Very sweet, very tasty,' said Sam.

'Now, Sam, you shall help me,' said Brock. 'Trim the logs while I build the walls. Here's a bill-hook. Do it like this.'

The Badger showed Sam how to swish off the

little branches and make the logs clean. Then he went on with the walls. Quite soon the little summerhouse was ready for its roof. Brock fastened branches across it, and there it was, a house in the forest ready for anyone who wanted to spend a night in comfort. There was a door with a wooden bolt and hinges of bark, and a knocker made out of a piece of oak. Brock had carved it in the shape of a fox's head, and Sam laughed when he saw how the jaw moved on a string.

'I met the Fox today,' said he to Brock. 'He said he would help me to make a hot-pot, a very good recipe, handed down to him by his grandmother.'

'His grandmother!' muttered Brock.

A few days later Sam met the Fox in the wood.

'Sam Pig, I'm ready to show you how to cook. I've got my grandmother's recipe in my pocket,' said the Fox, lightly skipping on one toe and swishing his brush like a fan.

'Come home with me now, Mister Fox,' invited Sam. 'There's nobody in the house.

They've all gone to see Brock's summerhouse
in the wood. Ann has made a carpet of rushes
for the floor and Bill and Tom are taking the
besoms to clean the leaves away.'

'I accept your invitation with great pleasure,'
simpered the Fox. Back to the cottage they ran,
the Fox leading the way, for he wanted to get
the cooking done before the family returned to
turn him out.

'Where are the scales?' he asked, as soon as
they entered the kitchen. 'You must weigh
everything carefully. It is most important.'

'We usually guesses,' said Sam, 'but we have
some scales somewhere for things like half a
pound of this and that.'

He got the little wooden see-saw which
balanced on a wedge of wood, and he showed
it to the Fox.

'You put a half-pound stone on one end, and
the thing to be weighed on the other. Then you
try and try till the two balance,' he explained.

'Very clever,' said the Fox. 'Show me the
half-pound weight.'

Sam looked everywhere, but he couldn't find

it, and the reason was that the Fox had seen it first and hidden it.

'Never mind, Sam. We can manage. I am full of ideas,' the Fox reassured the little Pig. 'I can do a half-pound press.'

He glanced at the sack of rice on the bench and the great tin of treacle which Brock had bought at the market.

'Half a pound of twopenny rice,' said the Fox. 'That's how my grandmother's recipe begins too. You put the rice on the see-saw – I mean the scales and I'll hold the other end.'

So Sam put a few fistfuls of rice on the long see-saw, and the Fox pressed down his end.

'More rice, Sam. It isn't half a pound yet. It doesn't make my end go down,' said the Fox.

Sam brought more and more, but the Fox pressed harder, and it wasn't till the sack was nearly emptied that at last the wooden scales balanced.

'It looks a big half-pound,' remarked Sam.

'Yes. It's the weather,' said the Fox. 'Some-times it makes half-pounds shrink to nothing and sometimes they grow. It all depends. Your scales are right, aren't they?'

'Oh yes,' said Sam. 'Tom and Ann use them.'

'Next get the treacle,' said the Fox, licking his lips. 'I think you might put the tin on the see-saw, and we shall see how much to take out.'

Sam carried the heavy tin and placed it carefully on the scales. The Fox pressed his end as before, and the two sides balanced.

'Exactly half a pound. Good guess,' said he.

'But – but – but –' began Sam.

'Exactly,' said the Fox. 'Now for the half-pound of what-you-like. That is the special part of my grandmother's receipe. Shut your eyes, Sam, while I look round for what-I-like.'

Obediently Sam shut his eyes and the Fox peered round. There were no ducks hanging in the larder, but there was a basket of new-laid eggs, and some golden butter which had just come from the farm. The Fox brought them out and put them on the table.

'This is what-I-like,' said he, calling to Sam.

'But those eggs have to last all week,' stammered Sam.

'My grandmother's recipe distinctly says eggs and butter for what-you-like,' replied the Fox coldly. 'We will now mix all together for the hot-pot, Sam. I think your bath would hold them comfortably.'

He weighed the butter and eggs on the scales, and of course they weighed half a pound when he pressed the end of the wood. Then he poured the rice, the treacle, the eggs and butter into Sam's bath and beat them with a wooden spoon. He heated them over the fire for a few minutes, and Sam stood watching with admiration. It was a hot-pot big enough for everybody to have a good helping, and then a second helping afterwards.

'Now for a pudding-cloth,' said the Fox.

'We haven't got one,' said Sam. 'No, not a pudding-cloth. We've got a dish-cloth to wash up, but no pudding-cloth.'

'Anything will do to boil the pudding in,' said the Fox gaily. 'A sheet from your bed, a blanket, a quilt. It is going to be a fine hot-pot of a pudding. Go and fetch the cloth, Sam.'

Sam went reluctantly upstairs. He felt uncomfortable as he dragged a sheet from his bed. Ann was very fussy about sheets. Usually Sam slept on straw, but lately he had a sheet. He didn't know what Ann would say when she found a pudding hot-pot wrapped up in it, as sticky as could be. Sam pulled the sheet after him and caught his foot in the folds. Downstairs he clattered, bumping and banging on every step.

When he disentangled himself the Fox had disappeared, with the bath and the pudding. Sam ran to the door. Away in the distance he saw the red figure of the sly fellow dragging the bath into the wood.

'Oh dear me!' sighed Sam. 'What will they say! Half a pound of twopenny rice gone, half a pound of treacle gone, half a pound of eggs and butter gone, and my bath too.'

He tidied away the mess and put the sheet back on the bed. Then he sat down, a miserable pigling, to wait for the return of the family.

Half an hour later they came in. Ann Pig came first with an armful of rushes to make another rug for the kitchen floor. Tom Pig came next with a bundle of firewood. Bill Pig carried a honey-comb from the wild bees' nest. Last of all came Brock, dragging Sam's bath with the great pudding hot-pot in it.

'Oh! Oh!' cried Sam. 'Where did you find that, Brock?'

'We heard a noise in the wood,' said Brock, 'and we went to see what it was. Such a squealing and squeaking as never was! There stood the Fox, with the bath, and a host of weasels leaping round, crying for their dinner. They said it was theirs, and he said it was his, because he had made it, so I went up and said it was mine.'

'And Brock won,' said Tom simply.

'Yes, I won,' said Brock.

That night they all ate the delicious pudding hot-pot, and they voted thanks to the Fox's grandmother for her nice recipe, although it had taken their week's store.

When they had finished they all sang the old song:

'Half a pound of twopenny rice,
Half a pound of treacle,

Half a pound of what-you-like,
Pop goes the weasel.'

'Why was the half-pound such a big one when the Fox weighed the rice?' asked Sam.

I leave you to guess Brock's answer.

Thursday's Child

Monday's child is fair of face,
Tuesday's child is full of grace,
Wednesday's child is full of woe,
Thursday's child has far to go.

Ann Pig was singing this old rhyme as she scrubbed the table, and Sam Pig carried buckets of water from the spring for her. Ann sprinkled sand from a little tin by her side, and then rubbed and scrubbed till the table was white as a bone.

'Whose child am I, Ann?' asked Sam.

'Whose do you think, Sam?' asked Ann, stopping a moment and laughing at the ugly little face that peered up at her.

'I don't think I am Monday's child, Ann,' said Sam, stooping over the bucket of clean water, and looking at his reflection in the rough mirror there.

'No. You are not fair of face, Sam,' said Ann. 'But your tail is curly and your ears are nice and long. Tuesday's child is full of grace,' said Ann.

Sam curved his right arm and stuck his little fist in an attitude he thought was graceful. He gave a delicate leap, just like a bird, but he knocked the bucket over and spilled the water.

'Oh, Sam! You're not a full-of-grace child, either,' said Ann. 'I am vexed. I am really.'

'Don't be vexed,' implored Sam, mopping up the water with his handkerchief and his scarf, and then sitting in the pool to finish off the drying.

'I think I must be Wednesday's child, that's full of woe,' said he mournfully, squeezing the water out of his trousers.

'No, you're not, Sam dear,' cried Ann, throwing her arms round him. 'You're not full of woe. You keep us cheerful and merry, Sam, although you sometimes do clumsy things, but you can't always be good, can you?'

'Then perhaps I am Thursday's child,' said Sam hopefully.

Before Ann could answer, Brock came in. The Badger threw his bundle down on the table, and sat on the table top, swinging his legs.

'I'm glad to get home. There's no place like home, Sam Pig, and don't you forget it.'

'No, I'll remember, Brock,' said Sam. He looked admiringly at old Brock perched so comfortably up there. Nobody else was allowed to sit on the table. Only the master of the house could sit where he liked.

'Look how white the table is, Brock,' said he. 'Ann scrubbed and sanded it and I rubbed some flour into it, and it is like snow.'

Brock sprang down and looked at his trousers. They were pasted with damp flour just as if he were going to be baked in the oven.

'Oh, Sam,' cried Ann. 'I didn't see you do that.'

Brock went to the door and shook himself and batted his trousers with twigs.

'Well, I can't go out for everybody will see me coming or going with these white patches,' said Brock rather sadly.

'Then you'll stay with us and tell us a tale, won't you?' cried Sam.

Brock groaned. 'I suppose so. I can't go out looking like a pie-bald Badger.'

'When was I born, Brock?' asked Sam. 'Whose child am I?'

Brock pulled his old brown notebook from his pocket and turned the pages. Sam got glimpses of strange pictures, of birds and beasts and flowers, of sun and stars and planets.

'You're Thursday's pigling, Sam. You were born on a Thursday. Here it is. Ann is Monday's child, fair of face. Tom is Tuesday's child, full of grace.'

Tom wriggled and grinned and kicked up his heels at this news.

'Bill is Wednesday's child, full of woe,' said Brock. Bill gave a frown and a shrug and tweaked Sam's ear.

'Sam is Thursday's child, far to go,' said Brock, and he closed the book, pulled the elastic band round it and put it in his pocket.

'It's quite true, that old rhyme,' squeaked Sam excitedly. 'Ann is the prettiest Pig in the family, and Tom isn't bad at dancing and leaping about, and Bill is a wonderful grumbler and grouser, and I'm the traveller. I went to market.'

'When were you born, Brock?' asked little Ann Pig.

Brock took out the notebook and turned the pages again.

'On a Saturday. Yes, I was born on a Saturday, long and long ago. Here it is.'

He read out to them the queerly printed words, and showed them the picture of a baby Badger alongside.

'Brock the Badger. Born on a Saturday night when the moon was full and the stars were shining and the North wind was blowing.'

'Saturday's child has to work hard for his living,' said little Ann.

'Yes, I am always working hard for my living,' said Brock, 'and now perhaps Mistress Ann Pig, pretty Ann Pig, who is Monday's child, will give me some tea and crumpets and oatcakes and boiled eggs, for I'm famished.'

They sat round the table feasting on all the good things Ann and Tom Pig had cooked for them. The eggs were nicely boiled, the crumpets were well buttered, the oatcakes were crisp as icicles and hot as fire, the celery was sweet as nuts. The four little pigs and Brock the Badger ate and ate till there wasn't a crumb left.

'You needn't do any washing up,' remarked Sam. 'I'll lick the plates clean.'

He took up the buttery crumpet dish and licked it, but Brock shook his head.

'No, Sam. Not done in the best families. It may be the manners of the pig-cote at the farm, but it isn't the thing for a family brought up by Brock the Badger.'

'Sorry, Brock,' said Sam. 'I thought I was saving work and saving butter too.'

'You can do the washing up tonight, Sam, if you want to save work,' suggested Bill. 'It's your turn.'

Sam filled the bowl with hot water from the

kettle, he put the dirty plates and cups inside it, and then washed up, using a bunch of twigs to clean the plates, a piece of sandstone to scour the pans, and a leafy towel to dry everything. Then he put them all on the shelf, five brown plates, with ferns and flowers marked round their rims, five mugs of earthenware, and the crumpet dish and saucepans.

Ann sat in the rocking-chair, darning the mittens and blankets; Tom was mending a broken wooden spoon, and carving a new one; Bill was sorting wild flower seeds into packets ready for sowing under the hedges, and Brock was smoking his pipe and staring at the fire. It was all very homely and comfortable, and happy as could be.

'Tell us a tale, Brock. I've finished double-quick, and not broke nuffin'. Tell us a tale, Brock.' Sam capered up, dragging his stool to the Badger's side.

'I've a bone in my leg,' grunted Brock, and he pretended to groan.

'Oh, where is it? Does it hurt?' asked Sam quickly.

'Silly,' scoffed Bill. 'All animals have bones in their legs.'

'Have I?' Sam looked alarmed, but Bill pinched his brother's fat little leg.

'Yes, you have. It's here. The hard thing inside you, holding you together.'

'It's nearly lost in the fat, Sam, but you've got a bone left,' said Tom, looking up from his wood-carving.

'Do tell us a story, Brock,' said Sam, wriggling away from his brother.

So Brock told the four little pigs the famous story of Dick Turpin's Ride to York. Dick was a highwayman, whom nobody could catch. With his bag of gold he rode away on his wonderful mare, Black Bess. From London to York he rode, leaping the tollgates, evading his pursuers, faster and faster, on that mare of great renown. But when he got to York, the gallant mare lay down and died.

When Brock finished, and Black Bess lay dead at York, there was a tear in Sam's eye.

'Oh, Brock! I wonder if Sally could go like that,' he cried. 'Black Bess must have been rather like Sally, don't you think so, Brock?'

'I shouldn't be surprised,' agreed Brock.

They lighted their candles and went upstairs to bed, to dream of Dick Turpin and his ride.

After breakfast the next day Sam went across the woods and fields to visit Sally the Mare. She was grazing in White Field, where all the little daisies powdered the grass, and she raised her head and whinnied with pleasure when she saw her friend coming towards her.

'Hello, Sally,' cried Sam, and he ran to her, and stroked her bent head, and plaited her thick lock of hair.

'Hello, Sam,' said Sally. 'What are you doing today?'

'I've come to see you, Sally. Have you been with the milk to the station?'

'Yes,' replied Sally, and she snatched a mouthful of sweet grass. 'Yes, I've done my first job of work, but in a few minutes they are coming for me. I've to go to the village with the Master this morning.'

'Do you think I could go, Sally?'

'I'm sure you can't. There'll be a load. We

are taking a calf to be sold to a farmer. Why do you want to go, Sam?'

'Because I'm Thursday's child. Thursday's child has far to go, and I feel I must be going somewhere. I feel it in my bones. I has bones in my legs, Sally.'

Sally glanced at little Sam's legs, but she went on eating for she was hungry and time was short.

'Whose child are you, Sally?' asked Sam.

'My mother was Grey Bess of Hardwick,' said Sally proudly.

'Grey Bess?' cried Sam. 'Did you say Grey Bess, Sally?'

'Yes. She was a famous mare, and she won a prize at the big horse show,' said Sally. She stood erect and arched her neck as she spoke of her mother.

'Black Bess galloped to York, Sally,' said Sam.

Sally blinked and went on with her breakfast. Sometimes Sam talked in a foolish way, and there was nothing to reply.

'I really meant to ask what day you were born, Sally,' said Sam.

'I was a Sunday's child,' said Sally simply.

'A child that is born on the Sabbath day,
Is merry and bright, and good and gay.'

said Sam. 'That's you, Sally. Oh, Sally, can you run to York?'

'To York? Why, Sam, that's a powerful way off. It's more than a hundred miles. Maybe two hundred, maybe three hundred. I can't go very far, I'm getting on in life. Over twenty I be, so Master says.'

The gate clicked and Farmer Greensleeves came across the field with a halter in his hand. Sam slipped under the hedge and stayed there till they had gone. Then he went off to think about it.

A few days later Sally went to the blacksmith's to be shod.

'Tie her outside when you've finished shoeing her, John Smith,' said Farmer Greensleeves to the blacksmith. 'I've got a few errands to do, and I'll come back in half an hour.'

'All right, Mister Greensleeves,' replied John Smith, and the farmer went off. The mare was shod, and the smith tied her to the iron ring in the wall a few yards from the smithy. Sally stood patiently staring at the wall, looking at the ivy and the moss, standing on three legs, and then idly stamping a foot, wondering how long the Master would be, then shutting one eye and drooping her head. She was dozing nicely and dreaming of the meadow down by the river, when she heard a shrill urgent whisper which made her jump.

'Sally! Sally!' said the wee small voice. There, between her forelegs, staring up at her, was little Sam Pig. He wore an odd three-cornered hat, and in his hand he held a large, bulging canvas bag. Sally looked at Sam and at the bag, which was familiar somehow.

'Sally, I've robbed the Bank,' whispered Sam. 'Help me to escape.'

'What! Robbed the Bank? The Bank of England?' Sally couldn't believe her ears.

'Yes. The Money Bank, not the Daisy Bank,' hissed Sam. 'Quick, Sally. They are after me! Law and Order's after me. Help me to escape.'

'Nay, Sam. Nay,' began Sally, but Sam

caught hold of the reins and dragged himself up to Sally's back. He leaned forward and untied the knot which held Sally to the wall. Then he kicked with his heels and chirruped to the mare.

'Gee up, Sally! Away we go! Gee up!'

The smith put his head out of the smithy door when he heard the clatter of hooves. When he saw Sam Pig instead of Farmer Greensleeves he raised a shout.

'Hey there! Stop thief! Stop thief!' he roared, and his voice was so powerful it rang through the market-place and brought all the shop-keepers to their doors. The grocer came running out with a sugar bag in his hand, waving his white apron at Sally. The butcher came out with a leg of mutton, and waved his blue-striped apron. The cobbler came out with his shoe and needle, and he waved his black apron at Sally. All the men shouted and waved, but the blacksmith's leather apron actually caught Sally's face so that she reared and nearly threw Sam off. Sally was frightened at all the fuss and noise, so she took to her heels and galloped as fast as she could down the road.

'Gee up, Black Bess, gee up!' cried Sam, flapping the reins, bouncing up and down like a little cork, and waving his three-cornered hat at the people who came from the cottages to see what was the matter.

'A thief! A horse-thief!' they said.

Farmer Greensleeves came hurrying out of the saddler's with a big leather horse-collar on his arm.

'Hey, Sally! Whoa! Whoa, lass!' he shouted. Sally heard his voice, she turned, but Sam kicked his heels into her ribs.

'Sally! Save me! Save your Sam Pig!' he cried, and Sally went on.

Then out of nowhere stepped the village policeman with a notebook in his hand.

'Stop thief!' he said in his deep voice, flinging himself at Sally, but the bewildered mare swayed aside and pushed through the hedge. She galloped across the field, and the policeman was left far behind.

'Is this the way to York?' asked Sam, who was now clinging to Sally's mane. The reins were dropped, but luckily they were twisted in a knot so they didn't trip Sally as she ran.

'It may be,' said Sally, and she bumped along, over ploughed fields, through gaps and over ditches, struggling her utmost to save little Sam Pig from the policeman.

'Can you jump over walls and over tollgates, Sally?' asked Sam anxiously.

'No, I can't,' said Sally shortly.

'There are several tollgates on the way, so I've heard,' said Sam in Sally's ear.

'Well, I can't leap them, so that's flat.'

Sally slackened her pace and stopped by a stream. She lowered her head and drank, and Sam slipped off and drank also.

Sally lay on her back and rolled in the grass. Sam kicked his heels and rolled too.

'Now tell me all about it, Sam. Whatever have you been a-doing of?' asked Sally, and she rose to her feet and nibbled a few blades of grass.

'I went to the Bank, and I saw a bag on the counter,' said Sam, 'so I carried it off, right under the Bank manager's nose. He was shovelling money at the back, and I walked off.'

'Why did you do that?' asked Sally, shaking her head at the bad little pig.

'Because it was full of gold of course,' said Sam. 'I'm taking it to York, like Dick Turpin, the famous highwayman. Can't you see my highwayman's hat, Sally? I made it out of rags and tatters.'

'Well, I must say –' began Sally, but she didn't finish her sentence, for there were shouts not far away.

'Hoy! Hoy! Hoy! Stop thief!' The two looked behind and there was the stout policeman running after them, with his truncheon in his hand. So Sam Pig climbed on Sally's back and they ambled away.

'Quick, Sally! Quick!' called Sam, shaking the reins. 'Off to York, Sally. To York.'

'Oh dear, Sam! I don't know the way to York,' complained Sally after a time, when she had crossed several more fields and left the policeman behind.

'There's a road over yonder,' said Sam, and they went through another hedge into a lane.

'This is the road to Merrytown Fair,' said Sally. 'I ought to be going home to my master. He wants me for ploughing this afternoon, and here I am gallumping across the country just as if I were out with the hounds.'

'You can't go ploughing, Sally. Would you

like to see me in prison, with chains on my legs? We must go to York,' cried Sam.

Grumbling a little but more cheerful as she saw country she knew, Sally trotted along the road. All who met her stared at the little figure in the three-cornered hat bobbing about on her broad back. Sam's sharp ear could detect the sound of galloping hooves coming after, so he turned Sally aside again into a wood. The moss was green, the trees hid them from sight, and Sally stopped.

'This looks like York,' said she. 'This must be York. I can't go any further. Are you satisfied, Sam Pig?'

'If you think it *is* York,' said Sam doubtfully, 'I am content.'

There was a rustle in the bushes and the Fox came out and winked at Sally.

'Hallo, Sam Pig! There's a hue and cry after you.'

'The police?' asked Sam hopefully.

'No. Brock the Badger is looking for you. You'll catch it when he finds you,' said the Fox, leering unpleasantly.

Sam and Sally went on in silence through the woods to the fields. There was something very familiar about everything.

'Oh, Sally! You're taking me home,' complained Sam.

'Well, Sam,' confessed Sally, 'I must go back to the farm for ploughing. Master will be fair mad at having to walk home from market without me, and he'll be madder still if I'm not at home when he gets there.'

Then Brock stepped out from the woodside, and laid hold of the bridle.

'Sam! Get down at once! What are you doing, play-acting like this?' said he indignantly.

Sam obediently slipped to the ground and stood in front of the stern Badger.

'Play-acting, Brock? I wasn't play-acting. I was riding to York like Dick Turpin with a bag of gold,' said Sam in his innocent way.

'Where did you get the gold?' asked Brock, looking at the canvas bag fastened to Sally.

'From the Bank. That's where gold is kept,' said Sam.

'What were you going to do with it when you got to York?' asked Brock.

'Give it to the poor children who have no pennies to spend,' said Sam, smiling his sweetest smile.

'Where is this bag of gold?' asked Brock very crossly and he didn't smile at all. Sam took the canvas bag from the saddle and gave it to Brock. Brock opened it and then he began to laugh.

'Gold!' he exclaimed. 'Gold! Yes, it's gold all right, but not the kind of gold you thought it was.' He poured some out on the ground for Sam and Sally to see. It lay there in a shining red-gold heap among the grasses.

'Why, it's corn,' exclaimed little Sam. 'It's only Indy corn for hens.'

'Yes, Sam. It's a bag of corn you are carrying off.'

'That's right, Mister Brock,' interrupted Sally. 'Master Greensleeves bought some Indy corn. That's our bag. I thought I knew it. He must have carried it to the Bank and forgotten it.'

'It was on the counter,' said Sam.

'Now, Sam. Home you come with me,' said Brock.

He tied the bag of corn on the mare's back and led her through the gate towards the farm. Sam Pig ran by her side, explaining all about Dick Turpin's ride to York.

'Off you go, Sally. Away you go to your stable,' said Brock.

Sally trotted away, very glad the ride was over, and when Farmer Greensleeves came home, hot and bothered because he had lost his mare and his bag of corn, there was Sally, looking round at him with her brown eyes, waiting for him outside the stable door.

'Sally my lass! I saw you galloping off with a little fellow on your back. Was it – could it be Sam Pig?'

Sally nodded her head and blinked her old eyes.

'The varmint! Well, after dinner we must go ploughing. You look as if you'd been roving, Sally. All mired. I must take the brush to you.'

Farmer Greensleeves brushed Sally's coat

and watered and fed her, and left her in the stable while he had his dinner.

'It beats me what that young Sam Pig wanted with our Sally,' he said to his wife.

In Brock's house sat Sam, also eating his dinner.

'Whatever made you act so silly-soft?' asked Brock.

'Thursday's child has far to go,' answered Sam.

'Oh! That's it. Then you'd best go upstairs to bed. That's where Thursday's child must go today,' said Brock.

Upstairs crept Sam, and into bed he crawled, for he felt very sore with the galloping.

'It was worth it,' he said. Then he fell asleep and didn't wake up till next morning.

'I can feel all the bones in my legs, Brock,' said he as he came stiffly into the room. 'Riding is very hurty for bones, isn't it? Especially riding all the way to York with a bag of gold on your saddle.'

Sam Pig Goes to School

One fine day Sam Pig went to school. He didn't mean to go. It was all a mistake. If Brock the Badger had said to him, 'Sam, I think it's time you got some learning. You must go to school,' then Sam would have gone quite willingly. But Brock didn't say anything of the kind. He knew that his own teaching about the ways of woods and fields was the best kind of knowledge for a young pigling. Brock would never have sent Sam to school. Sam had heard of a school, but he thought it was a jolly gathering of starlings in the trees, or a company of lambs playing in the fields. The starlings went to school when they met together in a great flock and chattered for hours in the evenings. The rooks went to school when they talked so much in the elm trees.

Sam went to Sally the Mare to discuss the subject with her. She was so wise, she would be sure to know all about schools.

He found Sally in the Home Pasture, leaning over the gate. Her chin rested on the top bar, her dark eyes were gazing towards the farm-house. Sam waited in silence for a moment, but Sally didn't utter a word.

'Hello, Sally,' said Sam, and he climbed on the gate and then hopped off again, bouncing on the ground.

'Hello, Sam,' said Sally, without turning her head.

'Is it home you are thinking of, Sally?' asked Sam.

'Yes. I'm thinking of the stable and the hay in the manger and the lantern in the corner. I do a lot of thinking, Sam. You are a gay little youngling, Sam Pig, but I am a sober old worker. For nigh twenty years I have dragged heavy loads up and down those hills yonder.'

Sam took a hop and a skip. He danced a step just to show Sally, and the shadows of the dancing leaves flickered on his trousers and head. Sally looked at him, at the leaf shadows, at the bars of shade made by the big white gate on the grass.

'That's right, Sam. You are a worker, too, in your own way. Like the leaves and sunshine, you work. Like the grasshoppers and butterflies, you have your place.'

'Yes,' agreed Sam, who didn't know what Sally was talking about. 'Have you ever been to school, Sally?'

'Not that I knows of. I've not had much learning, except when I was broken in,' said Sally cautiously. 'I've heard tell of school, and I've taken the children down in the cart on bad days when river was in flood, but I didn't go inside for lessons myself. I heard the talking of it, through open windows.'

'What did you hear?' asked Sam curiously.

'The Rat was on the mat, and the Fox was in a box,' said Sally.

'Ah! I think I should like that,' said Sam, and he pulled a blade of grass and nibbled it.

'You'd better keep away,' warned Sally. 'It's not for the likes of us. It suits little childer, but not old mares and young piglings.'

A few days later Sam Pig was walking through the village. He went rather fast, for he

had no business to be there all by himself
without Brock the Badger, or Sally the Mare,
or Farmer Greensleeves, but he had been to
gaze at the humbugs and peardrops in Mrs
Bunting's shop-window. They filled the glass
jars, and Sam stared at their beautiful shapes
and colours, and thought of the taste. Then he
started off home. He heard the sound of
laughter and singing as he went by a wide-
open iron gate, and he stopped a moment.

A crowd of little children, not much bigger
than himself, were dancing round in a ring,
singing a gay song:

> *Ring-a-ring of roses,*
> *Pocket full of posies.*
> *Atishoo! Atishoo!*
> *We all fall down!*

They rolled on the ground, laughing and
atishooing and Sam laughed and sneezed too
in the gateway.

Then they took hands and sang another
song, dancing round and singing shrilly:

There was a farmer had a dog,
And its name was Bobby Bingo.
B-I-N-G-O. B-I-N-G-O. B-I-N-G-O.
And its name was Bobby Bingo.

Sam crept through the gate and walked into the playground. Somebody held out a warm little fat hand, and Sam Pig took it. Somebody at the other side held out a thin little hand and Sam Pig took it. In a moment he was dancing round with the rest, singing very shrilly and laughing and leaping on his toes. The only difference was that his voice was higher, his laugh was softer, and his ears were longer and his feet were nimbler. Round and round went little Sam Pig, his head nodding, his wide hat flapping, his little toes tripping neatly.

Then they stood in a row, and one child counted them out with:

Higgledy, Piggledy, My Black Hen.
She lays eggs for Gentlemen.
One for you, and one for me,
O.U.T. spells out goes he.

And little Sam was left to be the catcher! How he ran! He caught somebody in a twinkling, for he was far quicker than the little children. He ran here and there, behind trees, over the stone bench, and nobody could catch little Sam Pig.

They shouted, they sang and danced and little Sam Pig shouted and sang and danced with them. Suddenly all the fun came to an end, for out of the long ivy-covered house came a lady all in a hurry and flurry. She rang a bell, ting-a-ling-a-ling, and clapped her hands. Everybody shuffled into a line and with them went Sam.

'The dinner-bell,' thought Sam. 'Now we're going to the farmhouse for buns and milk. Now we're going to have puddings and pies. Now we're going to have treacle dumplings.'

They went through the door into the infant school, and the children scrambled to their seats. Sam stayed with the little ones, and sat down at the end of a wooden form. Next to him was the little girl who had held his hand in the ring. She had yellow hair and eyes as blue as Sam's, but her ears were very small, not at all good for listening. She looked at Sam more closely and touched his plaid trousers with her forefinger.

'What's your name?' she asked, giggling a little at Sam.

'Sam Pig,' whispered Sam in his best voice. 'What's yours?'

'Betty Bywater,' she answered.

'Betty Bywater, stop talking,' said the teacher, turning round. Then she saw Sam Pig. Luckily she was short-sighted, and Sam's long ears and snout were misty to her eyes, but the others saw clearly enough.

'He's a little pigling, Miss. He's been playing with us,' said one.

'He's a pig, teacher. He's a pig,' said another.

'You mustn't say such rude things,' said the teacher severely.

The children shuffled and peeped and giggled. Never had they been so troublesome. They couldn't keep still. They peered at Sam and whispered and laughed. Sam laughed and blinked at them.

The teacher rapped on her desk and they all turned to her, although they kept peeping at Sam on the back row in the corner of the room.

'Say your poetry, children,' said the teacher.

The class chanted their poem in a sing-song manner, and little Sam tried to join in and then gave it up.

*I have a little shadow, that goes in and out
   with me.
And what can be the use of him is more than
   I can see.
He is very very like me from the heels up
   to the head,
And I see him jump before me when I jump
   on my bed.*

'I've got a shadow,' shouted Sam. 'I have, and I know what's the use of him. He's to keep me company when I go out adventuring. He fights, does my shadow.'

'Dear me,' said the teacher. 'You are very talkative.'

'I know a poem,' went on Sam rapidly, and before anyone could speak he recited his own bit of poetry, which Brock the Badger had taught him.

The Bat, the Bull, and the Bumble-bee,
The more you tease 'em the fiercer they be.
But treat 'em kindly and you will see,
How grateful to you they'll allays be,
They'll keep you in their memoree,
The Bat, the Bull, and the Bumble-bee.

'Very nice indeed,' said the teacher. 'Kindness to all animals. Yes, very nice.'

Sam sat down rather breathless after his effort, but triumphant.

'A is for apple,' said the teacher, pointing to a picture of a large letter A and a lot of little letter a's, on a sheet.

'A is for apple,' shouted the class.

'I like apples,' remarked Sam Pig conversationally. 'Farmer Greensleeves has lots of apples. I can go and get them. I helps with the hay. I helps the Irishmen, I do.'

'Silence, little boy,' said the teacher.

'B is for Bear,' she said, and everybody repeated 'B is for Bear'.

'Bees make honey,' said Sam. 'We've got Bees and Beetles and Bumble-bees and Butter-flies and all at our house. Me and Brock the Badger we finds 'em all, and knows 'em.'

There was silence. The teacher was coming to Sam with a stern look on her face, and all the children opened wide their eyes with excitement.

'Why are you still wearing your hat?' she asked, stretching out her hand to remove Sam's wide haymaking hat.

' 'Cos it's a nice hat, and I allays wears it when I come to the village because my ears is big Ann says. It's my haymaking hat. I went haymaking in it with the Irishmen. I rode to market with Farmer Greensleeves in it. I went in the big engine called George Washington, once upon a time, in this hat.'

Sam was breathless defending his hat. He feared the lady was going to take it from him, and he was ready to fight for it.

'You mustn't wear it in school,' she said gently.

'School?' echoed Sam, astonished. 'You

haven't talked about Fox in a box. I thought this was a bun-and-milk farm. I think I'll be going home. I think Brock wants me. I think I've made a mistake. Good morning.'

He sidled from his place, bowed politely, and marched off. The teacher looked after him, dumb with surprise. Nobody spoke for a whole minute, and then there was an uproar and everybody, including the teacher, ran to the door. There was little Sam Pig disappearing through the gate, running as fast as he could.

'Come children. We will go on with our lessons,' said the teacher quietly, but somehow the sunshine seemed to have gone along with little Sam Pig.

When Sam got home he told the family all about it.

'You went to school?' they cried. 'What did you learn?'

'I learned A is for crab-apple, and B is for honey-bee, and I said my poetry,' said Sam. 'I didn't learn C.'

'I'll teach you,' said Brock. 'I know an alphabet, and we'll learn it together.'

So Sam Pig and Brock went to the woods. There was a sandy patch of ground near the stream where the water had overflowed. It was smooth and clean, and only marked by the feet of a waterhen. With a couple of sticks they made letters in the sand, criss-crosses and curves. Brock chanted the alphabet to Sam, and they sang it together, with only the birds and rabbits listening. It was all about the things Sam knew. This is how it went.

A is for Ann, B is for Brock.

C is for Cabbage, D is for Dock (leaf).

E is for Egg, F is for Fox.

G is for Goblin, H Holly-hocks.

I is for Icicle, J is for Jam.

K is for Kitty, L is for Lamb.

M is for Mouse (Jemima), N is for Nest.

O is for Owl, P is for Pest (Weasels and Foxes).

Q is for Queen Bee, R is for Rain.

S is for Sam and Sally, T is for Train.

U is for Unicorn, V Velvety, W White.

X is for Xmas, Y Yuletide delight.

Z is a-crooked-little-path-going-from-

Sam

Pig's

house

across

the

fields

to

Farmer-Greensleeves'-Farm.

'Do you know which is the nicest letter, Brock?' asked Sam, as they surveyed the funny little twisty letters sprawling all over the ground.

'No,' said Brock. 'Which do you like the best?'

'S is the very jolliest of all,' said Sam. 'It's all curly like my tail, and it's like the little path that goes to the farm. It's S for Sally, you know.'

'I quite agree,' said Brock. 'I like letter S the best.'

'Now I'm going to teach Sally her letters. She says she hasn't had much learning, and I've been to school, haven't I, Brock?'

'You have indeed, Sam,' said Brock, smiling down at the small eager pigling.

Away ran Sam to tell Sally about the letters and to show her S for Sally.

'It's shape of a hook, Sam,' said Sally, when Sam scrawled the crooked letter on the ground. 'It's like the hooks at the farm they have for hanging up their lanterns and herbs. Farmer Greensleeves has a dozen or so like this lying on the shelves, and he slings many a thing aloft on them, on the hooks in the beams and ceilings.'

'Yes. S for Sam and Sally and S for hooks,' said Sam happily. 'I must tell that to Brock. I don't expect he knows.'

The Treasure

Sam Pig had never been a good climber of trees, except nice little apple trees with branches close to the ground. None of the family of Pigs could climb trees, and even Brock the Badger was better at digging beneath their roots than clambering among the boughs.

'Oh Brock!' said Sam one day. 'I wish I could climb trees, like Maldy the cat at the farmhouse. She runs up the trunk of the elm and looks down at me from the branches, and she puts her tongue out at me.'

'Now, Sam. You keep to the ground and behave yourself,' said Bill, interrupting. 'Don't give yourself airs. There's plenty to do down below, planting potatoes, or washing up, or sweeping the paths, without climbing trees.'

'I believe he wants to climb trees so that we can't find him,' said Tom Pig.

'No, I don't,' cried Sam, hotly defending himself. 'I want to look over the fields and woods. I'm only a very little pig, and I can't see far unless I climb a hill, or get on a gate, or find a tree with easy branches like steps.'

Brock put down his pocket-book which he had been reading. He made a few writing marks on the nearest tree, scratches on the bark, deep lines of secret message. Then he turned to the little family, who always wanted his advice and help.

'Of course,' said he kindly. 'We understand Sam's longing to get high up. Little Pigs have hard feet that run on the ground, but they are not made for tree-climbing.'

'Man climbs trees, and he wears boots,' objected Sam.

'How do you know that?' asked Ann. 'Have you seen him?'

'Oh yes,' answered Sam. 'I was in the wood yesterday, very early, and I saw a man coming along, so I hid myself.'

'Quite right,' said Brock. 'Very seldom does

any man come near our house.'

'He looked about him,' continued Sam, 'and I thought he would see me, so I crept into a hole among some brambles, and I never made a sound. Then I watched him. He carried a sack, all knobs and corners. He looked round again, as if he thought someone was coming. Then he began to climb an oak tree. It's my tree. It's the one I've always wanted to climb. The all-alone oak in the holly wood, Brock.'

'Yes, I know it. We all know it. The tree with a hole high up, where the Owl lived before it got too draughty. The tree with a flat bough, and a bare branch on top. Yes, we know it.'

'Well, this man climbed up the tree as easy as winking, and he took the sack with him. When he got to the hole he flashed a light down it, but he couldn't see far, for he grunted crossly. Then he dropped the sack inside, and he slipped down to the ground. He stared about for a bit, and looked hard at the tree, and looked around, but he didn't see me. Then he went away, walking fast and tip-toeing. He didn't crackle the sticks, he was the quietest man I've ever seen.'

'What was he like?' asked Ann Pig, shivering a little.

'He was rather like the Fox, with a pointed face, and crafty eyes. It wasn't a kind face like Farmer Greensleeves' or old Adam's. It was a twitchy face, and I didn't like it at all.'

'Mind he doesn't carry you off,' jeered Bill Pig.

'What do you think he hid there, Brock?' asked Tom.

'Maybe a store of food for the time when he is hungry,' said Brock. 'Tins of pineapple and salmon and treacle.'

'Oh my! Brock! I've never tasted those things except treacle. Could we have those tins?' asked Sam quickly. The other pigs licked their lips and crowded round the Badger.

'Certainly not! We mustn't rob man. The tree is his cupboard, his larder and pantry,' said Brock.

'Perhaps it wasn't food he hid there,' piped little Ann. 'Perhaps it was a musical box and a fiddle.'

'Well, we can't climb trees, so we shall never

know, and what does it matter?' said Brock. 'He lives his life, and we live ours, and the two ways of living are far apart.'

He took up some rushes and began to twist a rope. Sam Pig hesitated a moment.

'It's my tree, and my larder,' said he softly. He went outside and climbed the garden gate. The gate hinges squeaked in a friendly way, and Ann Pig came to join Sam on the gate. They all squeaked together, making a fine music, very cheering on a dull day.

'I believe it's something special,' said Sam. 'The man was very quick and sharp-looking. He wasn't like the farm men or the country folk you see at the market, Ann. I was scared of him.'

Squeak! Squeak! went the gate.

'Let's go and look at the tree,' suggested Ann.

Squeak! Squeak! went the gate.

'It says "Yes, yes",' laughed Sam.

They leapt down and ran through the woods for a mile or more to the great oak tree in the holly copse. There it stood, a grand old tree with ancient boughs outstretched. Half-way up

The Treasure

the trunk was a circular hole, partly concealed by a branch. Sam showed Ann where the moss had been scraped away by the man's boots, and they tracked his footprints and sniffed at the ground.

'Not a nice man,' said Ann, turning up her little nose.

They hopped and skipped round the tree, and sniffed again at a footprint.

'He doesn't smell of cow-cake or hayseeds or horses,' said Sam.

They stood on tiptoes; they lifted each other up; they put a pile of stones and climbed unsteadily upon them but the hole was too far away.

Sam fetched Jemima Mouse. She was a clever climber. She ran up the rugged tree trunk in a twinkling and looked into the hole.

'I daren't go inside, Sam,' she squeaked. 'If I did I couldn't get out. It's like a deep well.'

Sam and Ann Pig danced with impatience.

'Badger's rope,' cried Sam. 'Let's tie it to Jemima's waist and drop her into the hole.'

'I'll fetch it,' said Ann. She hurried home and

317

Sam remained by the tree, to talk to little Jemima.

Brock sat on a stump, with coils of green rushy rope plaited finely and neatly around him.

'Can we have that rope to drop Jemima down the tree?' asked Ann breathlessly.

'Nay, she would be hurt, the tiny mousekin,' said old Brock. 'I'll come with you and look at this hole.'

'And we'll come too,' cried Bill and Tom, hurrying up. 'We all want to see where the man climbed.'

So away they went, Brock the Badger, Bill Pig and Tom, and little Ann Pig puffing and panting by their side. When they got to the holly copse, where the great tree stood, there was no sign of Sam.

'Sam! Coo-oo! Where are you hiding?' they called.

'You needn't think you can play a trick on us, because you can't. We are all here, Brock too,' shouted Bill.

'Come out, Sam,' said Brock gruffly, and he

peered into the holly bushes and the hole where Sam had hidden when he watched the man.

A queer muffled sound came from the tree, a faint call.

'I'm here, Brock. I did it. I climbed the tree, and fell down the hole,' said the soft, far-away voice of Sam. 'I can't get out, Brock.'

'Yes, he's in the tree,' squeaked Jemima. 'He did it all by himself.'

'We'll get you, Sam. Don't be frightened,' said Brock in his deep, rich voice, which always comforted the little pigs.

'I'm all right, really, Brock. I'm not frightened a bit. It's warm down here. I've tored my trousers. Have you a bit of string to fasten them up?'

'Are you eating all the food down there?' asked Bill.

'Greedy Sam! Got into the hole to eat the treacle,' said Tom, calling through his hollowed fists.

'There ain't no food. It's all teapots and jugs and hard things. Nothing to eat,' said Sam. 'And they hurt me when I fell on top of them.

There's a lot of earwigs down here, and a bit-bat, Brock.'

'Hist, Sam! There's somebody coming. Don't speak, Sam.'

Brock stood motionless, his nose to the ground, every hair on end. He gave a low growl. The little pigs were frozen into silence.

'We must go into the bushes till he's gone. It's a man. I smell him. Quiet, Sam.' Brock spoke in hurried whispers which carried to the tree trunk and Sam crouched low.

The mouse ran home, and the three little pigs with Brock the Badger faded away into the brush-wood. Not a sound did they make as they followed Brock the hunter. They moved gently through the grasses and leaves, their toes felt for roots, their bodies were soft as they bent and turned. Brock covered them, as they lay down in the holly thicket. Then the old Badger crouched with his sharp eyes staring through the tiny green windows, and his harsh body deep in the shadows. The light fell through the branches, and Badger's black and white face was exactly like light and shade. He was invisible.

There was a strange silence as the man floundered through the bushes, breathing heavily, running, turning round, staring about him. He carried a rope with a large hook at the end, half concealed under his jacket.

When he got to the foot of the oak tree he straightened the rope, tested it, and put it round his shoulders. Then, with great agility, he started to climb the trunk. Brock edged nearer, but the little pigs could see nothing. They were out of sight among dead leaves. They could hear the man's movements, his quick-panting breath, his muttering voice, the scraping of his boots as he climbed, and the jingle of metal as the hook caught against the rough bark.

When the man reached the hole he rested for a moment, holding to the branch, and flashing a lamp into the hole.

Brock scarcely breathed. He was afraid little Sam would cry out, but Sam did nothing of the kind. Down in the hole sat Sam Pig, waiting. He too heard the man's deep breathing, he heard the scraping of his boots on the bark, and the grunts of exertion as the man came nearer. Sam looked up at the little round hole through which he had fallen. It was darkened by a white face, but Sam never said a word. Then a light flashed, but Sam was out of its reach in the shadows at the bottom of the deep hole. There was a moment of shuffling and down came the hook dangling loosely and hitting the trunk. When it got to the bundle it wavered about as the man sought to catch the cord which fastened the bag.

Sam took hold of the hook. With his tight little fist he clung to it, and to the bundle.

'Got it! First go! Blimey! Got it!' cried the man, and he was so excited he nearly fell from the tree.

Brock's hair stood on end. His heart beat steadily, his eyes glared, he was ready to spring to the rescue of little Sam.

In silence the bundle was pulled up. Sam was bumped to and fro, scratched and bruised, but he said never a word. The man carefully dragged the rope up the tree.

'It's heavier than I thought. Solid silver all of it. A goodish weight of solid stuff, better than I knew. My luck's in this time,' he muttered.

At last the hook was getting to the hole, and the man was ready to take his bundle. He stretched out his hand and to his horror it was grabbed by a sticky little paw. Out of the hole came, not his bundle of stolen silver, but the

two big ears, the long nose and the sharp white teeth of Sam Pig.

'Ow! Ow! Golly! Crikey! A goblin! A boggart!' The man shrieked and let go the rope. He tumbled down the tree, and fled. When he looked over his shoulder, there was Sam's face, black with the cobwebs and dust of the tree, staring at him from the hole, and Sam's black fist shaking at him.

'Haunted! Haunted!' screamed the man. 'I won't do it again. I'll go straight from now on. Ow!'

He ran through the woods to his bicycle hidden by the road, and away he rode to the town.

Sam Pig swung his leg over the edge of the hole and dragged the bundle out. Then he sat, laughing down at the family, while Brock and the three little pigs came out of hiding.

'Oh, Sam! You did scare him. How brave you are, coming up like a Jack-in-the-box! You look like a black goblin,' they cried, as they danced round the tree.

'Sam,' said Brock. 'I am proud of you.'

'It's nothing,' said Sam modestly. 'There was a hook, and I held on to it. I felt like a fish on a line, Brock.' He laughed and tossed the bundle down to Brock. Then he hung from the branch and dropped among the soft leaves.

'Open it, Brock. Open it,' cried the pigs impatiently. 'Let us see what the man hid.'

Brock opened the bundle and out fell a silver teapot, jugs and tankards, cups and spoons of beautiful old silver.

'Where did this stuff come from I wonder?' said Brock.

'From the Big House,' cried Sam excitedly. 'When I was there, in the kitchen, I saw that lovely teapot. I remember it. The Irish cook picked it up and gave it a polish. Yes, I saw it, Brock.'

'The Big House? The man must be a robber, like the Fox. We must send it back, Sam.'

They walked home, talking about Sam's adventure, and wonderful silver tankards with lids and all.

'I'll take it back myself,' said Sam. 'I want to see the Irish cook.'

'Then I'll come to the gates to carry it for you,' said Brock, looking down at the dirty happy pigling who danced by his side all the way home.

'Let's have tea in that teapot tonight,' said Ann. 'Can we, Brock?'

'I think we might,' said Brock. 'Yes, we'll have tea in a silver teapot and we'll drink from silver mugs and tankards.'

So Tom made the herb tea in the magnificent silver teapot from the Hall. It was the first time such a queer mixture of herbs had been brewed within its aristocratic body. Ann held it with both hands and tilted it, so that a fine brown stream came from the embossed spout. All the little pigs sat round, and sipped the tea from the silver mugs and tankards. Brock the Badger drank his own ale from the old Georgian tankard with a domed lid. They all laughed at the queer reflections of their faces, the crooked fat faces they saw in the sides of the mugs. They all enjoyed the taste of the brew, and thumped the mugs on the rough oak table. Really truly, it didn't taste quite as nice as in their own earthenware mugs, they thought privately, but they didn't say so, and the reflections were as ugly as goblins.

'Were you frightened, Sam, when you were dangling on the rope?' asked Brock curiously.

'Yes,' confessed Sam. 'I shivered so much I thought he would feel the rope shake.'

'How did you keep so quiet?' asked Bill scoffingly.

'I held my tongue.' Sam pertly stuck out his pink tongue at Bill and then grinned at his reflection in the silver.

'He would have carried you off if he had known you were only a little pig,' said Tom.

'But when he saw you, he ran away, and no wonder,' added Bill. 'You are a blackamoor, Sam.'

'How did you climb up the tree?' asked Ann.

'Oh, I just tried and tried,' said Sam airily, 'and the wind blowed me, and I tried again, and I did it.'

'Good for you,' said Brock, and he quaffed his ale and puffed at his pipe.

'Need I get washed?' asked Sam.

'No. You can stay dirty till tomorrow, Sam, for a special treat,' said Brock. 'I like a nice dirty pig sometimes.'

'Thank you. Thank you,' said Sam, and he picked up his silver mug and stared into its shining polished sides at his own little ugly face.

Sam Pig at the Circus

Sam Pig brought back the news. He had seen the picture on an old barn door down the lane. It was one of those ancient doors that act as newspapers or town criers for country folk. Upon its rough lichened weather-worn surface the auctioneer pasted his bills of sale, which stayed there for a year or more until the wind and rain tore them off. Those who passed by read the words, but as only three or four people went that way on the busiest day, the old door depended upon one telling another the news displayed there.

Now Sam couldn't read the printing, but he was glad the old paper bill had gone and this fresh new one hung on the door. It had brightly coloured letters, green, red and blue, and a picture. That was clear enough for anybody who couldn't read. Ladies leaping through paper hoops held up by clowns, piebald ponies dancing with their manes flowing, dogs with frills round their necks. Sam climbed the three mossy steps of the barn and stood with his nose close to the poster for a long, long time, smelling the odour of paste, tasting the print, staring at the words. Every detail he saw, every curl and flourish, and the rows of gay letters.

He spelled out the letters which he knew quite well. He didn't know what the word was, but he remembered the alphabet Brock had taught him down by the stream with sticks and pebbles for pen and ink. He said letters aloud, slowly, choosing the most important-looking word which ran across the poster.

'C for Cabbage. I for Icicle. R for Rain. C for another Cabbage. U for Unicorn. S for Sam and Sally.'

He was pondering this puzzle, of Sam and Sally going to take cabbages to the Unicorn, when he heard a merry sound of laughter. Some children were coming down the lane. Sam returned to the field, through the hedge. He could hear their joyous cries as they read the poster.

'A Circus! A Circus coming to Hemlock Meadow. Ten horses, an eques-es-trian act, a performing seal, a troupe of dogs, and Fairy Bell, the smallest rider in the world with Fairy.'

'I 'specks my Mum and Dad will take me!'

'Hurray! Hurray! I *know* my Dad will take me.'

Sam didn't stop for more.

'I *know* my Brock the Badger will take me,' said he to himself as he galloped over the fields. He ran full-tilt into the Fox and fell backward with the shock.

'Look where you are going,' said the Fox crossly, and he gave Sam a sharp cuff on his head.

'Very sorry,' said Sam. 'I was taking some important news home.'

'And what is that?' asked the Fox curiously.

'A Circus is coming. A Circus with performing dogs and horses and – and – C for Cabbages,' said Sam hurriedly.

'Indeed. Which night?' asked the Fox.

'Saturday, down in Hemlock Meadow.'

'Ah!' said the Fox. 'Ah! Farmer Greensleeves will doubtless go, and the hen-place perhaps – perhaps –'

Then he remembered Sam was listening.

'Yes. What about it?' asked Sam.

'Nothing, only that the hen-place will be locked as usual,' remarked the Fox casually, but Sam was sure that wasn't what he had intended to say.

Sam went on his way, running to tell Brock, saying it to himself. 'C for Cabbages. I for Icicle –' The family was curled up asleep on the rugs and Brock was dozing in his chair when Sam bounded in at the door.

'Brock! Ann! Tom! and Bill! All of you!' he cried, and the little pigs rubbed their eyes and yawned. Here was Sam excited, busy and talkative when they all wanted to sleep.

'There's a Circus coming to Hemlock Meadow!'

'A Circus? What's that? Why did you wake us?' asked the brothers lazily.

'A Circus?' cried Brock, sitting up wide awake.

'I saw the picture of it on the old door in Hedgesparrow Lane. There was a red C for Cabbage and a blue I for Icicle, and a white R for Rain, and another Cabbage, and a Unicorn and a – a Sam Pig and Sally the Mare.'

'Yes, Circus, Sam. Very good indeed,' said Brock, smiling at the panting, puffing little pigling.

'And a picture of a pretty little girl on a pony, and a crown on her hair, like Ann at the Maypole, and dogs with frills, and – oh Brock, such a lot of things,' said Sam.

'I must go and see this picture on our door,' said Brock. 'The old auction bill has been there for many months, and I'm glad they've changed it. I must find out about this Circus.'

'Can we go? Can we go to the Circus?' asked all the little pigs at once.

'We'll see,' said Brock, quietly puffing at his pipe. All around the countryside, in many a village and hamlet, children were asking the same question. Mary and Dick Greensleeves were asking their father, 'Can we go? Can we go?' and the blacksmith's daughter was asking her father and the grocer's little boys were asking their father, and the miller's boy was asking the miller, and the parents were replying, 'We'll see,' just like old Brock the Badger.

It seemed as though the family of little pigs couldn't go to the Circus, for when Brock looked in the money-box, there was one penny, very old and battered, and a crooked sixpence with a hole bored in it, and a medal that Sam had picked up. The box hadn't been touched for a long time, and a spider had put a fine web all over it.

'How I wish I had kept a bit of that hundred pounds reward for finding the treasure,' said Sam.

'Perhaps we could walk in without paying,' suggested Ann brightly. 'We went to the Flower Show and nobody stopped us.'

'They might think we were performing pigs,' said Bill.

'I shall go and hunt for a penny in the lanes,' said Sam. 'I'm a good spier, and sometimes there's a penny lost by somebody on the way to market.'

'You won't find enough money to take you to the Circus,' warned Brock. 'I'm afraid we must be content with looking at the outside and listening to the music from a distance.'

Sam Pig hunted and peeped in the flowery hedge bottom where sometimes a penny falls, but all he found was a dirty old half-penny, lost by a tramp a year ago. He washed it clean and put it in his pocket.

'If only they'd take Pig-money,' said Sam aloud. 'If only they'd take Penny-cress, and Penny-royal, and Penny-wort, then we could all go.'

'They won't, Sam,' said a throstle in the hedge. 'They like silver and copper that nobody can eat.'

At the farm the children were excited with the news of the Circus, and the rumours of its loveliness. They talked of it from morning till night. They were all going, except old Adam, who was staying to keep house while they were away. Even Mollie the dairymaid was invited by her young man.

Sally the Mare talked to Sam Pig about it. 'All of us, on Saturday night,' said she proudly.

Sam looked wistfully at Sally.

'I wish we were going. I do want to see a Circus. You are a lucky mare, Sally.'

'I'm not going *inside* the Circus,' said Sally, opening wide her eyes and shaking her head at the impetuous little pig. 'Nay, Sam lad, they don't let carthorses go *inside* the Circus tent. I shall wait at the Blue Boar, and have a chat with the horses in the stable there. I'm not going inside the show. Life's enough of a Circus without that, what with ducks on their heads in ponds, and that young colt galloping wild in the fields, and the cows pushing first to be milked, and hens chattering all day, not counting the antics of the pigs. Life's enough of a Circus for me.'

Sam sighed and kicked a stone with his toe.

'All the same, I want to go,' said he to the ground.

'Why don't you?' asked Sally.

'Because it costs money, and our money-box is nearly empty,' said Sam simply. 'That's why.'

'I'm certain sure Farmer Greensleeves would pay for you,' said Sally. 'He got some money out of the bank only yesterday. You're only little ones, you could sit low down.'

'Do you really think he would?' asked Sam.

'I bet he would,' said Sally, nodding her great head. 'He was saying to the Missis how well you gathered the stones from the fields. Much better than the miller's boy. He said he would like to do something for you, give you a bag of apples or cabbages. I should write to him, Sam. You do that, Sam.'

'I can't write a letter,' said Sam.

'Not write a letter? Why, I thought you were a scholar! I thought you'd been to school!' Sally nearly stepped on Sam, she was so much astonished.

'Only for one day, Sally.'

'And you didn't learn to write letters? No Reading and Writing and Sums? No French and Jogfy and t'other things?'

336

'No, Sally,' said Sam in a very little voice.

'Why, Sam Pig, I'm ashamed of you,' said Sally.

Sam's ears drooped, and he bent his head to hide a tear.

'I didn't learn nuffin 'scept A for – for Apple and then Brock said it was A for Ann.'

'Well, well,' said Sally, staring solemnly at the sad little pig. 'Well, write that, Sam. Write A for Ann.'

Sam went away and he began to write letters to Farmer Greensleeves. They were all the same. They lay on paths, in the grass, by walls, on doors, under gates, and wherever Sam could get room for his crooked little letters.

He picked up sticks and framed them into letters as Brock had showed him.

'C for Cabbage,' said he, and he made the letter C in the dust of the farmyard early in the morning when everyone was asleep.

'I for Icicle,' said he, and he added that nice easy letter.

'R for Rain,' said Sam, and he had a fine struggle with that awkward letter.

'C for another Cabbage,' said Sam, and he put a second curved C on the ground next to the R.

'U for Unicorn,' said Sam, and he twisted a slip of willow into a letter U.

'S for Sam and Sally,' cried Sam triumphantly, as he curled and bent the snakelike letter S.

He stood upright and regarded his work. CIRCUS was written in fine strong sticks, of willow and hazel, clear for anyone to read, if the cows didn't walk upon it.

Sam strutted off, very proud, and then he began again in another place. So he went on, writing his solitary word, sending his message with sticks and stones, and moss and seeds. He made it with dandelions and daisies, with nut leaves and snail shells. He wrote it with green rushes, and yellow straw and sweet hay. He used a chalky stone and made the crooked word on the barn door. He even wrote CIRCUS at the front door of the farm using white pebbles on the doorsill. For hours he worked, at dawn and after dusk, and the word CIRCUS was

planted everywhere about the farmhouse and
cart roads.

Farmer Greensleeves scratched his head when
he saw these queer twisted letters sprinkled over
the ground.

'Who's been writing Circus all over the
place?' he asked. 'Who's been putting sticks
and stones in a litter everywhere? It's main bad
writing, whoever did it. Must be somebody
playing a trick. What does it mean, this Circus
in the yard and down the lane?'

Nobody knew, and when little Dick and

Mary Greensleeves came running to say they had found the mysterious word by the pig-cote and in the cowhouse, they were quite puzzled.

They kept watch, and in the early dawn just before milking time, Farmer Greensleeves saw little Sam Pig kneeling in the stackyard laboriously making his crooked word with bits of rope.

'Sam Pig? What's to do? What's all this about Circus?' asked the farmer.

Sam leapt to his feet, startled at the voice.

'Please, Master, I did it, Master,' he stammered.

'Do you want to go to the Circus, Sam? Is that it?' asked Farmer Greensleeves kindly.

Sam nodded his head violently, not daring to speak.

'Well, I'll take you, Sam.'

'Oh, thank you, Master! Thank you! And Bill and Tom and Ann and Brock the Badger?'

'Yes, the whole caboodle of you. We are going and you shall go too. I've never taken a menagerie to a Circus, but I'll do it. You'll have to walk there, but I'll pay for you and see you through the turnstile, unless they won't admit you.'

'Oh, Master!' said Sam, smiling with an angelic smile.

'And mind you dress yourselves neat and tidy. I don't want to have folk talking,' added the Farmer. 'You meet me outside the Circus, at six o'clock. You'll see us all coming in.'

'Yes, Master, and you'll see us too,' said Sam gleefully.

'I bet I shall,' said the Farmer softly, and he went indoors to break the news to his wife.

'The whole caboodle of them,' said he again. 'The whole truck-load.'

Then he popped his head outside the kitchen door.

'Sam! No more writing Circus! I've seen that word enough for a lifetime,' said he, shaking his fist.

Sam grinned and ran into the stable to whisper to Sally.

'Sally! We're going. He's taking us. Oh, Sally!'

'I'm proud of you, Sam,' said Sally. 'You are

a scholar after all. You did learn something at school.'

Sam went home, turning cartwheels, swinging on gates, cheering and shouting till he had roused the woodland and scared the rabbits and annoyed the Fox, who was waiting to ambush them.

'Sam Pig, you are a foolish young pigling,' said he.

'Oh, Master Fox! I am a scholar, I am,' said Sam.

The family was filled with joy when Sam brought the good news, and Brock patted Sam's head.

'We must all behave well, and be a credit to the farm. Never before has this family gone like royalty to a show,' said Brock. 'We've always had to creep through back doors and here we are going like kings and a queen.'

The next day was Saturday and most of the time was spent in getting clean and getting dirty and starting all over again. Sam's trousers had been washed the night before by Sister Ann. The pattern of checks in red and blue came clear again when the dirt of a hundred days rolling in the mud was scrubbed away. They hung on the line to dry and Sam lay in bed waiting for them. Little Ann washed her own short skirt, and Brock brushed his coat and trousers. He found new feathers for hats and flowers for button-holes, and handkerchiefs for pockets. He cut good smooth hazel sticks for the little pigs to carry like all good country folk.

They had a big tea, and then it was time to start. Brock wore his silver watch, and Ann had her walnut-shell locket dangling round her slim neck.

'No falling in ditches, Sam, no chasing butterflies or fishing for trout, or climbing trees,' said Brock.

They locked the house and hid the key under the stone. Then off they went, chattering softly, squealing with tiny squeaks of glee, whistling and calling to the throstles and blackbirds and the proud cock pheasant, telling them where they were going.

Suddenly Sam stopped.

'Brock! I must go to the farm. I believe the

Fox is going to rob the hen-roost tonight. I must warn them,' said he.

'All right. We'll wait here, and you can nip across the fields,' said Brock.

Sam raced under the hedges and over the ditches, back to the farm. He panted into the farmyard, and there was the cart all ready with the farmer and the children in their Sunday best, and Sally all decked out with her horse-brasses, and the best whip with a blue ribbon tied on it.

'Come along, wife,' called the farmer. 'It's time we started.' Then he saw little Sam, all bedraggled and tousled, puffing at the gate.

'Hallo? What's this? Aren't you going to the Circus?' he asked.

'Please, Master, have you 'membered to double lock the hen-place?' asked Sam.

'I haven't,' cried the farmer, slapping his hand on his pocket. 'I forgot.'

'Fox will be about tonight,' whispered Sam.

'Thank ye kindly, Sam Pig,' said the farmer, and he got down from his seat and went to the hen-place.

Sam was starting off again, when the farmer called him back.

'I'll give you a lift part way till you catch up with the others,' he offered.

Mrs Greensleeves came out, dressed in her Sunday coat and skirt, and her Sunday hat. She was rather surprised when she saw Sam Pig and she gave a sigh.

'Sam's coming with us,' said Farmer Greensleeves. 'He can ride at the back with the childer.'

So away they went, and the two little children made room for Sam Pig at the back of the cart. When they reached the cross-road, Sam leapt down.

'We shall be there to meet you,' said he.

'You'll go the short cut over the hills, Sam, but I must drive round the valleys. You'll be first I reckon,' said the farmer.

Sam washed in the stream, and Brock brushed him with a handful of gorse, and Ann rubbed the spots of mud from his trousers. When the little pig was respectable again they went on their way over the hills, through the woods and high places, but far below they could see the white winding road running in and out of the folds of the green hills. Then they saw a glow of lights in the valley, and a cloud of smoke. They could hear the sound of music, and drums, and cries of a happy crowd of people.

'I'm glad we are meeting the farmer,' said Ann. 'I should be frightened to go there all alone.'

They dropped over the crest of the hill and ran down the green grassy slopes to the river. In Hemlock Meadow stood a great white tent, with a flag waving on the top, and many caravans and booths around it.

Crowds of people were walking about, falling over the tent pegs, staring at the caravans, gazing at the horses tethered in the field, watching the men carry water from the river for the beasts. The family of little pigs went quietly among them, not speaking a word, keeping very close to Brock, who looked like a little old countryman as he smoked his pipe. They were all very much excited with the smells of strange animals, the sounds of foreign voices, and the bewildering sights. Dogs barked and horses whinnied, and clowns looked out of tent door-ways. They got glimpses of gilded saddles and white-powdered faces, of clowns and beautiful piebald ponies. The band played inside the great tent, and a fine gentleman shouted at the entrance, asking the people to come in. A lady blazing with jewels took the money as the crowd slowly wended its way through the sacking corridor.

The little family stood on one side, trying not to be swept along with the others.

'Seems as if some of the Circus has escaped,' said a woman, pointing to Sam Pig.

'Performing pigs, they is,' said another.

'Put out here for advertisement,' said a third, and she gave Sam a poke with her umbrella.

There was a bustle and commotion, and stout Farmer Greensleeves pushed his way through with Mrs Greensleeves and the children.

'Here we are, Master,' squeaked Sam.

'Come along. Follow me and the Missis, next

to us, with the children last. Dick and Mary, you go after this lot,' said the farmer, hurriedly collecting them in a bunch.

They joined in the procession, and squeezed together very close, trying to make themselves as small as possible.

'Two half-crowns and two at half-price for the children and five seats at threepence for – for – for the rest of us,' said the farmer, taking his money-bag out of his pocket.

The jewelled woman peered over to see who was passing so low down, for the little pigs were nearly out of sight.

'Dwarfs,' she muttered. 'Midgets,' said she. 'Midgets, threepence each.'

'That's right,' said the farmer. 'Midgets threepence each.'

So they all walked into the Great Top, which is the Circus tent. The little family parted from the farmer, who went to the red baize-covered seats. The four little pigs and old Brock sat on the front row far away from the others, on a low wooden plank, and with them sat the poorest children, and a few farm boys. It was really the best seat of all. They had a beautiful view of everything, and their short legs rested comfortably on the green turf. It is true that nobody bowed to them, and the ring-master was facing the other way, but that made it all the better.

They saw the blacked feet of the sparkling piebald ponies, and they could nearly touch the scarlet bridles and gold tassels. The horses' hooves thundered close to them but they had no fear. The clowns took no notice of them, they were too busy telling their jokes to the rich people at the other side of the Circus, and so the four pigs could tell their own little jokes to a small pony who came close to them.

'Hallo,' said Sam, in a soft animal whisper. 'Would you like a lump of sugar?'

'Yes, please,' said the little pony, pushing its nose to Sam's pocket. Sam brought out a fistful of sugar and the pony feasted.

'Who are you?' asked the pony.

'Sam Pig and family, all come to the Circus,' whispered Sam.

'And I am Pepper the Pony,' said the small

pony, frisking and dancing on its hind legs to show Sam what it could do.

The ring-master saw there was something going on in that remote corner, and he cracked his whip. Away ran little Pepper, to gallop round the circle, and tell everyone that Sam Pig and family had come to the Circus.

After that every animal stopped near Sam and Brock for a word or two, for a grunt or a squeak of recognition.

Clowns tumbled about the ring, and the laughter of the four little pigs rang out, higher

than any other. Here was something they understood – rolling and playing and teasing. The clowns glanced towards these merry-makers, and one of them came up, and held out his pointed hat in mockery. Sam took it and put it on. Then he handed it back and the puzzled clown bowed to him.

'That's good,' said the people. 'They've got a pigling sitting down on the front row, trained to wear a hat.'

'See me afterwards,' muttered the clown to Sam.

'Behave yourself, Sam,' grumbled Brock. 'Don't shame Farmer Greensleeves. We haven't come here to see your tricks.'

Sam was abashed. He sat very still and quiet, but when a beautiful young girl with gold hair and a wreath of flowers came riding in, he sat up and smiled.

Round and round she went, bowing to the people and when she passed Sam she bowed to him too. Then she stood on the pony's back and danced lightly on one toe, while the animal galloped gently round the ring. The clown held out a paper hoop. Like a fairy she leapt through it, tearing the thin paper, and alighting on the broad back of her pony. Other clowns ran in with blue and yellow hoops of paper, and the girl danced through them all, leaving streamers like ribbons behind her. Sam leapt up in his seat. He grabbed a hoop from one of the clowns and held it high, dipping it as the pony ambled towards him.

'Jump,' he cried, and the girl leapt through it, but the pony was so startled by Sam's squeak, it swerved, and only just caught the girl in time.

Brock seized Sam by the trousers and hauled him back to the seat. Ann was jigging up and down, Tom and Bill were clapping like mad.

Farmer Greensleeves was looking at them. He shook his head and laughed.

'Those pigs are enjoying themselves and no mistake,' he observed to his wife.

Next came the jugglers, who threw up cups and balls and bottles and caught them. 'Brock is a far better juggler than these men,' thought Sam. Clever Brock who could outwit the

Leprechaun, and tease a fairy, was quicker with hand and eye than any human juggler.

A trapeze artist hung from the roof, and swung from ropes and ladders, as if he were in the branches of a high tree. He flung himself down and caught a swing half-way. Then came a dazzling display, as he leapt through the air, and swung by toes and fingers.

'He's like a squirrel,' said Ann Pig, staring up at the slim lithe man. 'I never knew man was like a squirrel before.'

'Man is like everything,' said Brock solemnly. 'He can swim in the sea and fly in the air. That's why he is dangerous.'

The little dogs came running in, excitedly barking, shaking the frills which decked their bodies, tossing their heads with the pointed hats. How the children laughed and shouted, and how the little pigs squeaked as they saw them! The dogs held up their paws and walked on their hind legs, they danced and smoked pipes and balanced on rolling barrels.

Sam bobbed about excitedly, and there was a sudden crack! He jigged again, and there was a crash! Down went the wooden form, and children and piglings and Brock all were thrown to the floor.

'Now see what you've done,' grumbled Bill Pig, scrambling out of the broken pieces. 'Upset us when we were comfortable.'

Everybody was laughing at the little legs in the air, and the squeals and cries as they rolled over together.

'Some people are enjoying themselves,' said a clown loudly. 'Doing circus tricks on their own.'

He ran up with a feather brush and tickled their faces, and set them in a row on the grass.

Next came a strange animal with no legs, who flip-flopped across the grass, and raised itself with flippers on a barrel.

'What is it?' asked Sam. 'Is it a kind of mermaid?'

'It's a seal,' whispered Brock the Badger.

The seal's sharp ears heard the animal voices and it turned its head towards the four little pigs.

'Solomon Seal, from the Ocean,' it said in a

deep gruff voice, and it barked huskily and grunted like an old sow.

The keeper gave it fish, and it clapped its flippers, and said, 'Solomon Seal. Solomon,' but of course only the pigs understood its language.

Then the man threw a ball to it, and it tossed it up, playing cleverly, balancing the ball on its nose. Sam Pig crept from his seat, and sidled away towards the seal. 'Catch,' barked the seal. Sam caught the ball and tossed it back, and then began a game of catch between Sam Pig and the seal.

The keeper stood aside, staring in astonishment, but Sam never dropped the ball, and the seal played with it and threw it to the little pig, and caught it again, so rapidly that everyone stood up and clapped.

Sam bowed and the seal clapped its flippers, and the keeper slapped Sam on the back.

'See me afterwards,' said he.

'Behave yourself,' muttered Brock crossly, as Sam ran back to his seat. 'You are disgracing the family by your bold antics, Sam. What will

Farmer Greensleeves say? What's the matter with you?'

Sam sat on the grass, half hidden, but his eyes were shining, and he was breathing quickly with the excitement of the ring.

So the Circus display went on, with new

delights every minute. Then came the great scene, when Fairy Bell, sitting in her little gold chariot, drove six diminutive grey ponies into the ring. The big black horses paced round with necks arched and legs lifted high, and among them went the tiny carriage with the small girl driving her team.

Everybody clapped, but Sam Pig, Ann Pig, Bill and Tom with Brock the Badger clapped their hands and stamped their hooves with excitement. Little Sam clapped so hard and so long that the clown who had been watching him suddenly picked him up and popped him in the carriage by Fairy Bell's side. Such a roar of cheering went up! Sam was frightened for a moment, and then he smiled and waved, and the little Fairy Bell smiled and bowed, too.

'Beauty and the Beast,' called the clown. 'Fairy Bell has now met Prince Charming.'

Everybody laughed, for Sam's ears stuck out, his hat was awry, and his little face was dirty. He didn't mind, and Fairy Bell was happy enough. Sometimes one of the dogs rode by her side, and now she had a small pigling for companion.

'Gee up! Gee up!' called Sam to the six little ponies, and when they heard Sam's voice they galloped quite fast. Brock the Badger sat in his seat, feeling rather anxious about Sam. He thought this was a kidnapping act and Sam was stolen away by the Circus people. He frowned and muttered to himself something about conceited piglings who have no sense, but Sam was smiling and waving and laughing in the little gold carriage, by the side of the charming young Fairy Bell.

When the ponies started for the doorway, Sam stood up.

'Goodbye, Fairy Bell,' said he, and he kissed the little girl and leapt down, just as if he were climbing from the farmer's cart. Then away he ran, padding very fast across the ring, and over the wooden border to the family.

The people cheered, again and again. It was all part of the fun of the Circus, and they thought it was the best act of all.

The band played God Save the King, Sam

stood up with everyone else, and Brock the Badger was stiff, with hair all bristled as if he would fight all the king's enemies. Sam could hear Brock growling and he thought the Badger was singing but in reality Brock was feeling very angry indeed.

'Do you want to join us? Circus life will suit you,' said the clown, running across and speaking to Sam. 'The manager will see you now. Follow me. You've got just the face for a Circus success.'

Sam hesitated a moment, for he could hear those growls like low thunder. Circus life would be beautiful, and he longed to ride again in the chariot with Fairy Bell, but there was Sally the Mare. He didn't want to leave Sally.

'Well,' said he slowly. 'It's very kind of you, and I should like to ride every night in Fairy Bell's little cart, and I can look after the ponies, but I know a big cart-horse called Sally the Mare, and if she can come too –'

'She can. Yes, she can,' said the clown.

Brock the Badger was growling like a lion. His deep growl grew louder, he snarled, and bared his teeth. The clown took a quick step backward, when he heard that horrid noise.

'Sam Pig! Come away home. No more nonsense,' said Brock in an angry voice, and he gave Sam a sharp nip. Sam didn't wait to say any more. Neither did the clown. He went back double-quick to the Circus folk to tell of the queer things he had seen and heard. Sam meekly followed the family out of the tent into the cold starlit night.

The fresh air brought him to his senses. They walked home across the hills, a little band wandering in the shadowed by-ways, unseen by any after their brief and exciting appearance in society. They chattered about the Circus all the way, but Sam was quiet. The others tried the tricks as they ran along the paths, they swung on the branch of an overhanging tree, and danced and galloped. They repeated the clown's jokes, and rolled over one another.

It wasn't till they reached home that Brock spoke to Sam.

'Why did you think of going with that clown?' asked Brock sternly.

'I thought it would be nice to be in a Circus,' faltered Sam. 'I should like to look after six ponies and Fairy Bell.'

'It isn't all riding in chariots, Sam. It's a hard life, and you are a lazy little fellow. Man's a hard task-master, little Sam. Besides, we can't do without our Sam Pig.'

'No,' whispered Sam. 'I won't go.'

For weeks the little pig family played at Circus. They made a tight-rope out of the washing-line, and tried to balance on it. They put frills round their necks and danced like the dogs. They skipped and pranced and turned somersaults, like the clowns. Sam even rode on Sally's back, and tried to leap through a hoop of twisted hazel that Ann Pig held out. Of course he caught his foot in it, and fell head-long, but he got up quickly and tried again.

'I sometimes wish I had gone, Sally,' confided Sam in the mare's ear. 'I might have been riding in a golden chariot now, by the side of the beautiful Fairy Bell.'

'And you might be scrubbing out an old caravan, and nobody caring a button about you,' said Sally. 'You be content and stay where you are wanted, Sam Pig. That Fox didn't get into the hen-roost. You stay here, Sam.'

'Yes,' said Sam meekly. 'Yes, Sally.'

Sam Pig Has a Bath

As soon as Sam awoke that morning he knew there was something doing. Bangs and clatters and scampering feet told him even if he hadn't heard a discussion about it the night before.

'Spring-cleaning time,' said Ann. 'Brock the Badger will be coming home after his long sleep in the woods, and we must get ready for him. I shall turn out his room tomorrow, and sweep away those great cobwebs in the rafters.'

'I shall do the white-washing,' said Tom quickly. 'I love white-washing, Ann. Sloshing the good lime about, and swishing the brush on the walls.'

'And I shall do the white-washing, too,' said Sam. 'It's my turn.'

'No, you're not big enough,' said Tom scornfully. 'You'd fall in the bucket and then we should have a white pig. No, Sam.'

'I shall clean out the pantry and kitchen and tidy the treacle tin and sugar crock and oatmeal barrel,' said Bill.

'I shall tidy the treacle tin and the sugar crock,' said Sam.

'Too late, Sam. You can scrub the floors,' said Bill. 'A low down job, for a small pigling.'

'I won't scrub floors,' sulked Sam.

Sam lay in bed listening to the riot of buckets and besoms. He liked spring-cleaning time, with its mat-beating, and its turnouts of treasures, and its dust and upset, but if there was no white-washing, then he would run away. No spring-cleaning, no white-washing.

He crept downstairs, and there was no hot breakfast on the table. The kitchen was in disorder, the table with its legs in the air. The white-wash bucket stood in the corner, and voices came from Brock's room. Swish! Swish! went the besom, and out flew a robin. Then a butterfly came fluttering from Brock's door, to

363

be followed by a blind bit-bat, dazed by the sunlight.

The cries and excitement grew, there was a clatter and out flew a large indignant owl.

'Brock let a part of his room to me. I'm a guest,' grumbled the owl, but it was no use saying anything. Tom and Bill and Ann were spring-cleaning.

Sam dived into the bread-mug and seized a loaf. He cut a slice of cheese and grabbed a few apples from the shelf. Then he stole out before anyone noticed him. As he scampered away he could hear their voices calling at his bedroom door.

'Sam! Sam! Get up and scrub the floors,' called Ann.

Ah! Sam's little feet pattered softly down the grassy path, he opened the gate, he waved his hand to anyone who might be looking, and away he went.

He walked with a gay lilting step across the woodlands, where the yellow-hammers were playing in the bushes, and the goldfinch swung on an old thistle head. A field-mouse spoke to him, and he stooped low to hear its words.

'Fine day for spring-cleaning,' it said.

'Pouff!' cried Sam.

He met a hedgehog hurrying back to its nest. It stopped when it saw Sam and waited for him.

'A nice spring-cleaning day,' it said.

'Piff!' snorted Sam.

The hedgehog looked surprised, and went on, with its little snout turned to right and to left as it sniffed at the sweet morning airs.

A red squirrel looked down from a tree. It scampered along a branch and darted down the smooth trunk to the ground. Then it raised its tiny paws and looked at Sam with beady eyes.

'A fine day for –' it began.

'Spring-cleaning?' snapped Sam.

'Spring-cleaning?' cried the squirrel. 'Oh no! Not for me! A fine day for paying visits, I was going to say.'

So Sam went on, through the woods, and there at the wood's edge waited the Fox.

'A fine day for spring-cleaning,' said the Fox, who knew everything.

'It isn't,' said Sam crossly.

'A fine day for spring-cleaning the hen-house and pig-cote, Sam,' it laughed and it lolloped off, like a red streak of fire.

'Everybody's crazy,' muttered Sam. 'Here we are, with the sun shining and the wind blowing and the primroses peeping out, and everybody thinks of work. I'll go and talk to the only sensible person I know, and that's Sally the Mare.'

Sally was in the field, pulling the great stone roller. It was heavy work, and she plodded steadily up and down the grass, making a pattern of dark green and light green, in lovely parallel lines. Sam sat on the gate and watched her, but Farmer Greensleeves had a busy look on his face, and Sam turned away.

He walked softly across the dew-spangled grass, with the scent of the white violets and pressed bruised grass and wet moss in his nostrils. He slipped through the half-open gate to the farmyard, and walked gingerly, peering about for strangers, towards the pig-cote. On the way he skirted the lawn of the farmhouse, and there, to his surprise, lay a carpet blooming with red roses and green leaves. Mollie was on her knees beating it with a carpet-beater, and old Adam was helping her. Mrs Greensleeves came to the door, with her dark hair wrapped up in a duster. Sam stared and backed away and went swiftly to the pig-cote.

There he found happiness and gaiety. The little farm pigs were talking so loudly they didn't hear Sam rattle the door. They gobbled their food, and pushed each other in the long pig trough, and squealed and quarrelled and

became friends again. Sam climbed up on the door ledge and looked down at them. Then he dropped a carrot among them.

'Goodness me! It's Sam Pig!' they cried, and they all ran to the door and held up their faces to him.

'Hello everybody! How are you this fine day?' asked Sam.

'Fine, Sam! We've just had a grand breakfast. Sharps and 'taters, and skinned milk, but we're still hungry. Have you brought anything else?'

'Well, I have,' said Sam, bringing the bread from his pocket. Regretfully he tossed it and the cheese and apples over the door and the little pigs fell upon the food with squeals of greedy hunger.

'Why is there such an upset at the farm?' asked Sam. 'Why is Mollie beating the carpet, and why are the chairs under the lilac tree?'

'It's spring-cleaning time,' laughed the little pigs.

'Oh dear!' cried Sam. 'I thought once that we were the only family who had spring-cleaning days. Well here I am, safe with you, for they won't white-wash the pig-cote, will they?'

'Yes, later on, but it will be when we are out in the orchard,' said the pigs.

'Hush! There's somebody coming,' whispered Sam. Footsteps came along the narrow paved path, and Sam jumped down from the door in alarm. The steps were coming nearer, heavy clumsy steps, not those of anyone whom Sam knew.

A stranger was there, a man with a face as black as night. He carried a big black sack on his back, and he staggered with the bulging bag heaved over his shoulders.

'Run,' cried the little pigs, who were peeping under the door. 'It's a black bogey-man. Run, or he'll catch you and put you in his bag.'

Sam didn't wait to hear any more; the sight of the man was enough for him. He ran in a great hurry, and, alas, there was nowhere to hide himself. He ran helter skelter round the little yard of the pig-cote, dodging behind the currant bushes and grindlestone. In the corner was a nice big tub, and Sam dashed for it. In a second he had scrambled up the sides and dropped into it.

'Lovely!' he muttered, as he sank into a fine cushion of soot, soft as velvet. He crouched low, but the footsteps came nearer, and the sack was emptied over him.

'Have you found the soot-barrel, Mr Sweep?' called Mrs Greensleeves from the back door. 'It's near the pig-cote.'

'Yes, Ma'am. You'll have a good supply for your garden when I've done.'

Sam curled up in a ball and waited. He was buried in the soot, but all the better for hiding.

'There's no place like a barrel of soot,' he hummed to himself, but the soot got in his nose so he had to stop his song.

The footsteps stamped about for a while, and then they went away. Sam waited, not daring to get out, and in a few minutes another bag of the soft velvety soot fell upon him.

'Just one more load,' muttered the sweep, and Sam waited. It was so warm and comfortable he nearly fell asleep. Then the third sackful was dropped upon him, the footsteps died away and all was quiet except for the distant beating of carpets and rattle of buckets.

'Sam Pig! Sam Pig! Are you there?' squeaked the small farm pigs. 'He's gone now, Sam.'

'I'm here,' said Sam very softly from the pile of soot. He tried to get out. Each time he fell to the bottom, and the soot curled over him like smoke and soaked into his skin as he paddled about in it, trying to make it hard.

'I can't get out. I'm stuck!' called Sam.

'We would help you if only somebody would open our door,' squeaked the little excitable pigs, and they kicked and scuffled, but nobody came. Sam would have been in the barrel of soot all day if Sally the Mare had not come home for tea.

She stood at the water-trough in the corner of the outer yard, supping the sweet spring water, raising her head and then lowering it as she drank.

'Sally, Sally, Sally,' called Sam. 'Sally, oh, Sally!'

'Who's that?' asked Sally, staring about her.

'It's Sam Pig, at the bottom of the soot-barrel,' said Sam.

Sally walked slowly across and pushed open the wicket-gate. She looked into the barrel in the corner, but she could see nothing of Sam. Everything was black as night in that deep barrel.

Sam waved a black fist and shuffled about.

'Push the barrel over, Sally,' he implored.

Sally gave the barrel a push with her foot, and a good kick. Over it went, and out of it rolled little Sam Pig.

'My goodness, Sam. You're coal-black!' cried Sally. 'You'll have to be scrubbed. Shall I dip you in the horse-trough?'

The little farm pigs had their eyes at the nicks of the door. They were laughing till their sides cracked at the sight of Sam.

'Oh, Sam! You'll never come white again, but never mind. You are just like our black cousin, and he's prize pig. He's considered very handsome.'

Sam trotted over to the horse-trough and leaned over to look at himself.

'I really am a black pig. I look quite nice, don't I?'

'You do indeed, Sam. Nobody will know you. You'd pass for a shadow in the night.'

'A little black goblin,' squealed the pigs with delight.

'Hallo,' cried Farmer Greensleeves, coming

down the path. 'What are you doing there, Sally? Who's upset the soot-barrel? Was it you, Sally? Whatever did you do that for?'

He didn't see the little black pig who sheered off and ran very fast among the tree shadows into the fields, and he led Sally away, grumbling at her clumsiness and her curiosity in looking at the soot-barrel.

'For an old mare, you've got the curiosity of a little child,' said he.

Sam scampered away, across the woods, to the garden path. He tiptoed up very quietly and tapped at the door, Rat-a-tat! Tat!

'Any rags and bones?' he called in a high little dusky voice.

Ann opened the door a crack and when she saw a strange black pig on the doorstep she gave a scream.

'Go away! Go away at once,' she cried, banging the door.

Sam rapped again, and unlatched the door.

'It's me, Ann,' he said, pushing his black head and ears round the corner.

'Go away at once! I shall call Brock the

Badger. He's on his way home. He'll send you packing, black pig!'

Sam laughed and laughed, and Ann recognized his gay laughter.

'Oh Sam! Is it really you?' she asked.

'Yes. It's me,' said Sam, and soot fell from him in a shower on the clean green rush rugs and scrubbed floor. His white teeth were shining in his black face, and his eyes twinkled.

'How did you get so black, Sam?' faltered Ann, staring wide-eyed at her young brother. 'We've just finished spring-cleaning the house.'

'I jumped into a barrel, Ann, and the sweep came along and emptied the farm soot over me, till I was buried entirely.'

'Hallo! Who's this black stranger?' cried Bill and Tom coming into the house. 'Who are you, sir, and why do you stand in our clean house? Who is he, Ann?'

'It's your brother Sam,' said Sam, pushing a dirty paw in Bill's face, and blacking his cheek.

'No, it isn't Sam. Sam's a pink pig – at

least comparatively pink. Out you go, young ruffian,' said Bill, who knew quite well it was Sam.

'Leave him alone, Bill. Don't tease him,' said Ann. 'Help me to get the bath ready.'

'Bath? Oh no! Don't make me have a bath, Sister Ann,' implored Sam.

'Bath!' echoed Bill. 'I had to scrub the floors for you, and now I shall have much pleasure in scrubbing you, young Sam.'

Then Brock the Badger came home, and when he saw Sam he took him by the scruff of the neck and carried him outside. He shook him and brushed him, but the soot wouldn't come off.

'The biggest bath ever known,' he commanded.

So the preparations for the biggest bath began.

Tom carried buckets of water from the spring and filled the kettles and pans. Bill Pig fetched the leather blow-bellows to blow up the fire. Brock the Badger carried the bath tub from the shed and put it on the hearth. Ann found towels and a piece of yellow soap that had lain on the top shelf for years, and a couple of scrubbing brushes they had used for the floors that day.

Sam sat looking at all this, filled with dismay. He felt that he was going to be baked and roasted and fried and boiled.

When the water was hot enough, Sam got into the bath, and everybody scrubbed him. Tom and Bill had the scrubbing brushes, and Brock used his own strong pad, while Ann squeezed water from the sponge over him. Soap suds lathered him, till he was covered with foam, but it was a black foam. He didn't come clean, and they emptied away the bath water and began all over again, with Sam groaning and protesting.

The steam curled up and swirled round the room in clouds. Soap got in Sam's eyes, so that they smarted. Every time he opened his mouth to say something, Bill pushed the soap suds there, and he had to be quiet.

Bill and Tom sang a little song and they scrubbed in time to it. This is how it went:

'Scrub, brothers, scrub,

Scrub little Sam,
Change him from a black sheep,
To a white lamb.'

'You can't change me to a white lamb,' spluttered Sam. 'I won't be a lamb.'

'Scrub, brothers, scrub,
Scrub a little pig,
Wash all his black hair
To a white wig,'

sang Bill and Tom, scrubbing with might and main.

A little patch of pink skin appeared, and gradually the soot was worn away.

'I'll never do it again,' vowed Sam to himself. 'Never have I been bathed so much! Five baths, one after another, and two scrubbing brushes, and Badger's paws, and Ann's sponge, all working at me at once. There won't be any of me left.'

'Are you there, Sam?' called Bill. 'Do I see my little pink brother coming out from under the black skin?'

'Yes, you do,' said Sam, 'and a savage brother, too!'

'The black has gone to his heart,' remarked Tom.

'Come, come,' said Badger. 'I believe he is clean. Now dry him and let him sit by the fire while we wash his trousers.'

Out of the bath crept a very small and a very pink pig. He was wrapped in the bath towel, and dried by the fire. Then he put a blanket over himself and sat on the floor, while Brock and Ann washed the poor plaid trousers. All that evening he had to wait till they were dry enough to put on.

'Of course I needn't have another bath for a whole year,' Sam boasted.

'We'll see,' said Brock. 'You've borne it very well, and I wonder there is any of you left. You are certainly thinner.'

'It all comes of running away and not helping with the spring-cleaning,' said Ann. 'So we've had to spring-clean you, Sam.'

'I'll make you a bowl of porridge, Sam,' said Tom kindly. 'Porridge with cream and sugar on the top. Now you are the pride of the family, the pink pearl of piglings.'

'The pink pearl of piglings,' echoed Ann and Bill Pig, clapping their hands.

'Thank you,' said Sam faintly.

Brock's Watch

One spring morning, when all the world was gay with flowers and growing grasses, Brock the Badger started to clean his silver watch. It was the old turnip watch, round and heavy, which used to be kept in the soup tureen in the farm kitchen. Farmer Greensleeves gave it to Sam Pig, and Sam gave it to his friend and guardian, Brock the Badger. That was long ago, and the watch had gone wonderfully well after Brock had oiled it and put a new hair-spring in it, made from one of Sally the Mare's own long black hairs.

However, an old watch won't go for ever, and one day it stopped. Even Brock's shaking wouldn't start it. So the Badger took it to pieces and laid all the little wheels on the table, while the family leaned over to look.

'Here's a wheel and there's a wheel, and lots and lots of tiny wheels,' said Bill Pig.

'It will take a clever person to put it together again,' said Ann.

'Like putting an egg back in its shell,' added Sam, 'but Brock can do it.'

'I suppose young Sam thinks he could easily mend a watch,' grunted Tom, pushing Sam aside as the small pig squeezed in the circle with his face near the wheels.

'I didn't say so, but perhaps I can,' muttered Sam, rather annoyed at being thrust out of the group round the wonderful collection of wheels.

He slipped out of doors for a few minutes and then returned, saying nothing.

'That'll teach 'em,' he thought.

'What day is it, Brock?' he asked, as he gazed fascinated at the glittering pile of wheels.

'It's Saturday,' replied Brock.

'I like Saturdays,' observed Sam, and he quite forgot his troubles. 'It's dumpling day at the farm and once I got a plateful. Oh-oo-oo! What a good taste!'

'Farmer Greensleeves goes to market on Saturdays, doesn't he, Sam?' asked Brock, glancing down at the small figure dodging under his arm.

'No, not this week,' said Sam eagerly. 'He's spreading mangold-wurzels for the sheep to eat and the lambs to nibble and me to nibble too. Sally the Mare will be drawing the cart, and I'm going to help.'

'Saturday, Sunday,' said Ann dreamily. 'On Sunday all good people go to church.'

'Not Sally the Mare. She has a holiday on Sundays. She stands in the fields and eats grass and listens to the church bells. Then she rolls on her back and kicks her heels. She does no work on Sundays, no work ever at all. It's her rest day.'

Sam stretched out a fist towards the wheels, but Tom gave him a cuff on his head.

'Now then, no touching, Sam,' said Tom sternly. 'These wheels mustn't be mixed up.'

Oh dear! It was a hard life to have a cross

brother! Just then there came a faint tap-tap at the door, and immediately Sam's spirits rose.

'Come in,' cried Brock. 'Come in.' Nobody entered.

'See who it is, Ann. I'm busy,' said he.

Ann ran to the door and opened it wide. Nobody was there, but a hare's foot was fastened to a string and it dangled against the door, tapping when the string was pulled. Sam grinned happily. The rapscallion of a rabbit he had bribed with a carrot had done the trick very neatly.

'It's a trick! Somebody's playing a joke on us,' cried Tom indignantly.

He ran out, followed by Bill and Ann. Then Brock went to the door and examined the furry paw which hung there. He sauntered away, after a suspicious glance at Sam, but Sam's head was bent and he seemed to know nothing about it.

Sam was left alone. He looked at the empty watch-case, and he remembered Tom's words. He began to put the wheels back.

'I can do this very well,' he thought. 'I'll give

old Brock a surprise. He'll know I'm a clever pigling. He will respect me. He'll say, "Sam, my lad, you are a bright Pigwiggin. You are far, far better than Tom and Bill. You are as clever as – as – Sally the Mare." '

Muttering to himself, Sam pushed the wheels together, fitting them as well as he could with shakings and pokings and grunts of excitement and exasperation.

'How did all these wheels ever get into the watch?' he whispered. 'They came out so they'll go in again, but, oh dear! They won't all go back. I *must* get them in somehow.'

He dropped the remaining wheels down the crannies, and he shook all together till they rattled.

'There! They're all inside and yet the watch won't go. It won't tick.'

He banged the watch and tapped on it and shook it once more. Then he climbed to the shelf where Brock kept his bottles of magic oil and ointments. This was absolutely forbidden, but Sam was desperately anxious to start the watch. He found some green oil in a bottle, and he dropped a few spots of it on the jumble of wheels. Instantly there was a movement among them; reluctantly, slowly, the watch began to tick as the wheels revolved.

Sam smiled broadly. 'Good old watch,' said he.

It went on ticking, faster, faster, then madly, wildly, and the hands moved round.

Sam climbed back to the shelf with Brock's bottle. He squinted over his shoulder, for something strange was going on below. The watch was singing in a small voice. It was sprouting a pair of tiny silver wings of little feathers on its sides. It was moving about the table all by itself, warbling in a tick-tock voice.

> *'Ticketty tick, Ticketty tick,*
> *Today is going, tomorrow's come quick.'*

sang the watch.

'Good heavens! What's the matter?' cried Sam, hastily scrambling down and running to the table.

The watch ambled across; it hesitated a moment on the brink.

It fluttered its small feathers, and flew down like a fledgling to the floor.

'Hey there! Stop a minute!' called Sam, trying to catch it, but it swung sideways out of his grasp. It dodged and it flicked its new wings, and then it went through the open door. It was too heavy to rise in the air, but the wings certainly helped it along and gave it speed. They beat and fluttered like the wings of a bird, and the watch swayed across the grass into the bushes.

'Now you've gone and done it,' said a voice, as Sam dashed into the garden. 'See what happens when you try to be too clever.'

Who can have spoken? Was it the wind in the apple tree or a mouse in the wall, or a spider dropping down on her thread? Everything was deeply interested in the flight of the watch and every insect, leaf, flower and bird opened wide its eyes.

Sam hadn't time to find out more, for the three pigs came hurrying back, followed by Brock the Badger.

'You'll catch it, Sam,' cried Tom, holding

his protesting little brother by the ear.

'You've led us a dance,' said Bill. 'Brock will be angry with you.'

'What have I done now?' asked Sam, bewildered by all the happenings.

'You know all about that knocking on the door,' said Ann.

'Me? Me?' cried Sam. What was a knocking on the door compared with a runaway watch, lost in the thicket?

'Yes, you,' growled Bill. 'Don't look so innocent. You bribed that rabbit to pull the string. We caught him and he confessed.'

'It was only April fooling,' explained Sam. 'I made April fools of you all. That's nothing.'

Brock walked into the house, and he patted Sam's shoulder as he passed.

'It was neatly done, Sam,' said he. 'That hare's foot was well-balanced and truly hung on the door. You took us all in.'

Sam waited breathlessly while Brock looked round the room. The badger turned slowly and stared at the empty table.

'Where's my watch, Sam?' he asked. 'I left it

all ready with the wheels laid out, and now it has gone. Where have you put it?'

'Oh Brock, I mended it for you,' began Sam.

'Yes? Yes?'

'And then – it just went away. It flew, Brock. It got a pair of wings, not very strong ones, and away it flew, Brock,' stammered Sam.

The little pigs gasped with horror at Sam's badness in even touching Brock's watch, but the old badger merely frowned.

'When you mended it, Sam, did you think I should say "Sam, you're a clever-my-lad"?' he asked quietly.

'Yes, Brock,' murmured Sam, hanging his head.

Brock glanced up at the shelf where his magic oil was kept, with the herbs and the wind's whistle and all.

'Did you use my green oil?' he asked.

'Yes, I did, Brock,' Sam whispered in a faint voice.

Ann's eyes were open very wide, and Tom and Bill hissed and snorted with annoyance at their young brother's impudence. Brock's things were never to be touched, but Sam had broken the rule. Surely there would be a dreadful punishment.

'He'll be packed off, and sent away from home for good,' said Bill to Tom.

'Serve him right,' said Tom to Bill.

'Please don't be cross with him, Brock,' pleaded Ann. 'I know he didn't mean any harm.'

Brock continued to regard Sam very solemnly, but Ann thought she saw a twinkle in his eye as he spoke.

'Them as use magic get their fingers cut. You are too clever, Sam. Now find the watch.'

So Sam hurried out, down the garden path to the thicket of hazel and blackthorn. He searched among the prickly branches and down in the bright petals of the yellow celandines, the primroses and violets that starred the grass. A glitter of silver came from the leaves, and the watch flicked its short wings and wobbled unsteadily away from its hiding-place, to the rougher pasture beyond.

'Stop! Stop! Badger's watch, you must not

fly away. Brock wants you,' shouted Sam.

'It's no use asking a watch to stop when you've set it going,' jeered Tom, leaning over the garden wall.

'It's running across the fields,' cried Bill. 'It's going back to the farm, Sam. Hurry after it.'

Sam ran fast, but the watch went faster, and the space between them increased.

The round, fat watch was half-flying, half-rolling through the blades of grass, disappearing from sight in the hollows, then shining like a lamp as the sun caught its polished back. It flew to the right and then to the left, it hovered like a butterfly, but Sam couldn't get near it. Sam scampered and dodged but the watch leapt and darted well ahead. One field was crossed and then another, and in the distance Sam saw some friends of his.

Farmer Greensleeves was carting mangold-wurzels for the sheep and Sally the Mare was in the shafts of the cart, standing very quietly with her head bent, thinking deeply of the scents and the fields she knew.

'Hello! Hello! Stop it! Stop the watch!' called

Sam, galloping along the path, and Sally slowly raised her head and sighed. The farmer didn't hear the high squeak of little Sam Pig. He was tossing the great pinky-orange mangolds down to the ground and the sheep were crowding round. The lambs bleated, the sheep answered 'Maa-aa-aa', and Sam's voice was lost in the babel of cries.

Through this bevy of animals rolled the silver watch, ticking furiously, and after it came Sam.

'Well, Sam? You seem to be in a hurry. What's the matter?' asked Farmer Greensleeves, as Sam came panting up to the cart. 'Do you want a mangold? Are you hungry, Sam, are you clemmed?'

Sally the Mare gave a little whinny, and she flicked her ears at Sam to say she couldn't go with him, she was busy.

'What's to-do, Sam?' asked Sally.

'It's your watch, Farmer Greensleeves, the watch you gave me, and I gave it to Brock the Badger,' puffed Sam.

'My old watch, as belonged to my grand-

father? What's it been doing? Is it going, Sam?' laughed the farmer.

'It's going too fast, Master. It's running away, it is. It won't stop ever at all,' said Sam, indignantly pointing to the gleam of silver moving across the field.

The farmer stared at Sam and then followed his gaze.

'I never knowed it to go at all, Sam. It was always stopped when I had it, on the dresser in the soup tureen. It's never gone in my lifetime, but it was a good watch in my father's time I believe.'

'I must run after it, Master,' said Sam. 'I want to catch it for Brock. Goodbye, Master. I'll come back and help you when I've got it.'

Sam waved his hand to the farmer and Sally, and he darted after the watch. Every tree shook its branches, every flower nodded its head as the silver watch danced along the way. Even the stones in the road glittered afresh and moved aside lest they should scratch it, and the birds sang very sweetly as if calling to the world to see the runaway watch.

But Farmer Greensleeves suddenly frowned, and scratched his head in amazement. He could hear the church bells ringing, and there he was in his weekday clothes, carting mangolds. There was a Sunday feeling in the air. All work had stopped. Sally the Mare had the same feeling. She set off towards the farm, but he called her back.

'Whoa, Sally! Here am I on a Sunday,' said he. 'I ought to be going to church, and I'm in my workday clothes in the field. The Missis will be vexed with me. Whatever have I been thinking of to mistake the day?'

Then Sam Pig came running back to him in a great state of unhappiness.

'It's gone,' said Sam. 'It flew very fast and I lost sight of it. I can't find it. It disappeared in the wood near the farm all among the bushes and nettles.'

'That's a pity, Sam. It was a good watch,' said Farmer Greensleeves, still puzzled, for he could see his neighbours going to church in the distance, and the choir-boys standing in their surplices at the church door and an old lady in her Sunday best with her prayer book in her hand, going up the churchyard.

'Yes, we liked it, all of us,' said Sam. 'Brock wore it on Sundays in his coat pocket. He showed us the works and we listened to the tick. Now it's ticking in a queer way, saying something about today going and tomorrow coming.'

'Sam, what day do you make it?' asked the farmer.

'It's Saturday. No, it feels like Sunday. It must be Sunday,' said Sam slowly.

'That's what I think, Sam,' agreed the farmer.

'It *is* Sunday,' remarked Sally the Mare. 'I don't work on Sundays. I'm going home.'

'Now, Sally. Steady, my lass,' interrupted the farmer, as Sally began to move away.

'It was Saturday a short time ago, but I think it's Sunday now,' said Sam. 'It has something to do with the watch. It sang – now I remember, it sang,

> *'Ticketty tick. Ticketty tick.*
> *Today is going, tomorrow's come quick.'*

'If that's the case, it is Sunday now and the church bells are ringing and parson's got his sermon ready and the Sunday dinner's cooking. Come back with me, Sam, and have a bite and we'll talk it over with the Missis.'

'I'll find the watch for you, Sam, if it's anywhere about here. I'll walk over the fields and look for it. Never you mind, Sam,' said Sally.

'Oh, thank you, Sally,' cried Sam gratefully. 'I expect you will see it caught in the bushes, poor thing.'

They went back to the farmhouse, and Farmer Greensleeves turned Sally out to the fields for her Sunday treat and her rest.

Sam dawdled about the farmyard, glancing now and then at the door of the house. He was not sure what Mrs Greensleeves would say when she saw him. She was not partial to a pig sitting in the same room with the family.

When the gate was shut and Sally was frisking in the meadow grass, the farmer returned and beckoned to Sam.

'Come along in, Sam Pig. You're welcome, surely,' said he.

'You're not bringing that pigling indoors, are you?' cried Mrs Greensleeves, when Sam stepped humbly over the doorsill with his hat in his hand. 'I'm quite upset this morning. I went and forgot it was Sunday, and here I am, in my everyday clothes, and church bells stopped ringing and sermon half done by now I expect, and psalms all sung without me.'

'We've both forgotten the day, it seems,' said the farmer. 'Don't take on, my dear. Sam Pig thinks it's on account of his runaway watch making time fly too fast.'

'Sam Pig? What has he to do with it? But I wouldn't be surprised at anything if he is mixed up in it,' said Mrs Greensleeves rather crossly.

Sam hung his head in shame, but he couldn't feel sorry, for he was too happy. It was bliss indeed to be invited to the farm kitchen for dinner.

Mollie the dairymaid set a stool by the kitchen fire on the sanded hearth.

'Sit right here, young Sam,' said she kindly. 'We'll give you your dinner to yourself.'

'There's no Sunday dinner ready,' said Mrs

Greensleeves. 'There's only Scotch broth today. It's very good broth, with plenty of turnips and carrots and potatoes in it, and barley as well, but this muddle about Sunday has put everything wrong.'

'I love Scotch broth,' murmured Sam. 'Sister Ann makes it for us, and she puts in nettles and dandelions and fat little snails.'

'Stop talking about snails, Sam Pig,' cried Mrs Greensleeves.

'Yes, Mrs Greensleeves,' said Sam politely. 'Sister Ann puts nice fat little caterpillars in it as well.'

'I'll play a hymn tune to you, Sam, a Sunday tune,' interrupted the farmer, reaching for his flute. 'It's the best I can do.'

So he played a happy little hymn tune and Sam sat listening with a blissful expression on his fat round face. Mrs Greensleeves set the table and Mollie warmed the soup plates and dishes, and the children came in to stand staring at Sam.

Then the big soup tureen was carried in with the steaming hot Scotch broth, which was poured into it from an enormous black sauce-pan. The family gathered round the table and Mr Greensleeves said grace.

'Ticketty tick. Ticketty tick!' came a tiny voice from the soup tureen and Sam Pig sprang to his feet.

'Master! Master!' he cried.

'Sit down, Sam Pig,' said Mrs Greensleeves sternly. 'If you are invited to dinner with us, you must learn to be quiet. Little pigs must be seen and not heard.'

So Sam sat down again, his eyes wide and his breath going excitedly.

'What's the matter, Sam?' asked Farmer Greensleeves in a loud whisper.

'Master, I can hear something,' began Sam, but Mrs Greensleeves shook her head at him.

'Not a word, Sam, or out you go. No talking at meal times.'

She ladled out the boiling soup and Sam Pig listened to the little voice talking. Nobody else seemed to hear it, but to Sam it was clear as a bell.

'Ticketty tock. Ticketty tock.
I'm too hot. I'm too hot,'

protested the familiar voice of the turnip-shaped watch.

When all had had their share, Sam Pig's little bowl was filled.

'This is yours, Sam,' said Mrs Greensleeves. 'You've been a good pigling on the whole and here's a nice helping. I'm sorry I spoke so sharply to you.'

Sam smiled angelically and lapped up his soup. There in the bottom of the bowl lay the silver watch, half drowned. He held it up in silence, and they all cried out.

'Well I never!' said Mrs Greensleeves. 'Fancy finding a watch in the soup!'

'It's the old ticker I gave to Sam once, and he lost it this morning, or yesterday morning, or tomorrow morning,' explained the farmer.

'It has found its way home,' said Sam proudly.

'Just like a cat or a dog,' added the farmer.

'I never noticed it when I poured the soup in

the tureen,' said Mrs Greensleeves, wiping the watch on a cloth. 'I was in such a fluster with Sunday coming all sudden-like, I emptied the soup very quickly.'

'It's got wings,' said Farmer Greensleeves, leaning over and taking the watch. 'Look, wings fastened to its sides.'

'They are to fly with,' said Sam softly. 'Brock will be glad it is found.'

'You put it in your trouser pocket, Sam, and keep it safe till you get home, or it may fly away again,' advised the farmer.

Sam put the silver watch deep in his pocket, and tied it with a piece of string. Then he waited for the spotted dick which Mollie brought into the room, all steaming on a dish.

He ate his large helping and then rose shyly.

'I must be going now. Thank you all very much,' said he. 'I must go home. Thank you for the nice dinner.'

'You know, Sam, I do believe it isn't Sunday after all,' said Farmer Greensleeves. 'It's Saturday now we've caught the watch. Poor old Sally will have to get back to work.'

'It *is* Saturday,' said Sam. 'The watch is ticking quite slowly now. I believe the hands are moving backward.'

'Best run home quickly, or it will be the day before yesterday,' laughed the farmer, and away Sam ran. He carried a basket of eggs from Mrs Greensleeves for Ann, and a mangold-wurzel from the cart for Tom.

Brock was delighted to see the watch again.

'I'll soon put it right,' said he, examining the case. 'See, the little wings are now engraved on the side, instead of waving and flying in the air. They are folded up, and it can't fly any more.'

'How pretty it is,' said Ann. 'It looks as if somebody had carved it with tiny feathers, like the wings of a cock-a-doodle-doo.'

Brock emptied out the wheels and fitted them back properly. He oiled the watch with one tiny drop of his precious oil and the watch began to tick. It ticked regularly and kept the right time. Brock compared it to the sun in the sky, and to the moon by night, and the planets wheeling up there, and the silver watch was always right. Neither too fast nor too slow, it ticked solemnly on, but sometimes it perhaps remembered its days of flying, for occasionally it flapped its engraved wings, and shook its tiny silver feathers, and crowed like a cock, and then it closed them again and went on with its serious work of keeping time.

The Hole in the Road

Winter was coming and the leaves were falling from the trees in drifts of gold and brown, and every one of the tumbling leaves carried a wish in its crinkled folds. There were thousands of wishes all dropping in the woods, smothering the ground in a tawny cloak. Sam Pig walked under the trees with his arms out, trying to catch a dancing leaf before it touched the earth. He leapt high and he stooped low, but the fluttering leaves slipped from his grasp. Every time he managed to hold one, he clutched it to his heart and made a wish. All his wishes were alike.

'I wish for a nice little house all to myself,

403

away from Tom and Bill and Ann, and even from Brock the Badger,' said he, as he caught a beech leaf, and then he added, 'but Brock can come and see me sometimes.'

'I wish for a dear little house with nobody in it, but Sally the Mare may look through the door,' said he, as his little fist closed on a yellow elm leaf.

'I want a little house where I can hide and go to sleep, with no washing up,' said he, as he grasped a gold oak leaf.

He caught so many leaves one day, he was sure his wish would come true, so when he left the wood he began to look for the house of his wishes.

First of all he hunted for a cottage with a thatched roof and white-washed walls and one room just big enough for Sam Pig. All the cottages he saw had people in them, with lots of furniture. Babies were crying and laughing in the gardens, and wheel-barrows were filled, and scrubbing brushes and brooms stood near the doors, and washing hung out in the orchards.

'Not that kind of house,' shuddered Sam Pig,

hurrying away.

He looked out for another kind of dwelling – a leafy one, with intertwined branches making a roof and a floor of grass, a door of oak and a tiny window – but there wasn't one at all.

The owl had a convenient house in a hollow tree, but the great bird stared down with a fierce expression when the pigling came tapping at the tree trunk.

'What do you want, Sam Pig?' he asked, fiercely snapping his beak.

'A house of my own,' answered Sam, who was startled to see anyone there.

'What's the matter with your own home, Sam? Aren't you happy?' asked the owl, blinking his large eyes.

'Not very, Mr Owl. They are all so busy. Tom makes me wash up and Bill makes me weed the garden, and Ann makes me wipe my feet on the mat. I want freedom.'

'Well, this is my house, and you must find freedom somewhere else,' said the owl abruptly, and he went back to the darkness of his room and fell asleep.

Sam tried to build a house of straw from the cornrick in the farmyard, but every time he put on the roof the wind came bustling round the corner.

'Puff! Puff!' went the wind with its fat cheeks swelling. It blew the house down and sent the straw flying.

Then Sam tried to make a house of brushwood, which he gathered in the hedgerows and copses. He got together a heap of sticks ready for the building and he made a rough little shanty in the corner of a field. Mollie the dairymaid came out to find firewood, and she was delighted when she saw it.

'Thank you, Sam Pig. Thank you for getting the kindling sticks for me. That was very thoughtful of you,' said she, as she picked up the firewood house and carried it off in a bundle to put on the kitchen fire.

Sam Pig did not like to disappoint her by telling her it was his private house she was taking. He liked Molly, so he kept his trouble to himself, but in time he got disheartened.

Even the little pigs in the pigsty at the farm had a nice cosy cottage with a yard and a garden, and he, Sam, had nowhere to call his own.

He began to think there was a mistake in the tale of the falling leaves. Perhaps they carried no wishes after all. Then, one night, he found a house, he tumbled into it, and there it was unoccupied and ready for him. It was a nice warm house with rosy lamps burning at the front door, and a soft cushion for a carpet. This is how he found it.

He was running along in the dusk, returning from the village, where he had been peering in the shop window. Evening was the best time to look in windows, for people didn't take so much notice of the queer little figure in plaid trousers and big hat when the shadows were out. He seemed to be part of them, as he slipped and glided among the bushes. He could gaze at the barley sugar and the humbugs, and imagine the sweet scent of them, and think of the joy of crunching their sugary hardness.

'If I had a penny, and of course I have not any,
I'd buy a little stick of lolly-pop,'

sang he in a thin squeak high as the bat's cry.

'I can't find a penny, indeed I have not any,
So I can't buy a lolly-lolly-pop,'

he squeaked.

Somebody stopped and stared at him. Somebody came near and touched his elbow. Sam Pig started with fright. It was the village policeman.

'I've seed you afore, now haven't I?' asked the policeman.

Sam didn't wait for any more. He ducked down and bolted between the blue trousers of the stout man. He ran swiftly along the road, past the solitary lamp flickering in the wind, and away down the dark lane. Then he saw some red lamps burning where men had been laying an electric cable to the Big House. The lamps glowed round a hole in the road, to warn away the carts and motors and late travellers.

'Dragon's eyes!' cried Sam in horror, starting

back, and then he laughed at himself.

'Silly Sam,' he scoffed. 'Them's lamps in front of somebody's house. I don't 'member a house here, but there must be one.'

He stepped softly up, but in a moment he fell over the edge and dropped to the bottom of the hole. He landed on a piece of sacking, comfortably placed there, all convenient for a pigling. He looked round the walls of rich brown earth, good-smelling of the clean soil, and he saw a pick-axe and a spade reared against the side of the house. By standing on the pick-axe he could peer over the top of the little house walls, to see the four red lamps glowing at the corners. He could even stretch out his hands and warm them.

'A nice little house all built for Sam Pig,' said he proudly. He drew the sacking over his head, crouched down at the bottom of the hole with his feet on the spade, and in a minute he fell fast asleep. His troubles were over, he had a house of his own.

Once in the night he awoke, but the lamps were burning and the house was safe, and the bed warm. Nobody drove down this lane in the night, there was no fear of discovery. Far away in the sky he could see his own favourite star, and Badger's moon, with a halo like a wide-brimmed hat around it, and Ann's little blue star.

'Everybody's star up there, to keep us from getting lonely,' he murmured softly. His thoughts flew to his brothers and sister in the house over the fields and across the woods.

'They are repenting of their crossness,' said he to himself. 'They are missing me tonight.'

He felt hungry, and he remembered he had had no supper. He climbed up the side of the hole and pattered softly back to the village. Every house was shut, every window was fastened. Sighing deeply, Sam walked away to the turnip field. Joe Scarecrow leaned sideways in the middle of the field, waiting to be taken indoors for the winter. He stared when Sam scrambled through the hedge.

Sam dug up a couple of turnips and put them under his arm.

'What are you doing, Sam Pig? I see you. I

see you,' called Joe, in his deep harsh voice.

'Hallo, Joe. Are you awake? I'm getting my supper,' said Sam.

'After midnight, Sam? You ought to be a-bed. Does the badger know you're out?'

'I've runned away, Joe. I'm living in a house of my own,' said Sam, puffing out his chest with importance. 'I've got a house down the road, with four red lanterns at the door.'

'Oh my goodness, Sam! You are a caution! I've a mind to see your house.' The scarecrow shook his straw arms and pulled at his foot to get it out of the earth.

'Well, come along with me. No birds will come tonight, and you can see for yourself how I am enjoying it.'

'Four red lamps,' murmured Joe, and out came his leg, and away he hopped with Sam Pig back to the hole in the road. Sam cooked a piece of turnip on one of the red lanterns, just to show how well it worked, and the scarecrow ate it. Then the scarecrow showed Sam how to catch the water that came trickling down the road.

Then Sam sat down on the sacking at the bottom of the hole, in his own little house, and he told Joe about the village shop and all the good things to be seen there – the besoms and hams, the clothes-pegs and tin whistles, the humbugs and barley rock.

Then the scarecrow told Sam all about a boggart he had seen one night wavering along in the moonlight, and Sam felt very grown up but rather uncomfortable.

So there they stayed, talking by the light of those four red lamps, and the stars began to fade in the sky, and Sam yawned and yawned, but still the scarecrow went on talking.

'As I was a-saying,' mumbled the scarecrow, 'I stood all quiet in our cornfield, and I heard a little shuffle and I heard a little scrunch, and what did I see, Sam Pig? What did I see, Sam Pig?'

There was no reply, only a snore from poor tired Sam, who had fallen asleep curled up on the sack.

'I'd best be going home,' said the scarecrow, and he heaved himself up, and climbed out of the hole without waking Sam. He strode down the lane, turning his head once to look at the four red lamps winking in the darkness.

'Good night, Sam. Good night. Sleep well,' he muttered, and he went back to the turnip field.

Sam didn't wake till morning, when the cloppetty-clop of hooves came along the road. Sally the Mare was taking the milk cart to the station. The wheels passed close to the hole, and Sam moved and sat up. Sally shied with sudden alarm when she saw the little figure of Sam deep in the ground.

'What's amiss, Sally?' called Farmer Greensleeves. 'Are you frightened at those lamps? Surely a good old mare like you knows that lamps can't hurt you!'

'It was Sam,' whinnied Sally, but the famer didn't hear or couldn't understand.

Sam leapt up and ran home for breakfast. He felt fresh and excited and very happy.

'Oh, Sam,' cried Ann Pig. 'Where have you been? I was so anxious about you, I cried, Sam. We've been up all night, waiting for you.'

413

'If Brock had been at home, he would have given you a belting,' said Tom sternly. 'You are a bad lad, Sam. Where have you been?'

'What do you mean by coming home in the morning and keeping us up all night?' asked Bill.

'Tom, Bill and Ann,' said Sam solemnly. 'Do you know where I've been and what I've found? I've got a little house all my own.'

'What do you mean? What kind of a house?' they asked.

'It has four walls and a carpet, and four lamps at the front door,' said Sam.

'Has it a roof?' asked Ann. 'A roof is very important.'

'The sky is the roof,' said Sam. 'It's a deep down house, in the earth, like Badger's castle where we've never been.'

'Oh, do take us, Sam,' begged Ann.

'All right,' said Sam forgivingly. 'I'll invite you all to come tonight when Man has gone away.'

'Oh, thank you, Sam. Thank you,' cried the little pigs, and they danced about the kitchen with joy, as Sam played a tune on the musical box.

> *'I've got a house,*
> *A cosy little hole,*
> *Down in the ground,*
> *Deep as a mole,'*

he chanted, and nobody was cross with him all that day.

He crept through the fields in the afternoon and peered through the hedge, just to make sure the house was still there. Men were digging, they were making more holes in the road. They were smoking real tobacco and laughing and drinking tea from blue cans and eating food from paper packets. Sam scampered home and told his family all about it. There were four holes in the road, enough for the family. Each of them would have a little snug house with red lamps at the door. The little pigs could hardly wait till night. They came out at dusk, and walked over the fields, laughing and whispering and dancing with glee. They looked through the hedge. A workman was lighting the lamps and putting them in place. They waited, and the man whistled a tune and settled the lamps and then got on his bicycle and departed.

The four little pigs squeezed through the hedge and explored the holes in the road.

Sam climbed down his own little hole. The pick-axe had gone, but the sack lay there, and, oh, wonderful, there was half a packet of bread-and-cheese sandwiches wrapped up in a piece of newspaper.

The rest of the little pigs scrambled into the hole, to share the sandwiches and to listen to Sam reading the news. They lifted down a red lamp, and baked some mushrooms over it. They puffed at a broken pipe they found thrown away, and they warmed their toes at the glowing flame. Then up came the scarecrow again, delighted to get an audience of four pigs to listen to his stories.

The moon shone down, the stars were in the sky, and the four little animals sat deep in the hole in the road with three lamps shining at the doorway and one lamp down below. The scarecrow perched himself on the edge of the hole and talked to them.

'Once upon a time,' began the scarecrow in a very scary voice, 'there was a boggart and it flapped its black wings and went "Whoo-oo-oo" in the deep dark night.'

'Oh dear, I'm frightened,' shivered little Ann Pig.

'Shall I stop?' asked the scarecrow.

'No, go on. We like being frightened when there's a nice red lamp,' said Sam, and he put his arm round Ann and kept her warm.

'Well, this boggart flipflopped down the lane one night and he met a witch riding on a broomstick,' said the scarecrow.

'Oh dear, I'm frightened,' said little Ann again.

'Shall I stop?' asked the scarecrow.

'No, go on,' they all cried.

' "Where are you going?" asked the boggart.

' "To find my supper," said the witch.

' "What do you have for supper?" asked the boggart.

' "Four fat little pigs," said the witch.'

'Oh,' wailed little Ann. 'I'm frightened.'

'Shall I go on?' asked the scarecrow.

'Yes, do,' they all cried. 'We like this tale.'

' "Then you won't get anything to eat," said the boggart, "for they are all as tough as leather." Then away flew the witch right up to the moon, and there she stayed.'

'That's a nice tale,' said Sam Pig. 'Please tell us another.'

'Yes, please tell us another, dear Joe Scarecrow,' added little Ann Pig. 'I liked that tale. I wasn't really frightened. I love sitting here in a hole in the road, with a red lamp burning and the moon up above.'

'Once upon a time,' began the scarecrow again, 'once upon a time there was a big giant. He came walking down the lane, going Sniff! Sniff! Sniff!'

'Oh dear,' cried little Ann, with a delicious shiver.

Then they all started, for they could hear footsteps coming down the lonely lane. The scarecrow put his hat on his head, snatched up his stick, and hobbled away as fast as he could go, right back to the field. The four little pigs tried to scramble out of the hole, but it was too late, they would be seen. Quickly they extinguished the lamp and lay very still. The remaining three lamps glowed warningly, to tell the traveller to keep away from the hole in the road.

But the footsteps came nearer.

'The boggart,' whispered Ann, clutching Sam's coat.

'The giant,' whispered Tom.

'The witch,' murmured Bill.

'The policeman,' said Sam.

It was indeed the village policeman. He walked heavily across the road and stared at the lamps.

'There ought to be four lamps guarding this hole,' he muttered. Then he caught sight of the four little pigs crouched in the shadow, and he flashed his little lamp into the hollow.

'Hallo! What's going on down here?' he asked.

'Please, sir – please, sir –' stammered Sam, gazing up at his round face from the bottom of the hole.

'You're fairly caught now,' said the policeman. 'Who are you?'

'Please, sir, Sam Pig, Tom Pig, Bill Pig, and Ann,' said Sam quickly, and the others grunted.

The policeman took out his notebook and sharpened his pencil, and the four little pigs trembled as they watched him, but Sam began to laugh, and the policeman stared again.

'Are you the friends of Farmer Greensleeves?' he asked.

'Yes, and friends of Sally the Mare,' said Sam.

'Was it you who found the silver from the Big House?' asked the policeman.

'Yes, hidden in a hollow tree,' said Sam.

The policeman put away his notebook and climbed down into the hole.

'I'll say nothing about the lamp, though you didn't ought to have moved it,' said he. 'I've got four children at home and they'll want to know about you. I'll report to them and not to the police-station.'

So Bill Pig gave him a taste of toasted mushroom, and Ann took charge of his helmet, and

Sam played a little tune on his whistle and Tom brushed the policeman's boots and polished them.

'Where's Brock the Badger?' asked the policeman, as he smoked the pipe Sam offered him.

'Brock's out hunting, and we came to see Sam's house,' confided Tom. 'When we are left alone we get into scrapes like this.'

'We've been hearing tales the scarecrow told us,' added Ann. 'We were scared when you came along. We thought you were a boggart or a witch or a giant.'

'Would you like us to tell you a tale, sir?' asked Sam.

The policeman said he would love to hear a story. So there they sat, and Sam told the tales of Joe Scarecrow, and of Sally and of Brock the Badger, and the policeman enjoyed them very much.

'I ought by rights to be looking for a burglar,' said he when Sam stopped to take breath. 'I must go now, but I think you ought to get back home where it's safe.'

'Oh, Sally the Mare will wake us in the

morning,' yawned Sam, who was getting very
tired.

'I'll move on,' said the policeman, but Sam
whispered, 'Hist! There's somebody coming.'

'I hear nothing,' said the policeman after a
few minutes' silence.

'We hear better than humans,' said Sam. 'There's somebody down the lane, and a queer padded soft noise he makes, not like your step.'

They all kept very still, and the footsteps came nearer, so that the policeman could hear them too. A man appeared, hurrying along, with his boots swathed in rags to keep them soundless, and round his face was wrapped a scarf.

'The burglar,' whispered Ann, and the policeman nodded.

The man trotted past, and quietly the policeman rose from the ground and followed. There was a scuffle and then a whistle.

'All right,' said the policeman, and off he went with his captive.

The little pigs stared over the edge of the hole and then lay down and went to sleep, till Sally the Mare trotted by.

'Time to wake up,' she whinnied. 'Milk train is coming and workmen are about.'

So away they all scuttled, back to their home, where Brock was sitting on the doorstep waiting for them.

'Where have you four been all night?' he asked.

'We've found a house, Sam's house, with four red lamps, and a policeman took care of us,' they said.

'I know,' said Brock calmly. 'I met him, with a burglar. Then I tiptoed along and peered down a hole in the road and saw four little pigs fast asleep, snoring loudly enough to wake all the burglars in the kingdom.'

'Oh, Brock! Did you see us! Did you like our house?' they asked.

'Very much indeed, Sam, but you won't be able to go there again. I heard the men talking at the "Dog and Badger", saying the cable was laid and the work would be finished today.'

'Did you go to the "Dog and Badger"?' asked Tom, alarmed.

'Yes, I went to talk to a friend of mine, but nobody took any notice of me. I went to get some little presents for four good little pigs, who never run away from home but always stay very quiet and good when Brock is away,' said the badger.

'Oh, Brock,' they exclaimed.

What did he bring them? There was a red handkerchief from the pedlar's pack for Sam, and a tin whistle for Bill, a nutmeg grater for Ann, and a knife for Tom.

Sam Pig in Love

Sam Pig danced across the fields with a daisy in his hand, and a goose feather stuck behind his ear. His plaid trousers were clean and patched with a new red and green patch, and his coat had a bright new button on it. He was singing as he danced and the words of the song floated high in the air till they came to Sally the Mare.

Sally stopped eating to listen. She gave a little grunt of astonishment, and a whinny of surprise, and then she walked slowly to the gate of the field and waited for her friend.

Sam bent down to gather another daisy, and then he started his song again, an octave higher, so that the shrill squeal of it made Sally open her brown eyes even wider.

'What's come over our Sam? Is he in love?' she murmured, for this is what she heard.

> 'Here comes I, little Sam Pig,
> Diddle diddle dee, Diddle diddle do.
> With a button on my coat and a feather in my
>   wig,
> Diddle diddle dee di do.'

Then Sam lowered his voice to gruff bass, like the tones of a man, and answered himself:

> 'What have you come for, little Sam Pig?
> Diddle diddle dee, Diddle diddle do.

*With a button on your coat and feather in your
    wig,
Diddle diddle dee di do.'*

Up went Sam's voice again, soaring to the skies:

*'I want to marry your little Polly Jane,
Diddle diddle dee, Diddle diddle do.
With a rose in her bonnet, she lives in your lane.
Diddle diddle dee di do.'*

In a gruff voice Sam went on with his song.

*'You can't marry Polly, little Sam Pig.
Diddle diddle dee, Diddle diddle do.
You haven't got a penny, you can only dance a
    jig.
Diddle diddle dee di do.'*

High up again floated the shrill fluting song of
Sam.

*'Then I don't want Polly, little Polly Jane,
Diddle diddle dee, Diddle diddle do.
I'll never never marry little Polly Jane.
I'll skip in the sunshine and dance in the rain,
You can keep your little Polly Jane.'*

'Sam Pig,' called Sally sternly, 'who's this Polly Jane you are singing about so loudly?'

Sam rushed up to Sally, and told the Mare all about her.

'She's a little girl with yellow curls who goes to the village school. I've seen her, Sally. She has curls over her head, curls like my own tail. She skips and dances just like one of us,' said he, the words tumbling out in his excitement.

'Have you talked to her, Sam? Do you know her?' asked the puzzled Mare, shaking her wise old head at the impetuous pigling.

'Oh no! Oh no! I daren't, Sally. I shouldn't know what to say. I want to marry her someday so I've made a song about her.'

'Sam, it won't do,' said Sally.

'I want her to run races and play with us,' said Sam.

'Where does this Polly Jane live, Sam?' asked Sally.

'Oh, Sally, what a lot of questions,' laughed Sam. 'She lives in a thatched cottage with a well in the garden and her father is the black-smith. I should like to be a relation of the smith's and make your shoes, Sally.'

'Put it out of your mind, Sam,' warned Sally. 'Little girls don't love little piglings.'

'Perhaps she will love this pigling,' said Sam. 'There was a lady loved a swine, Sally, and I'm not a swine.'

'Why do you really want to marry her, Sam?' asked Sally, after a pause.

'So as I can go to the smithy and tinkle on the anvil and make a hiss with a hot iron in water,' said Sam Pig. He seized a stick and tapped on the gate.

'Listen, Sally. Listen to the hammer making horse-shoes. Tink! Tink! Tink! That's the song of the smith.'

'Nay, Sam Pig,' said Sally. 'You come along o' me to the smith's tomorrow. I've got a loose shoe, and we'll see.'

So the next day Sally went to the blacksmith's forge, and Farmer Greensleeves rode on Sally's back, while little Sam Pig ran behind, puffing and panting, with his coat flapping open, and his hat flapping up and down and his scarf swinging in the wind. He was wearing his best clothes. Sam was disappointed Farmer Greensleeves had not driven in the cart, but the farmer was in a hurry to get back.

When they arrived, there was another horse in the shed, and Sally had to wait outside. The farmer went off to the saddler's to take a saddle to be stitched, and to visit the wheelwright's where a cart was being painted. Sally stood patiently waiting for Sam. She knew he was coming, she had seen him down the lane, and quite soon she heard the familiar little trot of his small hooves as he pranced along the road.

'School comes out soon,' said Sam. 'Then you will see Polly Jane. You will like her, Sally.'

The little pig stood close to Sally, stroking her downbent nose, and from the smithy came the joyful Tink! Tink! Tink! of the blacksmith's hammer.

When Sally was led into the dimly lighted forge, Sam followed on her heels.

'Please, sir, can I blow the bellows?' asked he.

'Who's this?' grunted the smith, peering down at the small figure. 'You be off.'

'Please sir, please sir, Sally's my mare,' said Sam.

'Is she? I thought she was Farmer Greensleeves',' said the man, but he rather grudgingly allowed Sam to help.

Sam swung on the long handle of the bellows, and pushed it wheezing up and down. The fire flickered, and the iron was made hot. Sally waited quietly while the smith hammered and bent the shoe.

Suddenly there were shouts and a rush of feet and the children came out of school. A little girl came dancing into the forge. She was like a beam of sunlight with her gold curls. No wonder Sam had fallen in love with her! Sally turned her great head and gazed kindly at her. Sam forgot to blow the bellows and the smith paused with Sally's hoof in his hand and looked up at his little daughter.

'Father! Father! Here I am,' cried little Polly Jane.

Then she noticed Sam in the background and she added, 'Who's that helping you?'

'It's a queer little fellow as sometimes works

for Farmer Greensleeves,' said the smith.

'He's a pig, Father. I can see his ears,' laughed Polly Jane. 'He's a darling little pig and I love him. He's the little pig who came to school one day and did lessons.'

Sam stood looking at little Polly Jane, and Polly Jane beamed at him. Sam put his fist in his

pocket, and brought out some sticks and stones, which he shuffled away out of sight, and then he fished up a necklace made of nuts threaded on a string, with little silver coins between them. Brock had found the hoard of coins buried in the Roman field, and Ann Pig had threaded them with the nuts to make a chain.

He held it out to Polly Jane, and then he put his fist in the other pocket. He brought from it a walnut shell, with a little carved pigling inside it, made by Tom one winter's night. He offered this also to the little girl.

'Oh, thank you. Thank you,' she said.

Sam turned very shy. He walked out of the smithy and began to hunt in the hedge for a stick. He wrote in the dust in crooked letters, POLLEE JAN.

'He knows my name,' cried the little girl excitedly. 'He can write it.'

'He's a scholar,' neighed Sally, but of course they could not understand Sally's language.

'POLLEE JAN' wrote Sam again, tracing the letters with his hoof, and then, very bashful, he ran joyfully home.

The smith took no notice – he was too busy with Sally – and even when later he looked at the letters he saw no sense in them.

'Your imagination, Polly,' said he. 'That's not writing. It's rubbidge. But it's a pretty necklace you've got there.'

Farmer Greensleeves returned, bustling in a hurry for the mare.

'Farmer Greensleeves,' piped Polly Jane. 'Your pig knows my name. Look what he gave me!'

'He's not my pig,' said the farmer. 'He's picked up scraps of things now and then, but he's not my pig. He's a born character, though.'

He paid for the shoeing, and rode away to the farm, and he thought no more about Sam or Polly Jane.

'Little Polly Jane loves me,' sang Sam, dashing into the house of the four pigs and Brock the Badger.

'Who is Polly Jane?' asked Tom coldly.

'She's a little girl with dandelion curls and cherry lips and forget-me-not eyes,' said Sam.

'She's not as pretty as me, is she?' asked Ann.

'She's just about equal with you, Ann,' said Sam tactfully. 'Not prettier but just the same prettiness.'

'We can't have little girls here,' said Bill crossly. 'We had enough with that water-maiden and the princess. We don't want any more fine females.'

Then Tom in a mocking voice began to sing:

> *'Can she spin and can she sew,*
> *Can she make a bannock cake?*
> *Can she knead the barley dough?*
> *Can she use a garden rake?'*

'No,' said Sam. 'She's only a little girl, very young.'

Then Bill took up the song:

> *'Can she mend and can she wash?*
> *Can she fetch and carry?*
> *Can she dig, for if she can't,*
> *She will never marry.'*

'No,' said Sam. 'She can't do those things.'

His ears drooped, he went sadly out of doors, across the fields to Sally the Mare.

'What's the matter, Sam?' asked Sally. 'You seemed happy enough when I saw you last.'

'Everybody laughs at me when I talk of little Polly Jane,' said Sam. 'Even you smile at me, and I do love Polly Jane.'

'What can I do to help you, Sam?' asked Sally, who was very sorry for the little pig.

'I don't know,' muttered Sam. 'I should like to write her a letter, but my writing isn't good enough. I can only write on the ground with bits of stick.'

'It's Saint Valentine's Day tomorrow,' said Sally. 'Why not send her a Valentine?'

'What's a Valentine? I've never heard of it. Is it something to eat?'

'It's a special kind of letter, and Brock will tell you about it,' Sally reassured the little pig. 'You send it to the one you love.'

'Oh, Sally! Thank you! Thank you!' cried Sam. 'I'll go straight home and ask Brock about it.'

He ran off down the crooked little winding path back to the cottage. Brock was standing near the gate, watching the birds singing to one another and flirting their tails to show off their bright feathers.

'Hush!' he whispered, as Sam came up. 'Don't disturb them. They're making love, for tomorrow is Saint Valentine's Day. The birds marry on Saint Valentine's Day, Sam. It is their wedding day.'

'That's just what I wanted to ask about,' Sam whispered back. 'Can I make a Valentine, Brock?'

'Who is it for, Sam?' he asked, rather surprised at Sam.

'For the one I love,' replied Sam cautiously.

Brock pondered this for a few moments. Was Sam thinking of Sally the Mare, or Mollie the dairymaid? he wondered. Or was it a tiny pigling in the farmer's pigsty? Whoever it was, Sam must make a nice Valentine, he decided.

'You must first find a strip of birch-paper, Sam, and then you must paint a picture on it, a heart with an arrow through it, or a cupid.'

'I won't put a heart with an arrow. I don't want to be shot,' said Sam. 'I'll make a cupid. What is a cupid, Brock?'

437

'A cupid is a someone with wings, who carries love,' said Brock.

'If I had wings, should I be a cupid?' asked Sam.

'Yes, perhaps,' returned Brock, squinting at the solemn little pig before him. He had never seen Sam so serious. 'Now run away, and see what you can do. You must send your Valentine to – to – whoever-it-is by tomorrow.'

Sam went off to the woods and stripped a square of bark from the silver birch tree. Silver-birch makes a good kind of paper, and Sam could easily draw on it with a pencil. Of course he had no ordinary pencil, but a fine stick, which he burnt in the fire. With the blackened tip he drew a heart on the white strip of birch-bark. Inside it he made a picture of a pig with wings. There was a nice long nose and two pointed ears, and two small eyes, and a pair of flapping wings.

Under it he managed to write, POLLEE JAN.

'That's the best Valentine anyone ever made,' said he proudly, and he hid it in the gorse bush. If Tom and Bill found it they would tease the life out of their brother. So Sam pushed it among the prickles of the green gorse and went home for tea.

'What have you been doing, Sam?' asked Bill suspiciously.

'Nothing,' stammered Sam. 'Only making a drawing.'

'Drawing what? What did you draw? A pail of water for my lady's daughter?' mocked Tom.

'No, I drawed a cupid,' said Sam bravely.

'Whatever is a cupid?' cried Ann.

'A pig with wings,' said Sam.

Tom and Bill rushed at their brother to find his wings. When Brock came in the three animals were rolling over and over, struggling and shouting.

'Sam's a cupid with wings,' cried Bill. 'We are trying to find Sam's feathers, but he hasn't any yet. I think they are sprouting.'

'I'm not a cupid,' panted Sam indignantly.

'Stop teasing your brother,' said Brock. 'Settle down quietly, and I'll tall you a tale.'

So they sat meekly by the fire, for it was a

chilly evening in February, and Brock told them about Saint Valentine's Day, on February the fourteenth.

Sam got up the next morning very early, and away he ran to the village, with his picture under his arm.

He knew where little Polly Jane lived, and he had to be his own postman. She lived in a cottage with two upstair windows under the golden thatch and two downstair windows and a door between. Sam crept softly up the garden path, between the grey little bushes of lavender.

He could hear the blacksmith snoring, but already the smith's wife was making the fire, and the glint of the flames came through the window. There was no letter-box, nobody ever wrote to the blacksmith, so Sam propped his Valentine on the doorstep.

Then he backed away and waited in the bushes. The village began to wake up. A labourer walked to work, the ploughman whistled, the baker unfastened his shutters, the cobbler unbolted his door, and the oatcake man threw open a window.

Then the cottage door opened and little Polly Jane stood on the doorstep with a basket in her hand.

'I'll get the eggs, Mother,' she called. 'There may be a Valentine egg for me, if the banty-hen has remembered.'

Then she saw Sam Pig's Valentine.

'What's this? An ugly little pig trying to fly! It's got my name! Oh, oh! Pigs can't fly. They can't spell either.'

She stamped her little foot and tossed the Valentine away.

'I don't want that silly old thing! Silly old thing! Silly old thing!' she cried, and she skipped away to the hen-house for the banty-egg.

Sam Pig crept out of his hiding-place. He felt very miserable as he picked up his rejected Valentine. He rubbed out POLLEE JAN and wrote SALLY. Then he hurried off to the farm and propped it outside the stable door. He was just in time. Farmer Greensleeves came out and picked it up.

The farmer stared at it and turned it over. Then he opened the stable door.

'A Valentine for you, Sally, and if I'm not mistaken it's from Sam Pig.'

'How beautiful it is,' said Sally, beaming at the Valentine which the farmer propped on her manger.

'How kind of Sam. I've never had a Valentine in all my twenty-one years. Nobody ever thought to give me one.'

Sam Pig listened behind the wall. Then he ran and threw his arms round Sally's neck.

'You are my Valentine, Sally! I want no Polly Jane. Never, never no more. Only Sally,' said he.

'What was that song I heard you sing?' asked Sally.

Then Sam, blushing for shame, sang the last verse of his song.

'I don't want Polly, little Polly Jane,
Diddle diddle dee, Diddle diddle do.
I'll skip in the sunshine and dance in the rain.
I'll never, never marry little Polly Jane,
For my heart belongs to Sally.'